HEADCASE

Peter Helton

CARROLL & GRAF PUBLISHERS
New York

Carroll & Graf Publishers
An imprint of Avalon Publishing Group, Inc.
245 W. 17th Street
New York
NY 10011-5300
www.carrollandgraf.com

First published in the UK by Constable,
an imprint of Constable & Robinson Ltd 2005

First Carroll & Graf edition 2005

ISBN 0-7867-1529-4

Printed and bound in the EU

Chapter One

Detective work is boring. Really really boring. It's boring when it goes well and even more boring when it doesn't. There is only one exception: the monumental, spectacular, energetically pursued and perfectly executed fuck-up. You know the kind I mean, the type that involves a startling amount of dead bodies and lands you on a cold stone floor in a pool of your own blood with even more bodies lying about, some with important bits missing.

Of course you can't expect to get up one morning and find it all there, ready for you. It comes at you in a quiet, crablike fashion, so you probably won't hear it coming. I certainly didn't, even though I switched off the music when I reached the wooden sign that points drunkenly up the pitted track to my house. Apart from the usual birdsong and the hum of the Citroën's engine it was near silent.

For me this silence marks the boundary between the reality of Bath and the quite different realities of my life in the valley, with its gentle morning rhythms, days of bovine slowness, its honeysuckled nights. I like to approach Mill House quietly, gauge its mood in the summery dusk, notice the pitch of the mill stream before it sinks into the background again.

With my head half outside the open window to sniff the evening air I swung the car on to the hard-baked mud of the yard, slid it beside the battered but eminently practical heap of Annis's Land Rover and killed the engine. The hydraulics sighed and the DS settled gratefully on to its haunches. Quiet.

Even though my stomach was growling, I was content for a moment just to stand and breathe in the dusk, listen to the small noises of the countryside. This was a rare summer, the kind that lets people forget their dreams of moving down under and consider cream teas instead; strawberries were selling out every day; street cafés were crowded; the spectre of a hosepipe ban stalked the city. And it was still only June.

The house and the outbuildings lay dark but a dim light came from the studio on the far side of the meadow – Annis was working late on her canvas, it seemed. With my arms full of shopping I pushed through the front door into the house and straight to the kitchen. The shopping deposited on the table, I prowled through the darkening ground floor, hall, sitting room, dining room, lighting the lamps as I went. The french windows were open and Annis in her painting gear was curled up in the big cane chair on the verandah.

'Hi, Chris.'

'Hi. Thought you were working. You left the lights on in the barn,' I said unnecessarily. You can see the studio from the verandah.

'I know. I was just taking a break. Have some orange juice?' Annis pointed to the glass jug on the table. 'Freshly squeezed.'

She looked tired, had probably put in a twelve-hour day in front of her easel. 'I will. Why don't you call it a day? You can't see a thing now anyway. And I'm fixing supper soon, I'm starving.'

Annis followed me into the kitchen carrying the jug. 'Need any help?' she offered.

'You can make the salad, I'll do the rest.' Then I saw it. She'd cut off half of her strawberry curls, they were now just touching her shoulders. 'You cut your hair. I like it,' I lied.

She screwed up her face and rolled her eyes to the ceiling. 'I had it cut three days ago. For a bloke who's a painter *and* a private eye you're very unobservant sometimes.'

'Sorry,' I said and busily unpacked the shopping.

'That's okay, you're not my lover. In which case you'd be dead now.' She waggled the big chopping knife at me.

I let that hang there for the moment. Not many people believe it but there was nothing going on between us. I mean there was lots going on between us but we weren't sharing a bed. We lived together and sometimes worked together and so far that seemed a good arrangement.

Annis simply turned up here four years ago when she was still a student. She sniffed around my studio, told some porkies about how she admired my work and asked if I'd take her on as an apprentice, like in the good old days before art colleges. She'd help in the studio, stretch canvases, clean my brushes, all very flattering. Then she showed me her work. She was supremely talented, that was instantly clear. I told her I had nothing to teach her but if she promised not to jack in her course she could work in my studio, it's a big old barn. Then I kept finding her asleep in front of her easel in the mornings so I gave her a room in the house.

Soon after that I slithered into detective work and Annis came slithering right behind. She's an excellent investigator, always gets the best out of people with her poise and her butterscotch voice. And if you saw her painting now you'd immediately assume that I was washing *her* brushes. She's nothing short of brilliant.

'So how did you get on with the Turner thing today?' she asked now, munching away at the cucumber. 'That's what you were doing today, wasn't it?'

'It was. Nothing suspicious at all. You're supposed to chop it not chew it.'

'Rule number one, don't piss off the girl with the knife,

7

you know that. So what *does* he get up to when he's not with Mrs Turner? See? I'm chopping.'

Mrs Turner had become suspicious of her husband's absences, his late hours at work, the sudden proliferation of meetings and conferences he had to attend.

'Nothing interesting so far,' I reported. 'I waited for him outside his architecture bureau in Brock Street until he knocked off work at twenty to six. Rang Mrs Turner on my mobile to check. Yes, he was "working late". I'd parked near his car in the Circus and never lost sight of his bumper across town and out towards Bathampton. Straight into the car park of the George Inn. He took to the towpath with a paper bag in his hand and strolled past the narrow boats for twenty minutes. Didn't talk to anyone, there were quite a few people out there. Opened the paper bag, fed the ducks with the remains of his last sandwich or whatever, then back to the George. Got himself a pint of lager shandy, the sad deluded man, and drank it sitting on the grass by the canal.'

'Didn't meet anyone?'

'Not a soul.'

'Any chance he clocked you following? Had you on?'

I didn't even answer that, just widened my eyes at her.

'Okay, of course he didn't. Perhaps he got stood up,' Annis suggested. 'Salad's done.'

I lit the grill and opened the wine. 'He didn't look around for anyone, just sat there, looking at the water. Returned the glass to the George like a good boy and drove home.'

'Then why tell his wife he's working late? Why not say I'm going for a walk by the Kennet-and-Avon after work, see you at – what?'

'Eight,' I supplied.

'At eight. Or was he thinking of chucking himself in? Does he seem depressed?'

'Thoughtful,' I conceded and shoved the prawn kebabs

under the grill. 'But why feed the ducks if you're thinking of feeding *yourself* to the ducks? Doesn't make sense.'

'Not to you but suicides aren't always rational.'

The prawns blushed pink after a couple of minutes so I whipped them on to the plates and tore off some olive bread and helped myself to salad.

Her eyebrows rose a fraction. '*You can help me with the salad, I'll do the rest*? What rest? You bought those kebabs ready-made. You didn't do a thing!'

'Exactly. Let Waitrose take the strain. Cheers.'

You have . . . four . . . messages. Called . . . Wednesday, 10.21 a.m. . . .

Every time I hear the silly voice I swear I'll get a decent answering machine but it took me forever to record my message so I always chicken out of that one.

Aqua Investigations is really an answerphone and a P.O. Box. There's an office in the attic of Mill House devoted to it but we never meet clients there. I arrange to meet at a café, a pub, a park bench even, but preferably at their own addresses, which usually teaches me more about the client. No one is ever allowed near our haven in the valley.

With my first coffee of the day steaming away on my desk I began ringing them back. First of the messages was from Simon Paris Fine Art promising good news, so I'd go and see him in person. The first client call turned out to be another unfaithful spouse, or rather her husband, and I turned him down politely. I'd only taken on the present one because the DS needs an MOT, and keeping a classic Citroën on the road is full of surprises, most of them nasty. Philanderers are our bread and butter but they are also boring, utterly predictable and time-consuming and I never enjoy handing over those videos and photographs. It's usually bad news and ill received. Talk about shooting the messenger.

Number two sounded quite promising if, naturally, boring. But the DS needed an urgent MOT and it sounded like a doddle. The silent partner of an antiques dealer in Walcot Street suspecting that business couldn't be quite as bad as he was led to believe. He gave us permission to bug the shop and the office, a job for Tim, so I fixed a meeting between the two.

Tim Bigwood is the third member of our little team. His primary job is an IT consultancy at Bath University so the easiest way to contact him is via e-mail. He's online twenty-four hours a day it seems. He even had a laptop built into his niftily modified Audi TT and can conduct Aqua business from there. He's our wires man. Anything to do with surveillance, pinhole cameras, sound-bugging, door-opening (and closing), and snooping around on other people's computers is Bigwood country.

Message number three sounded more promising still. From someone called Virginia Dufossee at Starfall House. Clear, precise voice. She would like to avail herself of my services. A request to turn up today, between twelve and one, at Starfall House, near somewhere called Compton Dando. Detailed instructions on how to get there from Bath. This was obviously someone used to giving instructions. She had also used my name which meant she hadn't just picked Aqua Investigations from the phone book, thinking like so many that a P.O. Box number meant cheap rates. We're not cheap. In fact we're barely competitive and we're choosy to boot. What Mrs Dufossee failed to mention was her reason for calling me. There was no answer when I rang back.

I had hoped to give our Mr Turner another shot during his lunch hour so I thought I'd better take a fresh cafetière of coffee with me when I went across to the studio.

Another cloudless sky roofed the valley. Five weeks without rain had depleted the mill stream but the water still rushed happily through the narrow channel along the house. As I crossed the dewy slope of the meadow the sun on my back confirmed it would be sticky work sitting in a car watching Turner.

Annis was perched on her stool staring at the six-foot square expanse of canvas she'd been working on for the last two months with the same expression I once saw her use on a bloke who was threatening us with a baseball bat. Needless to say the bloke packed it in. Only paintings never pack it in, they always have the last laugh. My own easel was mercifully empty. I had finished a painting three days earlier and was resting on fresh laurels. When they dry out they get uncomfortable, which would be soon enough.

'Trouble?' I suggested. 'Brought some coffee.' Annis is a hopeless addict.

'Been nothing but trouble from the start. You're not in your painting gear and you brought my poison, so spit it out.'

'I'm meeting an expensive voice at noon.'

'Hence the Armani shirt. Anything good?'

'I'll find out.' I poured a mug and held it out to her.

'Organic Colombian After Dinner in the morning? What do I have to do to earn it?'

'Keep an eye on Turner's lunch hour.'

She sniffed the coffee again, rabbit fashion, took one sip, just to make absolutely sure. 'Done.'

Compton Dando turned out to be an affluent village sleeping roughly halfway between Bath and Bristol. Its high hedges and double garages speak of commuting lifestyles and early retirement of highly paid professionals, though the odd tractor can still clog up the hectic rat-run lanes between the two cities, bringing the excitement of squealing brakes and festering impatience to the early morning racers trying to beat the crawling misery of the A4. The river Chew cuts through its northern half, another ten miles to go before it spends itself into the lake.

Turning left after the bridge I started following the instructions Mrs Dufossee had provided, up and out of the village past two farms then right into a small wooded dell. 'You can't miss Starfall from there.' She was right, I couldn't.

Whether modest manor or immodest villa, Starfall House was a solid piece of Georgian masonry shielded by a sentry of trees from the well-maintained private road that led down to it. A tiny yellow Lotus looked lonely in the oval of raked gravel. I gave it a wide berth and parked close to the ivy-choked front of the house. From what I could see of the gardens Mrs Dufossee was also used to giving instructions to more than one gardener. The swishing of unseen lawn sprinklers was the only sound I heard until I tried the old-fashioned black bell-pull. It responded with a fading knell deep inside the building.

I had expected a maid at the very least but the woman who opened the door and immediately turned her back on me had Lotus driver written all over her. Grey slacks, a silk top in a matching shimmer and pale grey heels that echoed across the cool chessboard floor of the hall.

When I caught up with her she was already smoking on a flowery two-seater by the fireplace in a reception room to the left of the hall. Very black, very short hair, high cheekbones and superb complexion. Her eyes were too blue to be true, coloured contacts sprang to mind. Now I could see the lawn sprinklers through the closed windows behind her but couldn't hear them. She pointed to an armchair a quarter of a mile away and frowned.

'How old are you, Mr Honeysett?' Surprisingly, clients rarely ask for my credentials. More rarely still for my birth date. I judged us to be of similar age.

'Mrs Dufossee –'

'Miss . . . Virginia Dufossee.'

'Any particular reason for asking?'

'Yes. I would like to know.'

This could go on forever so I told her.

She blew out smoke. 'You don't look it. Must be all that hair.'

'Is looking my age in any way relevant to your problem?'

'No, but acting your age might be.' She dismissed it with a wave of her cigarette. 'I have responsibilities and I need responsible help. Let's get on with it. Follow me.' She dropped her depleted cigarette into the ashtray without dirtying her fingernails by stubbing it out, picked up a thick plastic folder from the coffee table and led the way. Across the hall and through double doors into an even larger drawing room, sporting a black baby grand piano and more furniture that didn't go with the Lotus.

'One.' Virginia pointed to a faint empty square on the cream wallpaper. She wheeled around and pointed over my shoulder to a similar patch beside the door. 'Two.'

We continued our tour upstairs along a gallery, literally.

'Three.' Another bald patch.

I had made up my mind but this was too good to miss. Already she had wafted us past a drawing by Francesco Guardi, a small Constable watercolour and several Turner studies, glowing in their frames like jewellery. Into an impersonal bedroom at the end of the long corridor, probably a guest room.

'Four, five, six and seven. Smaller ones. Coffee?' She was off again.

Only reluctantly did I turn away from a small Pissarro in the hall. We descended to ground level and passed under the stairs into the Essential Country Kitchen, scrubbed oak table, Aga, copper-bottomed everything and dried bundles of herbs, purely for show, I decided.

She presented me with her folder and turned to the kettle. 'I assume they mean something to you? I hired you because you're also a painter. That's right, isn't it?'

Half of it was right, only no one had been hired yet.

'I marked the missing ones. Milk, sugar?' I fended off any such suggestions.

The list made impressive reading but something immediately bugged me about the stolen paintings, quite apart from the fact that they were missing, which bugged me a lot. People who steal paintings deserve to be shot. Not dead. Just shot, a lot. The coffee was instant and lousy. I wondered how you married a John Sims longcase clock in the front with Gold Blend in the back. Or perhaps they brought this stuff out for the hired help? I doubted it, since Virginia seemed quite happy to swill it down with her next cigarette. Maybe she had fried her taste buds with nicotine.

The paintings explained why she had picked on me. Any self-respecting PI would have turned her down but she was hoping I'd do it for art's sake. For art's sake I turned her down.

'Three Spencer Gores, two Harold Gilmans and a couple of Sickerts go astray from your house and you call *me*?'

'Why not?'

'Have you called the police?'

'No, that's why you're here.'

'If you really want them back then you'll go to the police. When did you discover the paintings were gone?'

'Yesterday. So I rang you.'

In my consternation I took another sip of imitation coffee. It didn't improve my mood. 'Only the police have the resources to recover stolen paintings, Miss Dufossee, and even they find it difficult. They've got specialist units for art theft, databases, the lot. Within hours the pictures will appear on the computer screens of every force in the country. Customs will keep their eyes open. The way the crime was carried out might point to who was involved. Not to speak of forensic evidence which might be deteriorating as we speak.'

'I need absolute discretion.' Her voice adamant.

'Then you're fonder of discretion than you are of your paintings.'

'Fonder of my father's health. I don't want him upset.'

14

Virginia twirled her cigarette in the ashtray. She spoke more softly now. 'My father is in Devon, at a private natural health clinic for a last ditch attempt to cure his cancer. He doesn't have long to live so he's going for a miracle cure. He'll be back in twenty days. If I go to the police one way or another it'll get into the papers and he'll hear about it. I don't want him distracted. They do a lot of meditation and things. It's hocus-pocus in my book but he's entitled to give it a shot without being sidetracked by this.'

'The collection is your father's?'

She nodded. 'This is his house.'

'It's an impressive collection. Eclectic, to a point, but impressive. I wouldn't mind a closer look later on.'

Her mouth twitched into a brief half-smile, possibly a half-smirk. Take the job, it said, and you can look all you like. If not, Nescafé and out.

'You don't live here?'

'I want to spend as much time with my father as possible while he's around. But no, I have a flat in Bath.'

'Your mother?'

She simply shook her head.

'So there's no one here at the moment? To look after the house?'

'My father's housekeeper took the opportunity to visit family while he's away. I look after the house in her absence but . . .' She didn't finish the sentence and I didn't ask. But I might later. The reproductions of the vanished canvases at the back of the catalogue made me nervous as well as angry. All of them were figurative, all but one of them nudes. I wondered about the thief's choice and taste. 'Has everything been left as it was? You didn't clear up any mess they made?'

'There was no mess. Everything is as I found it.'

I gave it one more try, to make sure.

'My chances of recovering these are very slim. It would

15

be a lucky break, no more.' I'm not known for lucky breaks. Breaks, yes. Lucky, no.

Her hand hovered over the ashtray, ready to drop the butt. 'But you'll have a go?'

'What will you do if I turn you down?' As if I didn't know.

'Nothing. I'll wait until my father gets back. I've tried ev . . .' She dropped the butt, spread her hands in surrender.

'You've asked everyone else and they all turned you down for the same reasons. Only someone said, "Try Aqua, they're a bunch of painters so might just be mad enough to take it on."'

She nodded. 'And are you?'

'Mad enough? I am now.'

There were two more things on my list for the day before I'd give the Dufossee paintings my undivided attention and both should be more pleasurable – to check on what exactly Simon Paris Fine Art meant by good news and to see Jenny at Somerset Lodge. Jenny first, I decided, since there was always a chance of food and by now I was ravenous. I drove to Poet's Corner.

Somerset Lodge, at the Alexandra Park end of Boswell Avenue, is a small residential place for recovering mental health patients, a kind of halfway house, run by the Culverhouse Trust, and Jenny Kickaldy is the long-suffering housekeeper.

When and where Jenny and I first met is now lost in the depths of time. She's always been there, it seems, and always been there for me when things get rough. I try to do the same for her but naturally she's much better at it.

So whenever things get on top of her and she needs to get away from it all for a day I step in and cook the meals and chat for a few hours with the residents. She hadn't called me for weeks so I thought I'd show my face. At the

16

front gate I nearly got bowled over by an eighteen-stone paper-girl who had just stuffed the *Chronicle* through the letter box. She managed to ram her overloaded bag into my stomach as she barrelled past me. I unjammed the paper from the letter box and let myself in with my key. I walked past the sitting room, with its perpetually burbling TV, through to the kitchen. It had been done up since I'd last been there. A brand-new electric oven and grill winked digitally across at me. Dave was there, lean and hectic, pacing the length of the kitchen and adjoining dining room, as is his habit.

I said hello.

'Hi, Chris.' He didn't stop. Jenny and I once worked out that Dave walks thirty miles a day pacing up and down, a cool ten thousand miles a year, which keeps him extremely fit and wears out the carpets.

'Are you cooking tonight?' he asked. The residents always ask me that of course. I've never worked out if they dread my cooking or if it's just a polite question.

'Don't know yet. Where's Jenny?'

Jenny was in the garden. I found her sitting cross-legged in the shade of the chestnut trees, blonde hair piled high on her head, sweating over paperwork that was spilling out around her on the grass. Linda, at nineteen the youngest resident, was saving the flower beds with the aid of an old-fashioned, tin watering can. Quite fragile and flower-like herself, she just smiled across. Linda is very shy.

Jenny lifted tired eyes from a thick file and also smiled, a tired smile. The shadows under her eyes were deeper than normal. Quickly she gathered some of the papers together, flipped one or two over. I help out but I'm not entitled to know medical details about the residents – unless they tell me themselves, which some of them do quite freely.

'You look worn out,' I said. 'Why didn't you ring?' I flopped on to the grass next to her. Perhaps it wasn't the nicest opening I could have thought of.

'Good morning to you too.'

'It's gone two o'clock.'

'Really?' Jenny puffed up her cheeks and slowly blew out the air. Then she seemed to snap out of it. 'Right,' she said breezily, gathering up her papers, 'in that case enough of this. I'll make some lunch. Want some? Stupid question. Let's go inside.' I have a reputation for being perpetually hungry, so people tend to offer me food a lot. Which is nice.

'If you need a day off I'm not too busy,' I suggested, following her across the lawn.

She stopped on the threshold of the back door. Checked no one was within earshot. 'We've got a bit of bother. A lot of bother actually. I've called a committee meeting, they'll have it here at Somerset Lodge on Saturday. So at the moment I've got to be here. Two more days. But after that, yes, please. I really could do with forgetting all about this place for a day or two.'

'You don't want to talk about it?' I asked, knowing the answer.

'I can't. You know how it is.' Jenny is fiercely protective of the residents' rights and privacy. Strictly 'need to know'. She was doing it now. 'There's one thing I ought to tell you if you're cooking next week.' She checked again that no one was listening. Linda was at the far end of the garden, just contemplating the bushes. 'I had a funny incident with Dave. It's nothing really but . . .' She nibbled at her lower lip. 'I think you're entitled to know. I was preparing supper a couple of days ago. Got it all in the oven. Had some garnish laid out to chop at the last minute. The big Sabatier knife next to it. Sat down and read the paper for a bit. Dave was pacing as per usual. When it was time to serve up I went to the chopping board and the knife was gone. Looked everywhere. Turned round and there was Dave, clutching the bloody thing in his right hand, like a dagger, pacing up and down like an assassin, right behind where I'd been sitting and reading.'

'Bloody hell. And?'

'And nothing. First I got scared, then I realized he probably didn't even know he had it. I said, "Dave, can I have the knife," and he just gave it to me.'

'Did you ask him what it was about?'

'I did, later, when I felt a bit calmer. He just said, "I don't know." So watch your back a bit but don't be obvious about it. You know what Dave's like, always on the boil. Talks about volcanoes and so on. Thank God I'm a post-Freudian.' She tried for a grin. 'The way I feel at the moment I'm post everything. And there's other stuff. Odd things go missing. Small change from the mantelpiece. A candlestick. Wanna play detective? Forget it. Let's eat.'

Dave had transferred his pacing to the living room so we could chat freely while Jenny threw together one of her famous buffet spreads in record time, despite her obvious tiredness. Since she insisted she worked quicker without my help I perched on the chest freezer and watched her whirl about, in her element now. Deep-fried chicken bits, tabouleh, dips and salads ran off the assembly line. Her hair was working loose and she blew wayward strands out of her field of vision while she worked and quizzed me about my day.

'Which hat are you wearing today, then?'

'Aqua business, I'm between paintings.'

'Is that like between chairs?'

'No, much more comfortable. Took on a new job today which looks like it'll run for a while and probably come to nothing. Art theft. Or you could call it a heist really, they got away with seven paintings.' Unable to resist the lemony smell of those chickeny things I reached for one and got my wrist slapped.

'You're as bad as the residents. Wait till it's on the table. I thought you didn't take on stuff like that. Isn't that a police job?'

'It will be, I'm sure. I've got twenty days to try to get them back before it goes official.'

'Your inspector friend isn't going to be too happy when he hears you've been holding out on him again,' she said with a certain relish.

'Needham? He's a detective superintendent now.'

'Even worse then, I should think.' Jenny always enjoyed my stories of the low-level feuding that's been going on between Needham and myself ever since my very first case. Then I was looking into some good old-fashioned sheep rustling when I stumbled into nasty goings-on in the meat industry which involved a deep-frozen meat inspector. Something which for my own reasons I failed to mention for a while since I naturally assumed the poor man would keep for another week or so while I sorted out the good guys from the not so nice. When I waltzed into Manvers Street police station one morning with all the evidence, terribly pleased with my own cleverness, the then Detective Inspector Needham made me sweat in a clapped-out interview room until long after last orders had been called. That 'stunt', as Needham called it, nearly cost me my brand new licence and set the tone for our relationship. Needham would give me a hard time, I knew. Especially if I failed. He's a proper copper, due process and all that. Some of the things Aqua get up to set his teeth on edge, particularly when Tim does his door opening/door closing routine. We call it checking things out, he calls it breaking and entering. Only Tim's far too good to ever break anything. Except codes.

'Can't be helped,' I summed up. 'My client won't go to the police for her own good reasons. So it's up to me.'

Jenny gave me one of her is-that-so looks and wiped her hands on her Short-Tempered-Short-Order-Cook apron. 'You just can't resist it, I expect. Paintings and all that. I know how you hate art thieves. I'm done. Want to sound the alarm?'

I did. Jenny knew I loved banging away at the big Chinese dinner gong in the hall. I took a good swing at it, making sure everyone in Boswell Avenue knew lunch was served at Somerset Lodge.

First to appear was Gavin, a spotty, slightly unsavoury-looking boy with thin, perpetually greasy hair. Was it grease or was it 'product'? I couldn't decide. He slithered in and stuck damply to the wall just by the door jamb, looking me up and down. Then he looked Jenny up and down, scratched his crotch and swallowed.

'Hi, Gav,' Jenny coaxed. Gavin hardly ever speaks, not unless he absolutely has to. He's twenty-two but his mind is stuck in his mid-teens somewhere, shy of girls, shy of the world. Only the pressures of bodily needs make him venture beyond his attic room. Food was one of those.

'Help yourself. We're having ours out on the lawn. You're welcome to join us,' she invited. Some hope. Gavin cleared his throat, laboriously and wetly. This meant he was going to speak, which is a rare occasion. We stood still.

'Is it . . . Thursday?' Gavin is also lost in time. Days, hours, weeks, all tenuous notions, all interchangeable. 'Is Gordon coming?' he squeezed out.

'No,' Jenny said firmly. 'Gordon won't be coming to see you.'

Gordon Hines is one of the more religious committee members of the Culverhouse Trust who looks after the spiritual welfare of the residents, especially the younger ones, the truly lost. Gavin didn't appear to be greatly put out on hearing that the visit was off.

Next into the room was the quiet Linda, rapidly outpaced by Dave. While we all heaped salads on to our plates Anne came clucking into the room, nervously chatting and fussing.

'Ooh look at all that food salads chicken I'm not so sure about chicken in this heat hi Chris did you make this it's a lovely spread we're so fortunate isn't it a scorcher today I'll just have a little bit of . . .' Despite her medication Anne is always a little bit hyper, always sweating a little in too

21

many layers of matronly clothing. She's thirty but she dresses sixty.

'One missing. Shall I go and look for Adrian?' I offered.

'He's in hospital again,' Jenny said, 'didn't I tell you?'

'Did he stop taking his medication again?'

'No. Fell off his skateboard. Again. Did it properly this time, broke his shoulder. They kept him in.'

Thus everyone was accounted for and we ate sitting outside on the grass, plates balanced on our laps. Through the window I could see Dave eating from his plate while pacing to and fro in the sitting room, never dropping a crumb on the worn carpet.

'You're doing an amazing job, Jenny,' I said, looking across at Anne chatting away, Linda nodding nodding nodding, Dave toing and froing. 'Would you look after me if I ever went a little gaga?'

'Sure, Chris, one more won't make any difference.' Jenny lifted her head to scrutinize my face. 'But you know what? Sometimes I think you're frighteningly sane.'

'Well finally! I've been going insane here trying to get hold of you. Don't you ever switch your mobile on? We've got work to do.' The austerely minimal premises of Simon Paris Fine Art echoed Simon's indignation. But he smiled at me. I smiled back and checked the walls. No red dots against any of my paintings, so where was the good news?

'The Saudis are back. Came in yesterday.' That was good news. 'And they do want to buy, they left a list.'

'They didn't want any of these?'

'Wrong size. Just like last time they're very specific. These are the sizes. They're all meant to fit into particular spaces in King Whatsit's old palace. Tell me you've got canvases in those sizes, Chris. If not, go and paint them. Like *now*?' Sometimes I think Simon must be bored out of his balding skull to get that excited but then I remember he gets fifty per cent commission on all my sales. I looked at the list he waved in front of me. It amounted to enough money to keep me in paint and Simon's son at Prior Park College for another year.

'If I have paintings in these sizes . . .' I began.

'Of course you have. And you know why? Because you took my advice and painted lots of different formats in the past three years since the Saudis last turned up. Tell me you have.'

'I'm not exactly sure of the dimensions, I'd have to check,' I mumbled.

'They can be an incy bit larger but not much. And don't sit down, you don't have time for that.'

'Even if I have the sizes it doesn't mean they'll want those particular paintings.' I tried to inject a few millilitres of caution into his optimism but I missed the vein.

'They will. They did last time. Last time they bought four, this time they're taking nine. They love your work. Being Muslims, with their injunctions against figurative art, you're right down their street. Apparently they find your work very spiritual. It's those deep blues and sumptuous pinks,' he enthused.

'Okay, I'll let you know.'

'Nothing of the sort. Here. Take my digital camera, get everything that fits the dimensions photographed and bring me the images pronto. They're only here for a few days.'

'No problem,' I said. 'But I need a favour. I've got a list of my own I'd like you to look at.' I handed him the sheet of paper with the missing Dufossee canvases. Simon sighed, produced a pair of gold reading glasses from his jacket pocket and studied the note for four and a half seconds.

'Very fine, Chris, but what? Buying or selling?'

'Neither, I hope. They've gone AWOL.'

Simon gave a low whistle and looked at the list again. 'Why show me?'

'You know every dealer in twentieth-century art in the West Country,' I flattered. Not enough.

A flash of his watery blue eyes over the top of his glasses. 'Not just the West Country, I'll have you know.'

'Ask around for me then, will you? Send a few faxes, make a few phone calls. If anyone's been offered any of them, even hears a rumour, I need to know.'

Simon slapped the note into his photocopier and ran off half a dozen copies.

'How much, do you reckon?'

'At auction? Two, two-fifty. Could run to more on a good day. It's the Sickert, you see?'

It was my turn to give a low whistle.

'Insured, one hopes,' Simon said laconically. He glanced once more at the note. 'There's something oddly familiar about this list.'

'You mean you've seen these paintings mentioned together before?'

'No, nothing like that. Can't think what, though. I'll get in touch if anything springs to mind or I hear something. Now get out of here and get cracking. On your own paintings.' He unceremoniously bundled me out of the door. Perhaps school fees had gone up this year.

A fat snake of double-decker tour buses was clogging up Brock Street as I stepped back into the late afternoon heat from Simon's air-conditioned emporium in Margarets Buildings. It slowed down to give their passengers a brief and oblique view of the sweeping majesty of the Royal Crescent before squeezing into Upper Church Street. The fortunate inhabitants of the Crescent have been made more fortunate still by being exempt from the diesel fumes and amplified commentary of the grinding tourist procession.

I turned the other way, inched the car out of its tight parking space in Catherine Place and zipped through Circus Mews and Bennett Street before rejoining the traffic stew at the bottom of Lansdown Road. I had no intention of getting infected with Simon's panic about the sale so

I settled into the inevitable crawl. There was one more thing to do before I returned to the valley: the meeting I had set up between Tim and the worried partner of the Walcot Street antiques dealer. Not that Tim needed me for this but the meeting took place, appropriately, in the beer garden of the Bell, not fifty yards from the premises of Austin Antiques, and I was ready for a drink.

A lucky parking space by the side of the charity shop, early eye contact with a hectic barmaid and I was equipped with an ice cold pint of Stella. The inside of the Bell appeared gloomy after the brightness of the street and was almost deserted apart from the scrum at the bar. Everyone had squeezed into the courtyard at the back. Tim and Carl Fishers, our worried client, were perched on upturned beer crates in a corner under some aphid-ridden bushes.

Fishers rose to greet me and we shook hands. A tiny black beard clung to the bottom of his sharp triangular face but his voice seemed to come from a broader chest than his gangly frame. It was deep and confident. He didn't seem to mind repeating his story to me while I pulled up a crate and sipped my Stella.

'I've been involved with Austin for two years now, sank quite a bit of money into it. His expertise, my money. It sounds naïve now but I don't really know anything about antiques. I just liked the idea of it, you know, not as impersonal as burying your money in other investments. Thought I might learn something, too. We met on the golf course a few years back, then one day I talked about investments and he suggested I come in with him. He was just starting up in Walcot.'

'And now you're thinking . . . what?'

'He's holding out. Things go through the shop and never turn up in the books. Return of sale, Geoff says, stuff he takes on from customers and when they don't sell after a time they go back. Business is bad, too much competition, he says. But I know he's making money.'

'Do any cash transactions show up?'

'Yes, some.'

'So we can't catch him out on that.'

'What I really want you to do is have a look on his computer. He puts everything on that but I wouldn't know how to switch one on. And put a camera and a microphone in his office, as Mr Bigfoot suggested before you arrived.'

This happens a lot to Mr Bigwood. He ran a broad hand through his woolly blond hair. 'Call me Tim,' he offered gracefully.

'And I don't want it done just for a limited time. I want to be able to permanently check what my friend Geoff gets up to,' Fishers said and gulped down his watery-looking pint.

'You want to buy surveillance equipment and want us to install it permanently?' Tim asked.

'I want to be able to keep tabs on him from now on,' Fishers confirmed.

I looked at Tim who nodded sagely. 'I've got the equipment in the car. Pricey to buy, but no problem.'

Fishers checked the time on his diminutive mobile. 'He'd have left by now. Shall we go, gentlemen?' He rose impatiently, couldn't wait to get at the guy. I hoovered up the rest of my pint and followed.

Fishers went ahead to double check the place was really empty, then waved us on. This was my kind of antiques shop. Geoff Austin had set it up two years ago yet the place gave the impression it had been here from the beginning of time. If Austin Antiques specialized in anything in particular then it was not apparent. Statuary; furniture; a musket, chained to the wall; rapiers and swords in a hollow elephant's foot; framed paintings and prints on the walls, against the walls, most of them dull; jewellery in vitrines; a stuffed fox in a glass case; figurines and china under lock and key, apparently valuable, definitely hideous. This was the kind of shop where you felt you could discover something exciting. The kind of shop where inevitably you discover that you can't afford your discoveries.

Tim lugged past me with a heavy stainless steel carry case, straight to the office. I followed reluctantly. A small room, now crowded with the three of us and Tim's equipment. A large mahogany desk, antique, held the computer, state of the art, according to Tim, who had already fired it up. A tall metal locker held more prints and some rare books, Fishers explained, the little safe in the corner the more expensive small pieces, including jewellery and watches, locked up every night. Fishers didn't have a key.

'An old Bruton Centurion,' Tim said with that dismissive tone that told me not to ask. He'd have it open in twenty minutes. I couldn't be of any real help here and left. I had pictures to take.

Chapter Two

An unfamiliar car was parked in the yard when I arrived at Mill House, something rare enough to make me curious. The scent of burning kindling and catching charcoal hung in the still air so I made my way straight to the back of the house. The barbecue was flaming. Under the ancient oak at the top of the meadow a girl or woman in khaki shorts and vest was pointing the long lens of a camera at me. Whether or not she took a picture of me I couldn't tell. She lowered the camera and skipped towards me. Very blonde hair held in a long ponytail, clear grey eyes and a slightly aquiline nose. I put her at early thirties.

'You're Chris Honeysett? I'm Gillian Pine.' She fished a business card from her back pocket where it had moulded itself into a slight curve against her behind. I would keep it for future reference. 'I'm a location finder for the BBC. Came across your house quite by accident. You do own this house? Miss Jordan said.'

Said Miss Jordan appeared with a tray of long glasses of orange juice and soda which lit up brightly in the sun. 'Hi, Chris, this is Gill,' Annis said. 'She's from the BBC. Fancies Mill House as a set for a drama.'

Gill made a mischievous face by half closing one eye and doing something curiously attractive with the corner of her mouth. 'And Miss Jordan . . .'

'You can call me Annis.'

'Okay, Annis told me exactly what you'd say to that.'

Both looked intently at me, expecting me to perform.

I obliged: 'Not bloody likely.' Both of them laughed. And that seemed to settle that.

We talked on the verandah. Gill entertained us with stories of her travels looking for suitable places to film, a job that seemed to have taken her everywhere I had ever heard of. Finding houses, streets, landscapes, facilities. 'I don't travel far afield any more though, only do Britain now. I've a son at home and don't want to be away so much.' She had one more light-hearted go at tempting me into handing over Mill House to a film crew, complete with cast and their trailers, BBC lorries and catering vans. 'They pay extremely well, are very well behaved. They'll pay for luxury accommodation if you need to move out for the duration and pay for any damage. Not that they'll do any,' she added quickly.

'What kind of programme is it?' I asked. Not that I was in the least tempted.

'Nothing in particular. I just couldn't resist photographing your house. I know I could sell them this place. No, I'm really out to find a large Georgian villa. Bath seemed the obvious place to come to. For a drama set at the turn of the century.'

'Any luck so far?'

'No.'

Then I remembered Starfall House and mentioned it to her. Then I remembered Mr Dufossee's illness. I doubted *he* wanted a film crew crawling all over his place. I added that I didn't think Starfall House was such a good idea after all, told her to be extra discreet. She promised.

Tim's eventual arrival at Mill House was the starting signal. Annis threw some red mullet on the grill, I cracked open near-frozen bottles of Stella and we were under way. Gill made to leave but we insisted she stay, at least for the food. Tim settled his broad back into a wicker chair next to Gill and gave us all the rundown on the Fishers job without mentioning any names. Tim is nothing if not discreet.

He installed a pinhole camera and microphone in the office and concealed the recorder in the basement, where Fishers could check whenever his partner was out. He had attacked the computer and found several files protected with encryption as well as passwords. Fishers didn't want Tim to spend all night trying to decrypt the files. The mere fact that they were this heavily protected seemed to confirm Austin's guilt for him. Fishers decided the camera would yield enough evidence. The old Centurion safe didn't hold out long but had no secrets to reveal.

'You're a safe cracker as well?' Gill's admiration for Tim's skills went up another notch. 'Where did you learn to do that sort of thing?'

Tim waved her question away with a fresh bottle of Stella. 'All part of the package.'

To this day I have no idea where Tim acquired his expertise in opening locks of all kind. Nor did I ever ask him how he can afford to drive a brand new Audi TT on the money he earns. And I don't intend to, in case I don't like the answers to my questions. I need Tim and don't want to have to let him go. One thing I do know. Whatever Tim gets up to he's never been caught. Superintendent Needham had all of us checked out and to his lasting surprise none of us had any 'previous'.

'So did we make any money?' I asked.

'Well, I did,' Tim declared. 'I sold him my own equipment. Wanted some new stuff anyway. Then there's time, of course.'

'Don't forget to fill in a time sheet then, I don't want another guesstimate.' Tim is even worse with paperwork than I am.

Annis now gave a quick account of her Turner-watching. He'd walked down Milsom Street, Burton Street and Union Street, bought his lunch at the sandwich shop by the abbey and sauntered on to Pulteney Bridge, down the

30

steps to the weir. There he consumed his sandwich sitting on the parched patch of grass below the café and made a call on his mobile which lasted half an hour. He smiled and laughed a lot. A social call. Then he went back to his office. *Nada*, in other words. Depending on who he was calling of course. Gill seemed fascinated by these workaday accounts.

Light was rapidly failing when I walked Gill to her car. We stood for a moment by the channel which gave off a cool, fresh scent that overlaid the darker smells of permanently wet wood and stone.

'I'm not sure I could live with the noise of your mill stream,' she said.

'Where in Bath are you staying?'

'At a B&B on the Upper Bristol Road.'

'I couldn't live with the noise of that.' It's a main thoroughfare with buses, lorries and whathaveyou bombing along.

'Mm. Point taken. If I'd known I'd have chosen somewhere else. But believe it or not, it's my first time in Bath.'

'Staying much longer?'

'A while.'

'Want to meet up again before you leave?' A question I hadn't planned to ask. Came out of nowhere. Impossible now to gauge her reaction in the dark. I concentrated on where the grey of her eyes shimmered indistinctly. She took her time.

'All right, let's.'

'Saturday lunch? At one? The Bathtub in Grove Street. Do you know it?'

'I'm a location finder, remember?'

She beeped her horn as she drove up the lane.

There are certain summer mornings that are just so. Mornings that seem to say, hey, I started it off perfectly, now the

31

rest is up to you. There are mornings that are so pristine it makes you afraid you might sully them with some clumsiness. A careless word. A less than graceful movement. There are mornings that later, when the nightmares arrive, when your life is irreversibly changed by the evil of the day, you wish you could simply crawl back to. And stay there forever. Hidden. Safe. Sane.

The sun licked languidly at the dew in the meadow when I wandered across to the barn with my first mug of coffee and Simon's camera. The birds were chiding in the trees behind the studio. The woodpecker was working, often heard, yet never seen. I flung open the broad double door and measured my canvases, propped the right sizes against the outside wall, away from direct sunlight. There were more than enough. I photographed them carefully and delivered the camera into Simon's eager hands in Bath.

Now I could devote some quality time to the missing Dufossee paintings. Virginia regretted she was too busy to meet me at Starfall House but would arrange for someone to be there and give me all the assistance – and presumably instant coffee – I'd require.

The sun was burning holes through the haze by the time I arrived at Starfall House. A silver Mercedes and a green BMW had got there before me. The man who greeted me on the doorstep might have been waiting behind the door for my arrival, so instant was his response to the bell.

'Mr Honeysett? Leonard Dufossee. My sister asked me to give you all the help you might need. Come inside.' I'd intended to.

He led me to the large drawing room with the baby grand and the empty spaces on the wall and flopped down on a sofa. His hair was short and wiry and black. His right eye was also black. 'A crate of wine caught me out, tumbled straight in my face,' he pre-empted my question. 'I run a mail order drinks business,' he added.

His irises were of the same intense blue as his sister's,

32

making me change my mind about the coloured contacts I had suspected her of wearing. The only other similarity I could find was the rate at which he smoked. Still only in his early thirties, I guessed, he had managed to grow a considerable paunch, suggesting that he might be ordering food in while mailing drinks out. The ashtray on the table was half full, the whole room reeked of the stuff. Leonard seemed far less sure of himself, had none of his sister's commanding air.

'Is there any news yet?'

I shook my head. 'I didn't expect there to be. Let's treat this as day one. I've put out a few feelers but as I told your sister the chances of clearing this up without the help of the police are slim. That doesn't mean I'm not going to give it my full attention. I'll start by photographing the place and lifting fingerprints.'

'Fingerprints? Surely burglars don't leave fingerprints any more.'

Leonard had a point of course. No halfway decent burglar would work without gloves. Only junkies do. And this had nothing to do with someone getting money for gear. The fingerprint lifting was more an insurance against the wrath of Superintendent Needham when he eventually found out that his forensic evidence had been trampled over by the time he and his boys got there. An empty gesture perhaps, but it would make me feel better about our inevitable run-in.

'There's always a small chance. Not so long ago a burglar was convicted by an ear print he had left on a window, where he'd listened to make sure the victim was out. So you never can tell.' I unpacked the equipment from my bag and started on the wall next to the empty square by the fireplace. 'Did you agree with your sister it was better to keep the police out for a while?' I asked while I worked.

Leonard cleared his throat. 'Mm, yes. It's better this way. Dad really isn't well. Though it does make me nervous, too. I grew up with these paintings. I'm very fond of them, especially the Spencer Gores – the nude in the garden and the one in the studio interior. Spent hours dreaming of girls in front of those canvases. But then I have to admit I can't actually remember when I last looked at them. You know, really looked? I regret that now.'

Leonard showed me where he thought the burglars had entered the house. A narrow window, originally a coal chute, in a cellar room had been forced. 'The connecting door to the hall should have been locked but it looks like it was left open by mistake. The alarm must have gone off when that door was opened, that's how it's set up. Then they disabled the alarm at the control box by the door.'

If the burglars already knew where the box was the alarm probably rang for no more than ten seconds. It had no relay to a police station, so once it fell silent they had all the time in the world. Upstairs, after I finished taking prints, I paid leisurely homage to the Pissarro – a village almost obscured by the russet foliage of the trees in the foreground. Pissarro could do trees all right. I could smell them. Leonard hovered nearby, not interrupting. Probably not wondering whether he was paying for the time I spent staring. I was sure his sister would have.

All the paintings were screwed into place with mirror plates, not wired into the wall or individually alarmed as they should have been. No smart alarms, no smart water. I could not imagine any insurance company being happy with these arrangements. Maybe ten, fifteen years ago but not today.

'The paintings are insured, naturally?' I asked.

'They are, but that's hardly the point, is it? It's not the money. At least not for me,' Leonard said, looking for a place to put out his cigarette and not finding one.

'Who has a key to the house?'

'Only my father, my sister and myself. And Mrs Ibbs, the housekeeper. She's away visiting relatives.'

'Does Mrs Ibbs live in?'

'No, in the village. She's a widow,' he added for some reason.

'Do you know when she'll be back? I'll have to talk to her.'

Leonard didn't know when she'd return but furnished me with her address and phone number in Compton Dando.

'The gardeners? Don't they have a key?'

'No need to, there is a shed with all the gear in it.'

'Do you trust Mrs Ibbs?'

Leonard seemed to find the question vaguely amusing. Yes he did trust Mrs Ibbs, she'd been looking after Starfall House and Mr Dufossee senior for years.

I thanked Leonard for his help and promised to keep his sister informed. He handed me his business card, asking me to ring him as soon as I had news. Perhaps Leonard and Virginia didn't communicate well. I declined to stay for a coffee. Starfall House had provided me with enough of a metaphorical headache, so I felt no need to add a real one.

My perfect morning was a little tarnished now but there was enough of it left in the hedges and fields around Compton Dando. Ever aware of the possibility of a tractor blocking the next bend I drove carefully through the narrow lanes, though I didn't really feel like it. Once I reached the A39 I put my foot down. The DS surged forward eagerly, oblivious to its impending MOT ordeal. The air blast through the open windows made no impact on the bad smell I had picked up at Starfall House. The whole thing stank, as they say. I just didn't quite know what of yet. I had to talk this over with Annis and give Tim some work to do as well, and then I'd see what I was left with. Not a straightforward burglary, of that I was certain. A window had been broken, sure enough, and it was certainly large enough to admit a person. But the dust on the frame was ancient. Nobody had squeezed their body through there. The window had been broken to make it look like a burglary. A burglary by someone without a key. An insurance scam? There was no way the Dufossees could collect insurance money without the police being involved, and they would know it. The insurer would never pay up without an official investigation. So what was left? Dufossee senior could not bear to be parted from these particular paintings and had taken them with him to the clinic without telling anyone. The window had nothing to do with it. Remotely possible. What was I saying? Bloody unlikely. But I would still ask Virginia about it. Did she visit him there? I'd find out. Next. One Leonard, two cars, one unstable crate of wine, one black eye. Which car was Leonard's? The Mercedes 500S or the BMW3 series job? Where, while I was lifting fingerprints and indulging my passion for Pissarro, was the other driver? Why weren't we introduced? Was it the gardener's? If so, I would consider retraining. One of the cars had to be Leonard's. Question was, how was I going to identify the owner of the other one without the help of Needham's boys? Well, I'd ask him, of course. Eventually. Did I buy the tumbling-crate-of-wine scenario? Not bloody likely. Next. The trusty Mrs Ibbs had after years of faithful service decided to furnish herself with a decent pension by carrying off some blue chip British art. Distinctly possible. Not knowing how old Mrs Ibbs was I nevertheless had a mental picture of a kindly woman of late middle age, even older perhaps. Maybe it was the mention of her widowhood that put the picture into my mind. I could also see a handbag, an unfashionable one, keys in that handbag. I could picture Mrs Ibbs in a deckchair in her own lovely garden while the keys were at the nearest Mister Minute, being copied. A son, a no-good nephew or similar, who had broken the window to deflect suspicion from his mum/auntie or similar. Mrs Ibbs got more interesting by the minute. Visiting relatives? Probably by now retired to a Costa somewhere. Next. A highly professional burglar who had done his research, knew where all the keys were

36

and when. Borrow keys, quick Mister Minute, return keys, goodbye paintings. Then why break the window? Inviting suspicion to concentrate on an insider job would suit him much better.

The A39 gave way to the A36. I slowed down. My driver's licence had acquired certain endorsements during a recent car chase along the Wells Road. Traffic division had been unimpressed. The precise terms they used to describe me at the hearing were 'Mr Honeysett is a danger to himself and a menace to other road users.' No one seemed to care that I got the guy, with only perfectly reparable damage to himself, his car, and a length of chain-link fence owned by the MOD. Ungrateful, see? But I needed my licence more than speed now.

Where was I? A highly professional burglar who walks straight past several Turners, a Francesco Guardi, a Constable and a Pissarro, their names engraved on brass plaques on each frame, to get to a Spencer Gore? Now in no way am I trying to detract from Mr Gore's artistic achievements but the Pissarro alone was worth more than Starfall House and all that was in it. Including the hand-held bronzes and the lustre ware cluttering up the place. The Guardi was priceless, the Constable a national treasure. The paintings might have been stolen to order but what burglar would not want to line his pockets with a few extra millions by taking out *four more screws*? To sum up, then. I'm looking for a man or woman who has a key, original or copy, who unscrews British art from other people's walls for the love of it. Whose exclusive interest is twentieth-century painting. Who doesn't want to enrich himself beyond measure *and who is cheap enough to take the screws with him when he leaves!* When I finally found this guy I'd have serious words.

I realized I was at the back of the railway station and made an odd decision. Perhaps it was the thought of housekeepers that made me do it. Maybe I was hungry

37

again. Perhaps I wasn't quite ready to present my fumbling thoughts to the crystal-sharp analysis of one Annis Jordan. Perhaps.

I turned the DS around. Drove up Wells Way, to Poet's Corner and turned into Boswell Avenue. Parked the car in the little off-road parking bay of Somerset Lodge. Opened the rickety wooden door that led from there directly into the garden. My perfect morning was fast receding into history, forever out of reach, impossible to reclaim.

I'd expected to find Jenny or one or two of the residents enjoying the sun on the lawn but the garden was deserted. Linda was still doing a good job with her watering can, it seemed. Annis and I are not great gardeners, we only just manage to hang on to my late father's herb garden, the rest is running pretty wild. Here a lot of quiet thought and effort had been expanded, creating an orderly profusion of life. The lawn had been mown in perfect stripes. At Mill House, when the meadow gets out of hand, we borrow a few black-faced sheep from our neighbour in the valley.

The aroma of Jenny's cooking greeted me when I walked in through the open back door. The television was burbling in the sitting room but I walked straight through to the kitchen to locate the source of the smell. It emanated from Jenny's new oven, its digital timer blinking nonsensical numbers at me. I couldn't resist it. I donned oven gloves, prayed I wasn't destroying a soufflé, and took a peek. A quiche, latticed with strips of bright red peppers and flecked with herbs. Feeling protective I prodded the centre with a fork. It would need a good ten minutes yet.

So Jenny was around somewhere. I found her in the sitting room. I briefly threw up on to the carpet. Not much, just a short heaving, a little liquid spilled out, then it stopped. Everything stopped, apart from a curious racing in my lungs and a tingling in my arms.

Jenny had crumpled between the two sofas, in front of the little table that held the residents' phone. Her body looked twisted, with one arm underneath her, but her face was turned towards the ceiling. I was quite sure it was Jenny. I recognized some of her features. Not too many were left. Her face appeared blue under the blood. There was a lot of blood. A great deal of it had soaked into the carpet, into her yellow dress, already drying in the lunchtime heat. There were streaks and splatters of blood on both sofas, turning the green covers black. I knelt next to her, circled her wrist with my fingers, feeling for a pulse. Her hand was cool, twisted back on itself. There was no pulse. One eye, her left eye, seemed to be half open, but I might have been mistaken. That part of her face had taken such a battering I couldn't be sure. But I was sure Jenny was dead.

Only after I'd made the call to the police did I notice that the right knee of my trousers had soaked up some of Jenny's blood when I knelt next to her to take her pulse. In the kitchen I switched off the oven. Poured myself a tumblerful of cheap brandy Jenny kept for cooking. On the mantelpiece in the dining room I found her cigarettes. I lit one, sucked the perfumed smoke deep inside myself and had to sit down immediately as the tingling in my arms returned. Only then did I remember the residents. I took up a smoking and drinking vigil sitting on the floor in the door frame of the sitting room, not wanting anyone to stumble on to her disfigured corpse. There just wasn't enough brandy to go around.

Some of the efficiency of the police machine that descended on Somerset Lodge eventually rubbed off on me. I stopped hitting the brandy and got behind Jenny's desk in her little upstairs office, with a very young uniformed constable sitting on a chair by the door. He tried to look bored but probably wasn't. Detective Superintendent Needham had snapped at him not to let me out of his sight in a way that suggested I might try to squeeze out of the office window as soon as his back was turned. Downstairs,

Scene of Crime Officers, the forensics team, uniformed police, Needham and Detective Inspector Deeks, his preferred sidekick, went through their routines. The pathologist was on his way from the Royal United Hospital. Of the residents only Linda and Anne could be found. Both were in Anne's room, with a WPC, and both were very upset. Anne was hyperactive, keeping up a loud and near hysterical lament, Linda just sat, rocking slightly, humming frightened little tunes and fixing and refixing the tight little ponytail she wears her hair in. The sooner they got some support the better.

I opened Jenny's big phone register and started ringing around. Most of the residents had different social workers, assigned to them in their original 'catchment areas'. I spoke to as many of them as I could get hold of and left messages for the rest. I informed the mental health team. A community psychiatric nurse was on her way.

After that I alerted the charity who ran the house, spoke to as many committee members as I could raise. Gordon Hines, whom I had met many times and who lived locally, promised to be at Somerset Lodge in twenty minutes. The more familiar faces the better.

For the moment I couldn't think of anything more to do for Somerset Lodge. The short spell of activity had done me good, had distracted me, given me a temporary purpose. The instant I put down the receiver my mind went dark again. Must take that quiche out of the oven, I thought ridiculously. Do something, do something. Anything.

'Thank you, Constable.' Needham dismissed the uniformed officer, making much-needed room for him and DI Deeks in the cramped office. Fortunately Deeks is tall and wiry. Needham takes up a lot of space, perhaps that's why he keeps Deeks around. I couldn't think of any other reason. DI Deeks always seemed slow and uninspired to me. Needham had lost weight since I'd last seen him but still showed the effects of too many canteen meals, fry-ups and takeaways around his waist and chins. He had probably lost a little more hair, too. Pushing fifty now, at the height of his power and probably his career. Deeks had taken the spare chair by the door but Needham eschewed the one in front of the desk. He hovered by the window, looked down at the clutter of police vans and cars in the street.

'Why don't you sit down, Mike?' I asked. Once, over a rare drink together, I had offered first-name terms, mainly because he kept calling me Mr Honeypott, and he had accepted. His face suggested he regretted that now. Mike dragged the chair away from the front of the desk and positioned himself at an oblique angle, didn't like the implication of behind-and-in-front-of-desk, letting me know who was boss here now.

'You reek of booze, Chris. Are you pissed?'

Was I? I didn't think so. Should have been after a few tumblers of brandy but decided I wasn't. I shook my head.

'Can we agree on verbal communication? Detective Inspector Deeks is taking notes, make it easy for him, will you?'

'Okay. No, I'm not.'

'Were you pissed when you got here by any chance?'

'I was perfectly sober. I'd just come from a client. I don't drink and drive.'

'I'm glad to hear it, your driving is bad enough when you're sober.' Presumably Mike was referring to my little car chase. Unfairly so, I thought. After all it was the other guy who crashed. 'And you were alone.'

'I already told you.'

'You didn't have the Jordan woman with you and send her home to keep her out of this? Or the Bigwood chap?'

'Nope.'

'Then tell me again what you were doing here, it doesn't seem your style somehow.'

I'd already given him the rundown on the whys and wherefores but when dealing with the police you have to get used to repeating yourself, they simply love hearing the same stories over and over, like children. But unlike children they don't like you to use the same words and expressions. It makes them think you've prepared a script. Which means they'll make you go through it ad infinitum. To be fair, my first account had probably been none too coherent. I told him again.

'Right, I forgot you're one of those blokes-who-cook. I blame television. All pukka food, I presume?' This was Needham at his wittiest. He doesn't get much funnier than that. 'Miss Kickaldy was dead when you found her?'

'Can we agree to call her Jenny? Yes, Jenny was dead.'

'How did you establish that?'

'I felt for her pulse.'

'So you touched the body.'

Deeks was scribbling on his pad, not his little notebook but a large spiral pad.

'Did you move her at all?'

'No, I didn't move her.'

'Are you absolutely sure? You were shocked. Could she have been lying face down and you turned her around? Natural thing to do.'

My thinking apparatus slowly engaged first gear. 'You mean she was moved after she died?'

'Let me ask the questions, we might solve a murder that way, all right? Did you move her?'

'I didn't.'

'You didn't see anybody at all, none of the residents, didn't hear a thing on the stairs?'

'That's what I said.'

'You arrived at one forty. Went to the kitchen, looked in the oven and poked the flan, then walked across to the sitting room and found Miss Kickaldy's body.'

'It's a quiche.'

'For Christ sakes, Chris, I'm not investigating a food crime. You called us straight away?'

'As soon as I was sure there was no pulse.'

'You certain about that? Last time you found a body it took you twelve days to pick up the phone. Uniform got here in six minutes, they inform me you appeared pretty blotto by then. How do you get pissed up in six minutes, Chris, unless you were drunk already when you got here?'

'Half a bottle of brandy.'

Mike used the back of his hand to wipe the perspiration from his forehead. 'Shit, Chris, I shouldn't even be talking to you. I should keep you incommunicado in a cell at Manvers Street until you sober up and work you over when your hangover has blossomed.'

That moment didn't seem too far off. My insides were rumbling and my mouth was full of feathers.

'The television was on when you found her?' This from Deeks.

'No, Deeks. I found Jenny's body, made sure she was properly dead, then thought I'd catch a bit of *Neighbours*. I'm a fan, see?'

Mike was about to give me a hard time about this when there was a tap on the door. Deeks opened it. The young constable stuck his head in.

'Professor Myers has finished,' was his message. All three of us piled out of the room and down the stairs to catch the busy pathologist before he disappeared.

Earnshaw Myers was somewhere in his sixties and white-haired. Needham always asked for Myers, considered him the best. He looked to be retirement age but had looked like this for a very long time, Mike had assured me. Myers was poised by the front door like a plane ready for take-off. I stood behind Deeks, for the moment forgotten. Myers gave no indication that he resented my presence. We had met before.

'Hi, Prof,' Mike started, 'what have you got for us?'

43

Myers lifted bushy eyebrows. 'Heavy object. Not too thick, perhaps a length of piping.' The eyebrows came all the way down now. 'Can't tell yet. Several blows. Delivered with considerable force.'

'Time of death?'

'Sometime before one forty,' came the smug reply.

'Don't play silly buggers, Prof, we know that, that's when Chris says he found her.'

'And I can confirm it. For the rest, read my report.' He relented, but not much, 'Okay, no longer than two hours before that. It probably won't get closer than that anyway but you never know your luck.'

'The bruising on her face. Around the nose. Was she beaten before she was attacked with a heavy object?'

'Could be. My guess is not, though. That's all I'm prepared to say.'

'Has the body been moved after death?' Mike quickly got in.

'Oh, the body has definitely been moved.' This with a firm look over Deeks' shoulder at me. 'And that's all I have for you at this stage. Goodbye, gentlemen.' Myers released his brakes and took off, swinging his aluminium case like a picnic hamper.

So it wasn't me who found the body. Or rather it was, only someone had discovered Jenny before me, had turned the body over to see who it was, which explained her twisted attitude, which I had taken for the result of her falling in an awkward position. It also meant that what had looked like bruising was probably lividity, where the blood had sunk to the lowest level of her body after she had died.

And whoever found her before me had not called the police.

The forensics team in their white paper overalls and galoshes were packing up too. A psychiatric nurse had arrived and called a doctor for Anne, who was feeling worse. Through the open door I spotted Gordon Hines sitting at the long dining table, looking forlorn. He rose as I entered the room and came towards me. 'Oh, Chris!' He awkwardly embraced me, patted my back. Not his usual style but he meant well. 'I only saw her this morning. I can't quite take it in. But to have found Jenny. It must have been ghastly. You look like you're about to keel over, better sit down.' He was right about that. It had been ghastly and still was. And I did need to sit down again.

Needham however was right behind me. 'Hey, we're not finished yet. And who are you?' he confronted Gordon. I introduced them, explained Gordon's function in the running of the house and the charity.

'All right then, let's all sit down together. Constable!' he called over his shoulder while he took a chair at the table. The forever nameless PC was dispatched to find out if forensics were finished with the kitchen, 'and if so put the kettle on, there's a good chap.' DI Deeks had pen and paper ready again for his superior's round two.

'Right, the residents.' Mike snapped his fingers a couple of times. Deeks didn't seem to mind, was probably used to it by now. He read out the names.

'Linda Kelly. Anne Gosling. Both accounted for. Adrian Febry.'

'Still in hospital with a broken shoulder,' I explained.

'He'll be out tomorrow,' Gordon added. 'Jenny told me.'

'That leaves Gavin Backhaus, absent, and Dave Cocksley, absent,' Deeks finished.

Needham set off again. 'So, two of the inmates seem to have absconded from your institution. Or what?'

Both Gordon and I took a deep breath. It was perhaps fortunate Gordon got in there first. His answer showed more restraint than I could have managed.

'First of all this isn't an institution. Somerset Lodge is a residential home where recovering patients learn to reintegrate, pick up life skills. So they can stand on their own feet again and live independent lives. There are no inmates here. Everyone's free to come and go as they please.'

45

'Is that so? Well, that's just changed. Until I know exactly where everybody is, and more to the point *was*, nobody is going anywhere without my permission. Any idea where our two absent friends may be?'

Both Gordon and I shook our heads. 'Supper is usually served at half past six,' I volunteered. 'Most residents show for that, but not necessarily.'

'Too long,' Mike said firmly. 'If one of them is a homicidal schizo I want to have him picked up now. Description.'

I let that pass for the moment, not feeling up to discussing mental health issues much further. At this point fainting seemed a more attractive and more likely alternative. 'I can do better than that,' I said. 'Follow me.' In the hall I showed Mike the picture board Jenny had made, with photographs from our last Christmas party here. There were pictures of all the residents, of me, of Jenny. I took down snapshots of Dave and Adrian, which despite the red eye effect of the flash were good enough for identification.

'Christmas pictures, eh?' Mike said. 'You were here at Christmas.'

'Uh-huh.'

'That's . . . that's rather good of you, Chris. I mean. To give up your Christmas for a bunch of . . .' He frowned, looking for an alternative word.

'Nutters?' I suggested.

Mike fanned himself with the photographs. 'You know what I mean. Can't have been much fun for you. It's an admirable thing to do. Really. Didn't think you were the type.'

I leant against the board for support, feeling distinctly iffy now. 'I didn't give up my Christmas for them, Mike. They were kind enough to have me. If I hadn't spent it here I'd have spent it alone at Mill House.'

Needham digested that for a moment with a pout and a nod. 'Still,' he concluded. 'Most people I know would prefer to spend Christmas alone rather than here. I know

46

I would. And I did, too.' He abruptly walked away to hand the pictures to DI Deeks who ran off with them to have them copied and disseminated.

In the downstairs toilet I splashed my face with water and drank copious amounts of it straight from the tap. That seemed to take care of the feathers in my mouth. Now I needed some aspirin for the rockslide behind my forehead.

Outside I slammed into the young constable, so I held the door open for him.

He nearly smiled. 'That's all right, sir.' It dawned on me that he was there to make sure I didn't flush myself down the toilet. Which I'd have gladly done if at all feasible. Instead I found some codeine tablets in the first aid box in the kitchen and washed them down with some more water, refusing the rather murky results of the constable's attempt at brewing tea.

Needham and Gordon were trying to establish whether anything had been stolen. So far it seemed everything was in place. I dialled Tim's number on my mobile. There was no way I could drive home, perhaps he could give me a lift when he finished at the uni.

'Who said you could make phone calls?' Needham snapped over his shoulder.

'Everyone's allowed one, aren't they?'

Mike just growled something incomprehensible and continued quizzing Gordon, asking for details on all the residents and everyone who worked here. I got through to Tim. He didn't ask for explanations, just said he'd be there. Cheers, Tim.

Everyone who worked here? That's when it hit me. Jenny was a one-woman outfit, with me standing in when she took a rare day off. The rest of the bunch, the support workers and social workers, were a peripatetic lot. So for the moment that left me. It was a sobering thought, unfortunately only in a metaphorical way. The implications had not escaped Gordon either. When Needham finally decided that I could go, not before warning me not to leave Bath without informing him, he cornered me in the hall.

'Quite apart from the tragedy itself, this puts us into a difficult situation. Ultimately the responsibility for looking after the residents lies with the committee members. I'm the only committee member who lives locally, and though I'll do everything I can to look after the place until we can draft in a replacement for Jenny, one thing I don't do at all well is cook . . .'

I can't have looked too enthusiastic because Gordon instantly amended: 'Obviously not for tonight, I'll get them a takeaway, if anyone feels like eating at all. Perhaps not even tomorrow but . . . We'll have to readvertise and after what's just happened it might take us a while to fill the vacancy.'

I wasn't sure I liked the expression, considering Jenny's body had only just been removed in an ambulance.

'And I know you're a busy man . . . it would only be for the cooking, and only until we find someone to take over. Please?' It was only then I noticed that Gordon was barely in a better state than myself. His skin looked ashen, his eyes seemed to be restlessly searching for solutions around the wall behind me. I realized he was looking at the pictures on the board, many of which showed a glimpse of Jenny. I promised to ring him at home when my head cleared enough to make decisions again. We had another awkward hug.

House-to-house enquiries had already started. Needham's boys had a van parked in the street where I could see two uniformed officers doing paperwork. Both looked up when I left the house. Tim's black Audi was parked nearby. He had Annis with him.

'We know. It's awful,' she said. 'Let's just get you home. You get in with Tim, I'll drive the DS.' Our little convoy of appropriately black cars was duly noted by the officers in the van. We made it to the sanctuary of the valley in record time.

Chapter Three

If Detective Superintendent Needham had hoped to lean on me during my blossoming hangover he had missed his chance. Most likely I had slept through it and felt, if not exactly sparkly, then at least reasonably in one piece. Annis had plonked what she considered a hearty breakfast in front of me – croissant, quince jam and one five-minute egg – on her way to the studio. I took it up to the old oak and ate it there. It's the best place from which to survey my domain in the valley. Immediately to my left stood the high barn of the studio. Annis had left the double door wide open to make the most of the tiny breeze that had started this morning. In front of me the meadow dropped away gently, Mill House sitting snugly at the bottom between the row of sagging outbuildings on the left, with the yard in between, and the mill pond, half visible behind the willows and the rise of the upper meadow, on the right. This morning I should have felt sadness, regret and the full pain of the realization that Jenny had been murdered, and brutally so. Instead I felt a curious elation at being alive, at simply sitting and breathing. And with it came a kind of guilt, as though I didn't deserve all this, should work harder, do something – what? – to atone for my unreasonably good fortune.

Shouldn't I be out there, trying to find Jenny's killer? Shouldn't I be tracking the Dufossee canvases before their trail – what trail? – went cold. And Mr Turner's extended lunch hours and after-work ramblings needed explaining.

My easel was still empty, my laurels wilting. Then, too, the shocking state of the outbuildings, especially their roofing, attracted my attention as if for the first time. So did the yard, which had only a few square feet of cobbling left here and there and turned into a quagmire each winter. I bitched about it every year. I promise I promise I promise I'll do it all, just let me sit here for a while longer and marvel at being alive. Not destroyed, crushed, shattered, pulped.

And that's what I did. I sat and breathed, listened to the lazy bickering of the birds in the trees behind, to the buzz of insects in the grasses; found and lost again the song of the mill stream. Until a car came down the lane and parked itself confidently in the entrance to the yard, blocking the exit. Old habits die hard. It was a grey Ford that should by rights have looked like any other grey Ford saloon ever made yet curiously managed to scream *police vehicle* as effectively as a siren. Needham got out, wearing a blinding white shirt and grey tie. He reached back inside the car. If he put on his jacket I'd know I was in trouble. But he just grabbed some papers and his phone, then got lost from view as he crossed the yard. I would let him find me, he knew his way around pretty well by now. After what seemed a very long time he reappeared on the ver-andah from inside the house, shielded his eyes against the sun with his papers and waved me down. He didn't feel like trysting under the big oak, it seemed.

Mike turned down my offer of an ice cold Stella, as I knew he had to. I just enjoy torturing him a bit from time to time but made up for it by equipping him with some juice. He drank it back in one long draught so I refilled it for him.

'You don't know how lucky you are, Chris. Living out here. It's stifling in Bath. Much fresher out here. You're bloody lucky,' he repeated. 'Look at this place.' Mike was sitting in the blue armchair in my sitting room, the chair my father chose to end his life in, and nodded at the beamed ceiling. 'You do sweet FA all day and you live like a king in your castle out here.'

I wasn't really in the mood to set Mike straight. My father was a doctor and had used his medical expertise to make sure he didn't get out of that chair alive. While I swanned around the Mediterranean, pretending to do research for future paintings, he had finally lost the fight against his depression. Deserted by his second wife and uncared-for by his feckless son he took a foolproof combination of drugs. In his suicide note he let me know exactly what he thought of me. He left Mill House to me precisely because I was a callous, uncaring sod who he was convinced would never amount to anything. If I wanted to hang on to Mill House I would have to start putting in an honest day's work, and if I lost the place it would be a fitting and highly visible monument to my failings. In the end, Mill House hadn't quite become the albatross he had hoped it would, though it had changed my life. Mike didn't know any of this, it happened long before he transferred to Bath.

'Did you know my house in Oldfield Park was built as cheap working-class accommodation a hundred-odd years ago? Now it takes all the overtime I can get to pay the bloody mortgage on it.'

I remembered. Mike's messy divorce had crippled his finances for the foreseeable future. Two daughters to provide for too, and his wife kept the children as well as the house, twice the size of his present one, in a leafy street in a suburb of Bristol.

Mike snapped out of it, slapped his thigh with the folder he had brought. I recognized it as one of Jenny's. 'Right, we've been through the house and garden and the neighbourhood. We found no weapon. Much more worrying, there is still no sign of Gavin Backhaus and Dave Cocksley. Tell me about them.'

'I don't know very much about Gavin. He's very shy, became very withdrawn when he was still at school, didn't

51

develop like other kids. Then he had an episode where he was sectioned, at the request of his parents, and spent time at Hill View Psychiatric Unit up at the RUH. Got better, was released home, got worse again. And so on. Everyone thought it was time to try something new. That's how he got to be at Somerset Lodge. He's been there a year.'

'Question: is he capable of killing? Has he ever been violent?'

'Not as far as I know. He's quite sweet really, in a pimply sort of way.'

Mike rolled his eyes and groaned. 'Quite sweet, give me a break. What about the other one?'

'Dave?' There was really no way I could avoid telling him about the knife incident Jenny had mentioned only two days earlier. I had a feeling I already knew how Mike, or any policeman for that matter, would react under these circumstances. And I didn't feel comfortable about it. 'Dave's very different. He's quite a nervy guy, paces up and down all day. He interacts with people but only on his own terms. Doesn't like being challenged on his opinions because he spends all day formulating them in his head, his day's work. If you contradict him he can get arsey about it.'

'Violent?'

'Until now only verbally.'

'Until now. You're bloody nonchalant about this. Oh, I forget, you like partying with these guys.'

By now I really didn't want to tell him about the knife thing but it would look bad later if I hadn't. So I dropped Dave in it. 'There was an incident a few days ago that Jenny mentioned to me on Thursday. Apparently he wandered around the house with a knife one day, you know, holding a knife while he was pacing.'

'What kind of a knife?'

'A chef's knife.'

'Did he threaten anyone with it?'

'No, Jenny thought he was probably not even aware he

was holding it.' Yet she had found it worth warning me about. What else had Jenny said?

'Why the hell didn't you mention this earlier? Look.' He whipped two sheets of paper out of the folder and waved them around in front of me, not as an invitation to read them but as some kind of proof. 'Both these geezers are on all sorts of drugs and also something called Haloperidol. I've been told that's an anti-psychotic drug. These guys are headcases, Chris, they're psychotic, schizophrenics. And they're on the loose!'

'Psychotic does not mean psychopathic, didn't they teach you that at policeman school?' I knew Mike was a lost cause but I had to try.

'That's splitting hairs as far as I'm concerned. Surely anyone psychopathic starts off as a psychotic.' Mike was getting into his stride now. 'Any normal person would have mentioned this knife thing straight away, oh, but not you, Chris. You find your friend brutally murdered but mention nothing about a knife-wielding psycho. What is it with you, Chris, whose side are you on? Can you please make up your mind about that once and for all?'

It was my turn to get huffy. 'You know exactly which side I'm on, Mike, I don't feel I have to prove that to you. But you've just confirmed what I was afraid of. You're jumping to conclusions. Dave and Gavin would not have been referred to Somerset Lodge if they'd been considered dangerous. They're no more dangerous than you or me.'

'Well, we all know *you* can be bloody dangerous.' Mike pointed an accusing finger. He was not happy.

Neither was I. 'Mentally ill people commit murder no more often than the rest of the population, that's a fact, Mike. Dave and Gavin are pretty harmless as long as they take their medication.'

'That's my bloody point! They've stopped taking their medication as far as we know. They've been missing overnight. Neither of them have taken their pills with them, so the longer they're out there the madder they'll get.'

'They're much more likely to harm themselves.'

Mike shot up out of the chair. 'What, are you a sodding psychiatrist now? Where do you get off making pronouncements like that?' He waved the papers about in a wide arc, indicating the size of his frustration. 'All I know is that if they had been locked up in the first place I wouldn't have every officer on my force looking for them now. Those two are top of our list, that should be bloody obvious. Prof Myers says the younger girl, Linda Kelly, may not have been capable, physically, of delivering those blows. I haven't interviewed either of them but it appears Anne Gosling was with Linda in her room, listening to CDs all lunchtime and neither of them saw or heard a thing until the police arrived. I got that much from the psychiatric nurse. That only leaves our two missing psychos or an outsider. Oh, and you of course.' He took a few determined strides out of the room on to the verandah as if to leave, then strode back just as determinedly and planted himself in front of me. I'd remained sitting on my sofa as before. 'One more thing.' He was speaking very quietly now. 'Jenny was your friend, right?'

I nodded.

'Now I know how I would feel. I would want to go after whoever did this. And the Assistant Chief Constable would instantly give the case to someone else because I'd be unable to keep it professional. I want you to stay out of this, Chris. Don't think I'll let you do your own separate investigation into Miss Kickaldy's murder. And don't for one instant think I've forgotten about the little matter of your mislaid gun. If I find out that you're withholding stuff from me, anything, any information at all, out of misguided philosophy or your so-called client confidentiality, I swear I'll send Deeks and a few boys down here and let them rip your mill apart until they find it. So remember, you're in deep shit just as soon as I want you to be.' He wheeled round again and made for the exit.

'What makes you think I haven't long chucked it in the

river?' I called after him. He stopped on the verandah and slowly tuned toward me. He was grinning.

'Because you're a sentimental fool, Honeysett. You love that old gun. Even though it'll probably blow up in your hand one day.'

The gun in question was an old army revolver, a Webley .38, which had once belonged to my uncle and came with the house. Perhaps the fact that the cartridges inside were over fifty years old had dissuaded my father from going down that road when he decided to end his life, yet he had kept the thing remarkably clean and well oiled. Needham knows I've used it and he also knows I don't have a licence for it. So I mislaid it and somehow managed to miss the gun amnesty in 1997. It got me out of trouble a couple of times and as Mike said, I'm very fond of it, even though it kicks like a mule and leaves my ears ringing each time I fire it.

I could hear Mike's car revving away and got another bottle of Stella from the fridge. Annis popped first her head, then the rest of herself around the door jamb.

'Is he gone? What did he want?'

'He asked me about Gavin and Dave. Even though he could get much clearer answers from Gordon Hines. He has the medical details. Gave me a hard time about my gun. Again. And he wants me to sit on my hands and wait for him to find Jenny's murderer. Fat chance. Even threatened to rip the house open to find my gun, which is really all he needs if he wants to shut us down.'

'He's right on that one, Chris. No, listen, listen. I think he secretly likes you but he also resents you. He thinks you've got it too easy. And even though he probably doesn't for one moment believe you killed Jenny you're on the prime suspect list until her killer is found. After all, six out of ten people who report a murder turn out to be responsible for that killing, you know that.'

I did. But how did Annis know that? I widened my eyes at her.

'I read in bed, all right? That okay with you? Anyway,' she said, shovelling coffee beans into the electric grinder, 'you two are in some sort of blokey competition, aren't you? Except that Needham thinks you're winning and you're winning because we bend the rules a little here and there.' She flicked on the noisy grinder with a gleeful grin, nodded away the precise seconds of enervating noise required to produce the Annis-approved fineness of ground Kenyan. 'He doesn't see that we've got rules too, different ones, admittedly. Stringent rules, a code of ethics. And we stick to them.'

'Above all Mike hates the fact that we made those rules for ourselves while his are imposed on him. He only embraces police rules with such fervour so that he doesn't need to feel resentful,' I said, pouring some Stella on to my own resentment.

Annis splashed boiling water into the cafetière. 'If we go after Jenny's killer, and I know you want to, it could jeopardize a conviction. Evidence has to be obtained in the correct way, not the way we usually go about it,' Annis said firmly and pressed the plunger.

She really had been reading in bed. Was she tired of the way we did things at Aqua? I couldn't quite picture Annis in police uniform. 'You think I should sit on my hands, too?'

'What would you do, Chris, if you found Jenny's killer? Be honest.'

'I'd hand him over to the police.'

'And if you knew they couldn't get a conviction because of some procedural mistake, some technicality?'

'I'd kill him.' I hadn't thought about what I was saying, it just came out like that. I'd shoot him. It was the honest answer.

'And I knew that too,' Annis said quietly.

We've always avoided hugging. It's one of the things that helps us to live at Mill House the way we do, one tiny part of the complicated dance we perform around each other, which we invented so that we don't end up in the same bed at night.

She gave me a shove instead. Not very hard but not entirely playful either. While I recovered my balance she emptied my Stella down the sink without comment. 'Now look at this.' She uncrumpled a letter from her back pocket, folded half of it over. 'What do you think? It's from Alison. Came yesterday.'

'Your friend? The Cornish painter?'

'She's not Cornish. But she inherited half a cottage in Cornwall and moved there a year or so after leaving art college. She was in the year above me.'

I read.

. . . even though I've been here quite a while now. Weird things keep happening, which freaks me out. I like living by myself, but the other day I thought I was being followed. Now I constantly feel watched. I get spooked sometimes, even though Mousehole is only a few minutes' drive away. Perhaps it's the solitude getting to me. I can't even think of giving up the cottage, I worked so hard to afford it, you have no idea how hard. It was kind of you to invite me up only I can't really get away right now. Of course you're always welcome to stay for a while. I know you're busy though, with painting and Aqua . . .

I handed the letter back. 'She wants you to come and hold her hand for a bit but doesn't know how to ask.'

'My feeling exactly. So we'll go. Get you away from here. If you feel as shit as you look then you deserve a couple of days off,' she said firmly.

'I've got the Dufossee thing to take care of.'

'Let Tim have a shot.'

'And Mr Turner.'

'Ditto. You'll really enjoy it, I guarantee. All that seafood, and her cottage is in a stunning location.'

Location. 'Shit. Location finder! I'm supposed to be meeting Gill for lunch. In about ten minutes.'

'Where?'

'The Bathtub.'

'Then you'd better get a move on.'

I got a move on. Weaving through side streets, then cutting across to the toll bridge, through Bathampton, choked with escapees from the city, down the Warminster Road. Why didn't I ring to say I was going to be a little late? Traffic was as insane as ever. I dumped the DS behind the Holburne Museum and legged it the rest of the way down Great Pulteney Street. I was still hideously late when I puffed into the little restaurant in Grove Street.

I've always liked the Bathtub, not just for its extremely edible food but also for the tucked-out-of-the-way atmosphere it manages to maintain, even though its premises are right in the centre of town. I often meet clients here, it's a good place to talk.

It only took one look to see that Gill wasn't there. 'That's unlike you, Chris,' said Clive, who owns the place, when I made imploring gestures at him. 'The lady regretted she had to go. But all is not lost, she left you this.' He handed me a Fuji print envelope and a folded note. Gill had another appointment too close to our lunch meeting and was leaving Bath later today. But she thought I might like to have prints of the pictures she took at Mill House. I felt surprisingly relieved. Whatever had triggered the impulsive lunch invitation to Gill had been expunged by Jenny's murder. Right now I was grateful that I didn't have to put a brave face on things or explain what had happened. Fortunately, with Clive I never had to explain.

'You look like shit, Chris,' he said delicately as he shoved a Stella at me across the tiny bar. 'Are you eating or can I give your table away? We're busy, in case you hadn't noticed.'

Might as well. 'Do you still do those scallops in garlic butter?'

'Anything for the Great Detective.'

Annis had been right, I wasn't firing on all cylinders and

needed to get away from Bath. Just thinking about what to do next seemed difficult. Physically doing what needed to be done seemed even harder. In my attic office at Mill House I found myself staring at the mess on the desk, at the silent phone, the pristine grey and blue of the computer screen, and felt dull and stupid. As soon as I reached for the receiver or stretched my hands towards the keyboard I was assailed by doubts. Was this the right thing to do? What if I did something wrong? Was I forgetting something important, did I remember things right, the conversations I had had, the conclusions I had drawn? Had I drawn conclusions?

Each time I stirred into action the same image flashed into my mind. Jenny, her twisted shape on the carpet, her face destroyed by many vicious blows, her hair caked with blood. The metallic smell of blood invaded my nostrils. My hands had developed a fine tremor, hovering over objects before grasping them. My mind appeared to be doing the same, fluttering, hovering, reluctant to grasp on to concrete thoughts.

Concentrate. I dialled the number for Mrs Ibbs, Starfall's holidaying housekeeper, was relieved when there was no answer. *Get a grip.* E-mails came easier. I mailed Tim and brought him up-to-date with the Turner case, such as it was; told him to keep an eye on the man without expanding too much energy on it and instructed him to place a half-page advertisement in the *Antiques Trade Gazette* in the Stolen Section, then faxed him the details and photographs. *Keep it together.* Found the website and put the stolen Dufossee paintings on the Art Loss Register, which every reputable dealer would consult if he was offered paintings with a less than perfect provenance and documentation. This was a pretty public way of going about it but I was banking on Mr Dufossee senior being too busy meditating to read the *Antiques Gazette* or surf the net.

Annis had packed my bags as well as her own and shoved me downstairs and into the driver's seat of the DS.

She loves her thirty-year-old Land Rover but quite apart from the fact that it's permanently stuck in four-wheel-drive my equally ancient Citroën beats it at long distance comfort without even trying. The CD player I had installed might offend classic car purists but I was glad for the supply of soothing Fugazi tracks – I find Fugazi soothing, okay? – that Annis craftily fed into it.

No amount of guitar play however could gloss over the fact that I was in trouble. Driving suddenly scared me. Witless. As soon as I hit the M5 I felt we were doomed. While I crawled along at 50 mph huge container lorries, loath to shift through endless gears to accommodate my geriatric style, loomed improbably large in my mirrors. Everything seemed to happen at a phenomenally threatening pace, everything felt dangerous. Sweat erupted from every pore of my body, trickled down my spine, stung in my eyes. My hands were in danger of slipping on the wheel. I wound down the window. The roar of air rushing in only helped to emphasize the speed with which I was hurtling towards sure destruction, inevitable doom. My stomach began to revolt, my bowels were not far behind.

'Pull over. Hard shoulder. Pull over when the coach has passed us,' Annis said, laying a rare hand on my buzzing arm. A National Express coach slammed past, I winced in the turbulence of its bulk. When I checked the speedometer I found the indicator fretting at 40. It took me another shaky mile or so before I unfroze enough to make the manoeuvre and brake ineptly on the hard shoulder, near an orange emergency phone. I wanted to run to it and call for help, any kind of help. Someone help me.

'Well done, Chris.' Annis didn't ask, she told. 'Get in the back seat and lie down. I'll get you there. Just have a lie-down while I drive.'

It's a left-hand drive so while Annis slipped behind the wheel I managed to squeeze out on the near side and fumbled into the back.

'Close your eyes, Honeysett. We're off on a holiday. Can I change the music?'

'Help yourself.' The first thing that came up on the radio was Kate Bush, *The Red Shoes*. Perfect. By now I was wearing them.

I woke up as abruptly as I must have fallen asleep, surfaced from apparently dreamless oblivion into a moment of disorientation and vague dread.

'Welcome back,' Annis said as I pulled myself into a sitting position. 'That was Tredannik.'

'What was?'

'The village we just went through.'

'So we're nearly there?'

'Mm-hm. You were out for hours. How are things inside Chris Honeysett?'

'Fine.' And I meant it. I felt safe and cosy here on the back seat, with Annis competently swinging the DS between the hedgerows on the steadily rising narrow lane. I wound down the rear window and stuck my nose out to smell the Cornish summer. It smelled entirely different from the valley, clearer, sharper, somehow. 'I'm sorry I lost it back there. Everything seemed impossible suddenly. Can't explain it.'

'No need to apologize, though you did scare the hell out of me. I think that might have been your brain telling you to give it a rest after the shock you had. And that's what we're here for. The Resting of Honeysett. Right, get ready for the view, coming up . . . now.'

As we reached a broken gate at a narrow turn-off and the lane and hedgerows fell away to the left the view opened out ahead and to the right. The track – it wasn't much more than that – dipped briefly, then rose again in a gentle curve up to a large but squat cottage, solitary and exposed on the cliff top. From the lane it had been utterly invisible.

I stretched luxuriously and shrugged off the journey in the few seconds it took to fill my lungs with the ozone-laced air. A ragged cluster of rocks a quarter of a mile out to sea was the only real feature in the expanse of ultramarine and silver below. Here the coast turned sharply back on itself to either side so that, apart from a similarly barren point far away to the south on my right, I could entertain the notion of riding in the prow of an enormous and very solid ship.

But it was far from shipshape. Back in the valley we like to pretend that the slight air of dilapidation, mainly in the outbuildings, gives Mill House a certain out-of-time charm that adds to its hideaway character. This place was a shambles. Annis had parked the DS on the grass, since the only clear space near the house which wasn't cluttered by some kind of junk was occupied by a battered off-white VW Beetle, which clearly aspired to junk status itself. The front of the house, sensibly facing out of the wind, could only be approached through a minefield of wooden crates, broken white goods and half-used building materials. Some of the roof-slates had slipped or were missing. Annis's head-scratching and disappearing eyebrows meant this wasn't what she had expected either. She led me around the back where a beautifully old-fashioned conservatory in the twilight years of its existence served as a painting studio, surrounded by the type of painting detritus I recognized and approved of: buckets, cans and jars, discarded canvases weighed down with rocks, broken stretchers and frames.

Alison caught sight of movement in the corner of her eyes, jumped clear of her easel and through the open door leading back into the house. As soon as she recognized Annis she re-emerged, making apologetic gestures. Come in, come in.

'You gave me such a fright, I didn't hear your car or anything.' Alison wiped her hands on her spattered painting shirt, then the legs of her jeans, and awkwardly pushed her dark, tired hair off her face. Her welcoming smile did nothing to eradicate the expression of sheer terror I had seen on her face when at first she fled from us into the house. She gave Annis a prolonged hug while I discreetly checked out the painting on the easel. A sombre Cornish landscape, a storm brewing on the horizon. Very assured, extremely competent. Before I could work out what bugged me about it my attention was claimed by the how-do-you-dos.

Introductions over, Alison ushered us nervously inside, through a crowded and surprisingly dark sitting room into which drawings, paintings and art materials had spilled, along a short corridor with worn floor tiles and into the large stone-flagged kitchen. It was an evil-smelling extension of the junkyard in the front. Alison's narrow frame appeared to be fluttering, along with her voice, while she filled the whistling-kettle at the overcrowded sink. She flustered about for matches, found only spent ones. I produced my lighter and took the kettle from her. There was no telling what would light first, the lazily hissing gas or the encrustation of fat on the cooker.

'Oh God, I know what you must be thinking, I really meant to clear all this up before you arrived.' She waved a tremulous hand at the mouldy dishes, festering bin, scrap-littered surfaces and the astonishing amount of empty wine and beer bottles in every corner. Her voice shook. 'I'm, I've . . . been struggling a bit.'

The place gave the impression that she had stopped struggling quite a while ago. I got the gas to light without setting fire to anything else. 'Don't worry, between the three of us we'll have this kitchen sorted in no time at all,' I said with as much cheer in my voice as I could muster.

The chaos was sharply familiar, a fair reproduction of the kitchen my father left behind when he killed himself. Although I was in Istanbul when a British Embassy official informed me of what had happened I managed to arrive at Mill House before anyone had thought of tackling the mess in the house. The smell of furry dishes, month-old garbage and stagnant dishwater I rediscovered in Alison's kitchen was one I have always equated with desperation, with losing the fight. Yet the fact that she was still painting surely meant not all was lost. What had Needham said about playing at being a sodding psychiatrist?

The kitchen eventually yielded three damp-stained tea-bags and after I'd been warned against opening the fridge we had black tea, Turkish style in water glasses, on the wind-snatched patch of grass in front of the conservatory. In the protective half-circle of Annis's arm around her bony shoulder, Alison finally stopped apologizing.

'I don't sleep properly. And ever since that *bastard* forced me off the road I've been stuck here, more or less. I mean I can walk into Tredannik but there's nothing there really, even the sodding post office has shut down.'

'Someone forced you off the road? How? When?' My own driving terror came buzzing back.

'A few days ago. Monday? My new Peugeot 106, too, practically written off. I'm lucky I didn't go over the cliff, it was *that* close.'

'You think it was deliberate? What did the police have to say?'

Annis shot me a don't-interrogate-her glance but Alison didn't seem to mind.

'Either he was pissed as a fart and didn't want to lose his licence or he actually tried to run me over that cliff. Oh, what am I saying, I'm getting so paranoid. It was pitch dark, after midnight. Came out of nowhere, I swear. Suddenly I had nothing but dazzle in my mirrors and then, wham! Some kind of delivery van, big thing. I didn't report it until well into the next day because I was way over the limit myself.' She pulled a pained face. 'Literally drinking and driving, with a bottle of Merlot between my legs. I know, I know, it was stupid and irresponsible but it wouldn't have made any difference.'

'Were you hurt?' I asked, trying to hide my useless disapproval behind concern.

Lifting a handful of lank hair she revealed a scabbed scar

high on her temple. 'I banged my head on the door, got winded and threw up all over the dashboard but that was it. Then I was too scared to move for ages. I could hear the sodding sea below me. When I got back to the car the next day I really freaked, it was so close to the edge. The towtruck people were shit-scared of going near it, said it might go any second.'

'Are you in trouble, sweetie?' Annis managed to ask the obvious question that had hovered over us ever since we arrived.

Alison responded by shrugging off the protective arm and got up, smiling a bright forced smile. 'I'm all right now *you're* here. But there's nothing to eat in the house, so we'd better go out somewhere for our tea. There's the Loaves and Fishes in Mousehole, that's pretty good.' She gave me a conspiratorial look. 'Annis told me you need regular injections of fish or you get grouchy.'

Somehow the thought of getting back into the car and of later returning from a restaurant meal to the chaos of the cottage felt like a recipe for gloom. 'I've a better idea. You two go off and go shopping while I blitz the kitchen and we'll have supper here.'

The two of them looked at each other, then at me, said 'Okay' in unison and legged it out of there.

'What have I done?' I asked the kitchen, once the sound of the car engine had faded. What I really needed to clear this properly was a stick of dynamite and a shovel but I made do with what I could find.

The amount of empties was truly staggering – all of it red, mostly French and expensive. I approved. The beer bottles were all large, Czech and, as far as pilsener goes, pretty posh too. Alison was going down with a certain amount of style. I stacked the lot of them in crates and boxes in the junkyard at the front of the house. In the absence of bin liners her large and varied collection of carrier bags had to do. I dived in, scooped, stuffed, shoved

65

and scraped. The appliances, though covered with historical layers of gunge, were fairly new, hence the old white goods in the junkyard. The fridge was the saddest place I had visited in a while, and that included a council estate north of Bristol. Only a field archaeologist could have done it full justice. I decided to junk the lot: milk turned to a solid piece of cheese, cheese turned to a solid piece of mould, open tins of botulism and blobs of unknown origin and purpose. Alison appeared to have taken the principle of self-cleaning oven quite literally, too. I soaked, chiselled, scoured and scrubbed, then washed, wiped and Window-leened. At the end I poured a vintage bottle of bleach over the last pockets of resistance, swept and mopped the floor and retreated from the ensuing fumes into the sitting room. During my cleaning blitz I had removed the remnants of meals and mouldy piles of teabags from the ashtrays here and filled several bags with garbage. Now I just cleared a space among the books on the sofa and folded myself wearily into one corner, convinced that I had done my good deed for the day.

What exactly was happening here? It seemed obvious that Alison was in some kind of trouble. But was it anything more than a bit of paranoia brought on by a lonely and highly alcoholic lifestyle? I hoped that in my absence Alison would open up to Annis and feared that, apart from being a damn good cleaner, I was probably surplus to requirements here.

The sound of the sea, some eighty feet below, was faint but ever present. The late afternoon light slanting through the conservatory door created sharp shadows inside the room. Suddenly the shadows faded, the room fell into gloomy dusk. I turned, unsure of what had created the sudden shift in the light. A solid bank of dark cloud was pushing in from the sea, the weather was turning, gardeners were rejoicing. Abruptly the wind picked up. I unfolded myself from the sofa and tried the glass door to the conservatory. It was locked and there was no key. That meant Alison locked it before she went off with Annis, which for a moment made me scratch my head but then it might just have been part of her routine when leaving the house. Peering around the corner I could see that all the paintings were turned to the wall except for the one on show on top of the easel. The darkness of the picture seemed to echo the rainstorm that relentlessly approached outside. At first glance I had assumed it was a painting Alison was just finishing but looking at it again I realized what had first bugged me about it. The fresh-looking paint on her palette, chrome yellow, emerald green and a range of reds, didn't tally with the colours of the landscape painting on the easel. She had to be working on something far sunnier than this. So she was looking at an older painting, so what? Perhaps her work wasn't going too well and the painting, which was certainly accomplished, represented a kind of touchstone for her. With satisfaction I noted that Alison, like myself, preferred an old-fashioned type of oil paint. Some of the paints I saw lying around in tubes or ranged about the easel in glass jars were of the finest handmade quality. I was just telling myself to give the detective's brain a rest from idle speculation when Annis and Alison tumbled through the front door, laden with shopping. Alison made the appropriate noises of appreciation for my handiwork in the kitchen.

'Okay, Chris, you can stay,' she said, and that out of the way we all fell on the shopping bags, and got the oven and kettle going. Alison was in better spirits, suggesting countless places we just had to visit together, walks we simply couldn't miss. Despite the darkening skies outside it felt like a new beginning in here and by the time I whipped the sea bream out of the oven and the cork had popped on the Sancerre my brain was pleasantly idling in neutral.

I woke parched from desert dreams in my cramped camp on the sofa – I had drawn a very short straw when beds were raffled – and took my time unfolding brain and body. The wind was still tearing at the house but judging by the weak moonlight in the windows the storm clouds had passed. The storm had lasted a few wild hours. In the end we had toasted each thunderclap at the kitchen table until the last bottle was finished.

Half past three. Dead of night. Still a little unsteady from my fair share of five bottles of wine I padded over the pleasantly cool floor to the kitchen sink and gulped down a couple of tumblerfuls of water. I filled another one to take back to camp and turned my back on the window over the sink. A movement in the corner of my eye made me wheel around and spill water over my bare feet. Nothing. It's nothing. Just moonshadows. Then why did my spine continue to tingle and my heart continue to pound? I topped up the glass from the tap and carefully peered out into the small stretch of cliff-top meadow I could make out by the side of the house. Still nothing. So get a grip. Annoyed with myself for being so jumpy I padded back towards my lair and froze by the door. Something. A small nasty tearing sound I couldn't at first place came from the conservatory. A solid black shadow not made from clouds crouched beyond the outside door. Someone. Then I recognized the tearing sound. Glass cutter. Whoever was out there would very soon be inside the studio and not long after that in the house, if that was where they wanted to be. But the locked connecting door, though entirely made from glass, would buy me time. I gulped the water, left the tumbler on the floor, tiptoed back through the hall and squeezed quietly out of the front door. The night air was cool and I was suddenly wide awake. Still drunk but wide awake. A slender moon rode high through scudding clouds on my left so I turned right, just as our visitor had done when he slipped past the kitchen window a moment ago. Carefully I threaded through the debris of the yard, armed myself in passing with a piece of copper piping. It wasn't much of a weapon but went some way towards compensating for the fact that I didn't have my gun to hand. In this situation I felt naked without it. The fact that I wasn't wearing any clothes at all didn't help much either. As I shivered closer to the seaward corner of the house I was struck by my lack of planning. Was I really attempting to apprehend a burglar in the nude, armed with a one-foot piece of copper piping? For a moment I was tempted to return inside, hit the lights and simply scare him off but by that time my dark visitor might already have got whatever he came for. I took a deep breath and peered around the corner. The dark shape moved about inside the studio, directing the torch beam here and there as he moved from painting to painting. Another art thief. Didn't anyone pay for paintings any more? I crouched low and crept closer. My mind still refused to furnish me with even a half-decent plan of action but somehow I intended to teach the man the current market value of Cornish painting.

Picking my way through the clutter along the glass front was slow work, too slow. The dark figure had completed his inspection along one wall and moved to the next batch just as I reached the open half of the double door. As he became aware of me he wheeled around and stopped dead, but just for a split second. Then he pointed the torch straight at my face. Just before the dazzle hit my eyes I could make out the bright shimmer in the eye holes of his balaclava. As I straightened up his boot found my face. I toppled back into a nest of glass jars, several of which shattered under my back. My assailant used the few seconds it took me to struggle up out of the shards of broken glass to put about twenty feet between us. I could taste blood in my mouth and my teeth felt a bit on the shaky side. Anger propelled me forwards. I lifted the copper pipe and advanced until his torch flicked on again. This time he pointed it not at me but at his own left hand. He was far more sensibly armed than myself, which was what he was showing me. His left hand held a shiny machete. He wasn't even threatening me with it, merely showing it to

69

me, holding it vertically with his outstretched arm, like an archaic warning. Then the beam flicked off. He turned his back on me and walked away, quickly but confidently, just as the lights snapped on inside the house and footsteps rattled on the stairs.

Seconds later, while I felt for loose teeth with one hand and gingerly probed my behind for splinters with the other, Annis came flying around the corner swinging a piece of two-by-one which she dropped when she recognized my rattling frame. I was shivering uncontrollably by now.

'What's up? Sleepwalking?' she wanted to know.

'Scaring off a burglar. Only he wasn't that scared.'

'Naked men are rarely scary. You're certainly not,' she said. Unkindly, I thought. 'Let's get you inside and have a look at you.'

Annis had managed to jump into jeans and a T-shirt at least and Alison, who was waiting for us inside in a classic rolling-pin-at-the-ready pose, had managed a dark blue bathrobe. Naked and dribbling blood from each end I felt more than a bit foolish. At least I got a little more sympathy once the extent of the damage was revealed in the light. What it really amounted to was a bleeding nose and a split lip and eyebrow. The more painful item was my lacerated backside. Lying on the sofa with my bum in the air I gave an account of events while Annis dabbed away with cotton wool and iodine and Alison sucked air through her teeth in empathy with my behind.

'He went through your paintings,' I informed her, 'but as far as I can tell he left empty-handed.'

Alison seemed a little shaken by the event but curiously unconcerned about her paintings. She didn't make any move to check out her studio to see whether or not I was right. 'Did you see his face?' was what she wanted to know.

'Balaclava. Quite the commando raider, in fact. Have you called the police yet?'

'What's the point?' Alison shrugged impatiently. 'Nothing nicked, no evidence except a hole in the glass and no description? All I get is another lecture by the local plod about security and how I'm asking for it living alone in an isolated spot like this. Had it before, don't need it again.'

'You had a break-in before?'

'No. Just prowlers. Someone trying the doors. Falling over stuff in the yard. I called the police a couple of times. They took twenty minutes to get here and did sod all. Coffee, anyone?'

No wonder she felt happier with us around.

'Did she give you a clue what all this might be about?' I asked Annis while Alison was busy in the kitchen.

'No, not a word. I tried to get at least a hint but she said it was probably nothing. Changed the subject pronto each time. She's scared though. I think we should stay a while, see if we can't sort it out somehow. She might open up eventually.'

'Did she talk about her work at all? That landscape on the easel . . .'

'That's an old one, I've seen it before. No, that's the other odd thing. Normally she'd drag out every canvas and ask my opinion, talk about it incessantly, but she was positively secretive about her work today. First I thought she was a bit overawed at having you here, you're quite a name now, you know? But it's not that. She said she hadn't done anything for a while yet I can smell she's been painting.'

'There's freshly used paint on her palette, lots of used brushes in that turps jar. She's been painting all right. But what? And our visitor was definitely after paintings only he didn't seem to find what he was looking for. Quite ferociously armed as well.'

'He was armed?'

I hadn't mentioned this before so as not to alarm Alison any further. 'Machete.'

'Did he . . .?'

'No, he just showed it to me, as in "Don't follow me, mate." I took the hint.'

'I'm glad. But this is serious, Chris. Your average burglar doesn't come armed with long knives unless he expects resistance or wants to ask pertinent questions about the whereabouts of the family silver. This wasn't a spontaneous visit. He was after something specific. He must have seen your car but he didn't want to postpone his break-in. Pretty determined, if you ask me.'

'Ask you what?' Alison returned with a tray of coffees.

I decided to try the blunt approach. 'What are they after, Alison? Your prowlers and burglars. I'm sure you know. Only we can't help you if you don't tell us. And we can't stay here forever.'

Alison set down the tray harder than she had intended, rocking the mugs. 'They're after paintings, I guess.' She shrugged. 'Only this one doesn't seem to like my work. I'm not going to have coffee after all, I think I'll try and get some more sleep instead. Laters.'

So much for the blunt approach.

When I woke again it was to the electronic warbling of the telephone. It took me a while to prise my eyes open and become aware of Alison, her arms folded in front of her, staring at the phone with dread in her eyes, letting it ring and ring.

'You want me to answer that?' I offered, as much to save my hung-over head as from any desire to be helpful.

'Would you? I don't want to talk to anyone.'

I hobbled across with my duvet around me and picked up the receiver, watched by Alison with a worried frown.

'About time. That you, Honeysett?' Detective Superintendent Needham sounded as rough as I felt. I mouthed 'It's for me' to Alison who smiled her relief.

'We found Dave,' Needham bellowed, managing to make it sound like 'You are surrounded.' 'Now get your scrawny arse back to Bath and be quick about it. If you're not here in three hours I'll issue a warrant for your arrest. And I might still do it then. That clear?'

'Engraved on my mind. Where did you find Dave?'

'In the canal,' said Needham and slammed the phone down.

I suddenly felt very tired again. Jenny dead, now Dave. One death was tragic, two were sinister. Unless it turned out to be suicide.

'You didn't want to answer the phone just now. How come?'

Alison shook her head. 'Some weird phone calls, that's all.'

'What, heavy breathing? Threats?'

She turned her back on me and walked across to the window, stared out over the sea, her arms still defensively folded. But she didn't elaborate.

I scrambled into my clothes, gingerly easing my jeans over said scrawny behind.

'You could use an answerphone,' I suggested. 'Or, failing that, record your conversations. The police can tell a lot from a tape if you ever decide to call them about it. It would give them a head start. Here, I'll leave you my dictaphone, it's perfect for that.' I set the little gadget by the phone and checked into the kitchen for some breakfast. Annis was already on the case, squeezing juice and warming bagels under the grill.

'That was Needham. He wants me back in Bath. Dave is dead.'

'Dead? How?'

'They fished him out of the Kennet-and-Avon canal, that's all he said. Threatened to arrest me if I didn't show my face pronto.'

'If Dave was also murdered that'll nudge you back up the suspect list,' Annis said helpfully and pushed a plate of bagels, cream cheese and cucumber in front of me. 'How're you feeling this morning?'

I tried my first experimental sit-down since last night and nearly shot up again. 'Not so bad. And you?'

'Rough as a bird's arse,' she assured me with a smile. Just to make me feel better. She looked as fresh as a daisy.

We decided that Annis couldn't possibly leave Alison alone. Ten minutes later my bag was in the boot of the car and I cautiously eased myself into the driver's seat.

'Will you be all right driving? And I don't mean your posterior.'

'I'll stay off the motorway and I should be fine. More importantly, are you two going to be all right here? I'd be happier if you took my gun.'

'You've got it here? I thought it was hidden at Mill House.'

I reached under the dashboard where Tim had constructed a neat gun holder for me, and handed her the revolver.

'Cheers, Chris, it might come in handy.'

'If you do have to use it hold tight, it's got quite a kick on it. Oh, and after you've fired it don't stick it in your waistband or anything like that. It gets bloody hot.'

'Silly me, and I thought that was an appendix scar.'

'Well, it ain't,' I said, remembering the painful episode without relish. I knew Annis was more than capable of defending the cottage against all comers, especially with a noisy Webley .38 to back her up. What I didn't know was that soon I would wish I had Annis – and the gun – with me in Bath.

With a Bartok concerto on the radio to keep me sharp and the pain in my behind keeping my mind from wandering

74

far I drove fast and made it to Bath with time to spare. Not that I had taken Mike's threat all that seriously. What really spurred me on was the uncomfortable feeling that all manner of things had been happening while my back was turned. I don't like playing catch-up.

Since I was here by special invitation I parked the DS in a vacant slot smack in front of Manvers Street police station. Wedged as it was between St John's and the Manvers Street Baptist churches the thing could never be anything but an eyesore. When it was built in the sixties it must have looked menacingly modern and efficient. Today, despite its recent renovation, it looked fit only for dynamiting.

As soon as I'd been buzzed in I could feel that the air conditioning was either on the blink or had been turned off due to another economy drive. Whatever it was, the atmosphere in the building was cloying and, along with probably everyone else in the station, I couldn't think of a worse place to be on a hot summer's day. A perspiring sergeant invited me to wait for Needham where he could keep an eye on me from behind his desk, on a moulded plastic chair (painful) next to a watercooler (empty).

I had expected Needham to keep me waiting around a while and then grill me on medium heat in one of the bleak interview rooms but he appeared after five minutes.

'Let's get out of here and find a pub,' he suggested grimly. He looked worn and disgruntled. The first few days of any murder investigation are pretty hectic, so two dead bodies in so many days had piled the pressure on the Superintendent and it showed. The one crisp thing about him was his immaculate shirt, of which he kept several in his office.

'There isn't a decent pub within a mile of here, Mike,' I reminded him.

'Don't I know it. Let's make it Garfunkle's then, in the old Empire Hotel, at least we might get some air.'

We were lucky with a table on the terrace and Mike

dropped heavily into a plastic chair behind his pint of industrial bitter while I sat down more delicately with my Stella. The journey back hadn't been kind to my behind.

'Dave surfaced yesterday, in lock number ten of the Kennet-and-Avon in Widcombe. A family on a rented narrow boat found his body nudging the gate early in the morning. Really made their holiday.'

'Has the autopsy been done yet?'

'No, but there were no visible marks on the body. Could be a simple drowning.' Needham's present drinking style gave a fair illustration of the dangers of drowning – he drained his pint in a couple of swigs.

'Another one?' I offered.

'No, I'd better not. But thanks, Chris.'

'So what's the assumption? Accident? Suicide? You think there's a connection between Jenny's death and Dave's?'

'Oh, there's a connection all right. We found what we think is the weapon used to kill Jenny Kickaldy when we drained and dredged the lock this morning. It's a sharpening steel with a horn handle. Gordon Hines, you know, the bloke who's looking after Somerset Lodge at the moment, identified it as belonging to the house.'

I remembered the rifled length of steel, had used it many times myself. A perfect impromptu weapon. I also remembered having promised to do the cooking at Somerset Lodge until Gordon found someone to take Jenny's place.

'So you reckon Dave killed Jenny, then tried to throw away the murder weapon and fell in after it.'

'Either that or suicide. He became lucid long enough to realize what he had done and drowned himself. At least that's what I'm hoping it'll turn out to be. The last thing I need is two separate perpetrators. That's the stuff of nightmares.'

'You have a time of death yet?'

'Are you kidding? Prof Myers said wet ones are notoriously difficult and walked off in a huff. He'll come through

76

in the end of course. And when he does we'll go over your movements in such loving detail, by the time we're through I'll know when you breathed in and out.'

So the slow roasting was still to come. Needham shook his head and let out a groan.

'Be right back.' When he returned he was carrying two pints, one of them a Stella. 'What the hell,' he said. 'The last one simply evaporated.'

'Cheers, Mike. So why am I here?'

'Because the Assistant Chief Constable won't let *me* let *you* take holidays in Cornwall with two bodies on the slab, while you're a witness as well as a suspect. Can you believe that? Personally I'd much rather you were at Land's End where you can't stick your nose where it's not wanted. Sorry about your holiday.'

I was thinking that it hadn't exactly been the restful break I'd had in mind but kept that to myself.

'Who identified the body?' I asked instead.

'Dave's parents. Poor sods didn't have far to go, they live right by the Royal United.'

Dave had parents living in Bath? This inconspicuous item of news somehow shocked me, but why? I had never thought of Dave even having parents. As far as I was aware they had never visited him at Somerset Lodge. Come to think of it, I had never seen anybody visiting anyone at Somerset Lodge. All the residents seemed to exist only as singular units, alone, with little history apart from their psychiatric one. If you had asked Dave where he originally came from he probably would have told you the name of the first psychiatric institution he had spent time in. Even Gavin, who was only twenty-two . . . The first thing that sprang to my mind was that I must ask Jenny about it sometime. Suddenly I felt curiously alone myself. Though not as alone as Jenny must have felt in those last moments when the blows rained down on her head.

I drained my Stella and set the empty glass carefully in

front of me because just now I felt like flinging it across the wrought-iron barrier into the traffic circulating on Orange Grove. With a kind of relief I realized that I was angry. I had, as they say, snapped out of it.

'Are we finished here, Mike? I've got things to do now.'

'For the time being yes. But stick around in Bath.'

'So who else is on your hit list?' I asked on the way back to the station.

'Anyone connected with Somerset Lodge. It does look likely that Dave did his nut, killed Jenny and then chucked himself in the canal. Now it's wait and see if we find any forensic on him to link him with Jenny or vice versa. Don't forget though, Gavin Backhaus is still missing. Perhaps they did it together. I'm keeping an open mind.'

I didn't say that he only kept an open mind in the hope an original idea might come flying in one day. I also didn't offer to eat my hat if the shy Gavin and the ever-pacing Dave had killed Jenny together. Or had done anything together for that matter. Gavin was a follower, that was true. When he first arrived at Somerset Lodge he silently followed Dave wherever his pacing took him but Dave would have none of that. Jenny suspected that he secretly despised the spotty youth and wouldn't give him the time of day. So why was Gavin missing? Was he alive or would he turn up in lock number seven or eight?

None of these thoughts were very conducive to making the kind of choices in the supermarket that would lead to an edible meal later on. Finding myself contemplating plastic-wrapped mince meat, quietly oozing blood on a cooler shelf, I quickly turned away. Who wanted to cook in this weather anyway? I came away with salad leaves, feta cheese (Greek, not the horrible French stuff) and a handful of crevettes. Supper would take exactly two minutes to prepare tonight.

Standing in the middle of my kitchen I thought how quiet Mill House seemed, unusually quiet, even for an empty house. The faint electronic bleeping of my answering machine far away in the attic office only helped to enhance the sense of silent hollowness. I opened the kitchen door wide and chucked some water on the suffering herb garden, then climbed up to my office. All my messages were from Simon. I'd forgotten him and the Saudis. The first message was enthusiastic and polite: Messrs Nadeem Khawaja and Salah Ahmet Al-Omari had chosen a staggering nine paintings from the photographs. He gave the titles. Could I bring them around asap. The formality of the phone call probably meant the buyers were at the gallery at the time. The next one was a lot more urgent and all the others were apoplectic silences followed by the crash of the receiver being slammed down, which spoke eloquently of my popularity rating at Simon Paris Fine Art. Guessing that Simon had shut up shop for the day I left a palliative message, promising delivery first thing in the morning. Then I rang Tim and invited him over for supper.

'What's on the menu?' he asked suspiciously. I told him.

'Rabbit food. Stick the barbecue on, I'll bring the rest. Half an hour.'

I was on my way down when I heard a thud. Followed by a rustling sound. Followed by silence. When I heard the noise I had stopped on the stairs, now I had to prise my hand loose from the banister. I've never played the hero. As a private investigator you take calculated risks but stay alert, that way you get thumped less. But being jumpy is definitely not in the manual. Being jumpy invites trouble. And I had jumped in my own house, which was more worrying still. I stuck my hands in my pockets and made myself saunter into the kitchen, from where I thought the sound had come. It had. My shopping bag had slumped off the table and emptied itself over the floor, presumably without anyone's help. Never having worked out how to kick myself I kicked the table instead and got on with preparing the salad and the barbecue. By the time Tim arrived with a couple of carrier bags the coals had burned down nicely. I set an armful of Stellas in a bucket of ice ('saves us running to and fro') and Tim started throwing food on the barbecue: marinated chicken, spare ribs (Cajun *and* Chinese), lamb kebabs and steak.

'Tim, did I mention it was just you and me?'

Tim sprawled on a wicker chair in the evening sunshine. 'Yup, you did.' He flipped open a couple of Stellas. 'Can't have a decent session on nothing but a handful of lollo rosso and a couple of crustaceans, mate. So how was Cornwall?'

I left out nothing, not even the pitiful state of my behind, then told him about the news from Needham.

'Two murders. Tricky. What do you think, Chris?'

'I don't know. Gavin is still missing. And where's the motive? Needham seems to assume that mentally ill people don't need a motive, they're mad and that's that. But Dave liked Jenny, they got on very well, and he wasn't the impulsive type. He'd think and pace and then pace some more before he'd make even the decision to make a decision.'

'From what you told me he'd been pacing for quite a few years. Could have finally made up his mind. What about Gavin? Is he alive, d'you reckon?'

'I'm asking myself that. Problem is I can't really say I know him. He can't have said more than ten words to me since he got to Somerset Lodge. Needham has his money on Dave with Gavin as a willing follower. Or his other victim. Can't see it myself. Perhaps I'll stick my oar in just a bit after all, preferably where our Superintendent can't see it. By the way, did you get anything on our wandering Mr Turner?'

Tim finished dispatching a sticky rib and licked his fingers before angling for a sheet of paper inside his jacket.

Within seconds it had grease stains all over it. 'I know what you're thinking, Chris,' he headed me off. 'I also mailed it to you, so you can have a nice clean printout of my report, just the way you like it. Well, I wouldn't exactly call it a result. He did go wandering about. His wife phoned me, as we had agreed, as soon as he'd called to say that he was working into the afternoon on Saturday. Normally the office shuts at two. I only just made it there in time. He set off downtown, had a cappuccino at the Café Retro, then walked down Manvers Street, through the tunnel by the side of the railway station and across Ha'penny Bridge . . .'

'In other words you lost him.'

Tim grinned sheepishly. 'My, my, you are the detective. How did you guess?'

'Too much boring detail for a start. What went wrong?'

'Hang on, you might still get to like it. He went along Rossiter Road, then crossed and went on to the towpath along the Kennet-and-Avon.'

'By the locks where Dave was found?'

'Uh-huh.'

'You've got my attention.'

'Thought I might. Unfortunately that's it. I hung back since there was no one else and nothing to hide behind. He went up on to the bridge where Horseshoe Walk curves around and I thought I'd be able to pick him up again on the towpath further down. But he was gone. Didn't even leave a puff of smoke.'

'Very inconsiderate.'

'I thought so at the time. I hung around for a while but you'd said not to spend too much time on it, so I didn't. Of course I didn't know then that Dave would take his final dip right there. Do you think there's a connection? If so, what?'

'Beats me.' Scores of people had to have walked there

over the weekend and the police were probably interviewing all they could find right now. It was just that I had
heard Widcombe and Kennet-and-Avon once too often that
day to let this one go.

Tim admired the pictures of Mill House Gill had left for
me at the Bathtub and promised to have them blown up
cheaply at the college for me. We finished the bucket of
Stellas (predictably) and all the food (incredibly). When
I woke later in the night and heard faint footsteps on the
stairs I knew it was only Tim, who slept over in the spare
room, ghosting about for a glass of water. Of course
I didn't ask him about it, or he would have told me that he
had slept through the night without waking once.

Chapter Four

The Great English Breakfast is great only if someone else plonks it in front of you. And even then only if that person lovingly grills tomatoes to perfection, fries mushrooms without getting them soggy, cooks real sausages slowly, doesn't try to fob you off with Danish bacon, doesn't let the beans cool down on the way to the table and has checked first how you like your eggs. I didn't feel I'd make it alive to the nearest place where such a marvel was available. My need for resuscitation was so urgent I simply baked up some frozen petits pains and stuffed them with an indecent amount of smoked salmon, which then allowed me to reintroduce the principle of non-alcoholic beverages to my insides. Then I took stock.

My Existential Fear Factor only ran at about 5/10 and the General Decrepitude Index was surprisingly low but my Accumulated Guilt Quotient was going through the roof. I had promised Simon the paintings for first thing in the morning which, by anyone's definition, was several hours ago. Severe grovelling would be required later. But first I rang Gordon Hines to make good my promise to look after the house and kitchen at Somerset Lodge. He said he would meet me for lunch at a place called Bonghy-Bo.

A hectic hour later, with the hastily bubble-wrapped paintings squeezed into every corner of the car, I parked the DS in Catherine Place, then ran at full tilt down

Margarets Buildings, less to save time than to appear sufficiently breathless when I burst into Simon Paris Fine Art, excuses at the ready. My prayers had been answered, Simon had company, so he couldn't savage me there and then. He was on the phone and hung up as soon as I came in.

'I was just ringing you at home. Glad you could join us,' he said pleasantly, but the look he flashed me bounced off my head like a Carl Andre firebrick.

I had never met the buyers whom Simon and I had, for shorthand, always referred to as 'the Saudis'. Simon introduced us with some ceremony.

'Salah Ahmet Al-Omari, Mr Nadeem Khawaja, may I introduce the artist, Chris Honeysett.'

Al-Omari and I exchanged pleased-to-meet-yous while Nadeem responded with a barely noticeable inclination of the head. Both looked undeniably Arab, yet wore sharp Western business suits. Apart from that they couldn't have looked more different. Nadeem suffered from a full moustache combined with designer stubble on the rest of his broad face. His suit strained to contain the kind of muscles only genetics combined with slavish attendance at the gym can produce. Al-Omari by contrast sported the sharpest little salt and pepper beard I had ever seen, and while slight as well as shorter than all of us his regal bearing marked him out as being in charge, an impression which got stronger when he addressed me.

'I do admire your work and am pleased to make your acquaintance at last. Unfortunately time is short or I should take great pleasure in conversing with you on the subject of the inspiration behind the individual works I have purchased. Perhaps we shall succeed in doing so on another occasion. Nadeem will assist you, we have a suitable vehicle nearby.'

Simon merely smiled serenely. It was the gallery assistant's day off, but this didn't mean he was going to start shifting paintings around.

The suitable vehicle turned out to be a black luxury van with blue windows. Since it was also parked in the leafy little square Nadeem and I made light work of shifting the canvases and securing them upright in the back. When I'd asked Nadeem where his vehicle was he'd merely pointed and didn't say a word there and back to the gallery. Whether it was lack of English, natural reserve or contempt for art and artists I found hard to fathom, though he handled the paintings with a delicacy I hadn't expected of him. Not many people know how to carry paintings. He didn't re-enter the gallery either but stayed outside as if he knew that Al-Omari would leave as soon as we returned, which he did. He shook my hand again, said, 'I thank you,' and walked off quickly with Nadeem up Margarets Buildings.

I felt like doing the same but decided to face the music.

'One minute later and I'd have throttled you, you realize that?' was Simon's opening shot. 'Those gentlemen spent hours hanging around because you wouldn't come through with the goods. I even drove them up to your house yesterday morning thinking you might be working in the studio or simply be too drunk to come to the phone, both of which was equally likely of course. Not a sign of you or Annis, it was most embarrassing. God knows I try, Chris, but you don't make it easy sometimes.' He followed this up with a few reminiscences of my past misdeeds while I studied my own canvases on the walls, discovering a flaw here, a missed opportunity there. I really shouldn't look at my work once it's been framed . . .

'Where exactly are they from?' I interrupted his flow.

'I haven't got the foggiest, Chris. I believe they mentioned Saudi Arabia when they first showed up. What does it matter?'

I wasn't sure it did, I just wanted to change the subject. 'You've been paid?'

'Half cash half cheque, or I wouldn't have let the paintings out of my hands, Chris.'

'If their cheque's no good the cash is mine,' I said flippantly.

'Don't be impertinent. And their money has always been good before.'

'Who are they banking with?'

Simon sighed his disapproval but put on his spectacles and picked up the cheque from his desk. 'Sainsbury's,' he said, slightly startled. Even he had imagined a more glamorous arrangement.

Bonghy-bo in Upper Borough Walls, a queue-at-the-counter café that shares a sunny courtyard with Laura Ashley, Habitat and Zucci, was a first for me. Call me old-fashioned but I'd always thought that my reputation as a serious investigator might suffer if I suggested meeting clients at a place with a silly name. People are startled enough when I ask them if they'd like to join me for a chat in the Bathtub.

Gordon Hines was already there, sheltering under a sunshade and nursing an Earl Grey. He was sweating away in a lemon yellow shirt, sky blue tie and thick brown corduroy trousers. I knew corduroy was meant to be fashionable again but a summer fabric it wasn't.

'It's good of you to come, Chris,' he said as I joined him with my iced orange juice, still pursuing rehydration. He didn't get up. I had always liked Gordon but was glad hugging had not become a permanent feature of our relationship. 'I've had such a time. The police have interviewed me twice, wanting to know all sorts of things.'

'Like what?' I was curious to know what kind of lines Needham was pursuing.

'You name it, they asked it.' He ran a damp hand through his thinning hair, leaving it shiny and limp. 'What was my relationship to Jenny. I ask you. Did we have a fight. What had I been doing at Somerset Lodge earlier that day. And when they found Dave dead as well they started on me all over again, as if they thought I personally killed both of them.'

'It's what they laughably call keeping an open mind. So you saw Jenny earlier that day? Any particular reason? Did she seem okay?'

'Don't you start, that's exactly what they wanted to know. It was completely routine, we were arranging a date for the committee meeting, as we do every month. Everything was just normal. Jenny was fine and Dave didn't seem any different either. But would they take my word for it? They went on and on at me. Especially that thin cadaverous one.'

'Deeks,' I supplied.

'That's the one. Minute details of nothing.' He gulped some tea as if trying to wash down the memory of his interrogation. 'I really appreciate you coming to do the cooking, we all do. We haven't had a full committee meeting yet but I spoke to everyone concerned on the phone. The residents will be glad as well, I've been feeding them takeaways, Chinese and such. Not very healthy, too much salt apparently. All I can make is omelettes, I'm afraid.'

'Don't knock it, making a good omelette is quite an art.'

'I didn't say I made *good* omelettes.'

'Ah.'

All this talk of food reminded us we were here for lunch. Gordon went for lamb cutlets which he declared acceptable, I had the seafood tagliatelle (a risky order outside Italy), which was surprisingly good. I was warming to Bonghy-bo.

'This time you'll have to do your own shopping, I'm afraid, I hope that won't be a problem,' Gordon said through a mouthful of food. 'The budget is three pounds per head per day, but I expect you knew that.'

This was complete news to me. I added miracle worker to Jenny's many virtues.

'Oh, we won't shoot you if you go a bit over. Under the circumstances. We're lucky to have you.'

Our bill, which Gordon had paid, came to three times the daily allowance for a full complement of residents. I half regretted having agreed to play housekeeper.

'There'll only be Anne and Linda to cook for,' he said on our way out, 'we'll take a while before filling Dave's place and of course Gavin is still missing.'

'What about Adrian? I thought he was back from hospital?'

'Oh, didn't I say? He's back inside. Got on to his skateboard, broken shoulder no object, and skated into the roadworks on Wells Road.' Gordon pulled his lip in thought for a moment. 'He's crazy as well as mad, if you know what I mean.'

I said I knew exactly what he meant.

I approached Somerset Lodge, as on the day I found Jenny, from the back and through the garden, carrying the shopping. The lawn was yellowing and many blooms in the borders had succumbed to the heat. The back door, normally wide open on a fine day like this, was firmly bolted from the inside. Nearby, the old zinc watering can lay on its side, a cobweb already spanning its shadowy opening.

Letting myself in through the front door instead I stepped into a silence as thick and dark as molasses. No voices, no burbling television, no sounds at all. And of course no inviting cooking smells. The curtains were still closed in the dining room. Somerset Lodge had once more drawn around itself the leaden cloak of mental institution Jenny had worked so hard to strip away from it.

I set the bags down in the kitchen, feeling weighted down by the palpable air of depression in the house. As I sorted fish, cheese and milk into the fridge, vegetables into the poignantly empty rack by the freezer, I realized that I had managed to walk past the living room without even glancing inside, automatically avoiding the place where Jenny had been beaten to death with her own sharpening steel. I stopped what I was doing and marched straight back through the dining room and hall and went inside. Here the wine red curtains were also drawn, allowing a trickle of pink-filtered light into the room. The cream carpet that had soaked up so much of Jenny's blood had been ripped out and replaced with a fake Persian rug. The bespattered sofa covers were missing. I opened the curtains and the window, letting in light and air and birdsong, then kicked on the television which came to life with a children's news programme. Then I made myself walk across the spot where I had found Jenny, to destroy the shrine-like quality the room had tried to take on while my back was turned. I was already living with a ghost, I'd be damned if I was going to cook with one as well.

In the kitchen I tuned the crumb-covered radio by the battered toaster to the awesomely awful Radio Bristol and turned the volume up loud enough to be heard throughout the house. Opening curtains and windows as I went I unbolted the door to the garden with as much banging as I could manage. The spider got chased out of the watering can, then I filled it with water, ready to be used. It all felt satisfyingly like playing football in church.

With the whistling-kettle filled and on the stove I clattered upstairs to Jenny's office. It had recently been lovingly ransacked by Needham's boys and put together again. If it ever held a clue to Jenny's or Dave's death the police would probably have found it. They were awfully good at things like that. Yet it was the first place I made myself look, saving her room for later.

Jenny had had no current lover or boyfriend I knew of. She had lived over the shop in an attic room and having overnight visitors was not encouraged by the Trust, on the grounds that it created jealousies and confusion for the residents, as well as being an unnecessary risk to their mental stability. What this had done for Jenny's stability I could only guess. I tried to remember when I'd last seen her outside this house and drew a blank. Her social life had been so restricted, having to be present at the house each night without fail, except during her holidays, when a sleepover was arranged with a local agency and someone stepped in to cook the meals. The sleepover staff were usually young nursing assistants with just enough training to scream down the phone for a psychiatric nurse if anything went wrong, the cooks were ill-tempered house-keepers who came briefly out of retirement to supplement their exiguous pensions. Somerset Lodge was not a popular assignment.

To give them their due the officers had left no visible trace of their search. The place looked as tidy as ever. Jenny's big phone book was on her desk, her electric typewriter on a separate little table to the right of the window, a wall chart of the month of June above it, with her handwritten notes of residents' appointments with psychiatrists and social workers neatly written into the square of the day.

I had no idea what I was looking for. Both Gavin's and Dave's notes were still with the police. I pulled out the remaining three. Being used to sticking my nose into people's affairs I felt only vaguely guilty about invading the privacy of the residents that Jenny had so fiercely sought to protect. I skimmed each file, looking for anything out of the ordinary, finding only the depressingly familiar.

Anne Gosling had cracked under the strain of her law studies and begun to hear voices urging her to walk naked in nature to let the tree spirits suck the evil from her body. She had been found, clad only in dried mud, building a nest of leaves in a stretch of woodland near the university. That was eleven years ago. The voices still came back on her bad days but the medication helped her to cope better.

Two years ago Linda Kelly had been cramming for her A levels when she went for a blow-out at a club in Bristol with her friends. It appeared she mixed a couple of E's with alcohol and at least one other drug and had woken up screaming in hospital the following Monday. When the screaming stopped and the medication took hold Linda became very quiet, very withdrawn. Periodically she got worse, then seemed to even out again. Without medication the banshee she had acquired that Saturday night would instantly make herself heard again.

I only briefly skipped through Adrian Febry's notes. He had been in hospital at the time of the murder, so all I needed was to make sure I didn't miss anything glaringly obvious. Adrian also periodically heard accusing voices that seemed to start far away and come closer over time. His symbolic way of coping was to keep moving, on in-line skates or skateboards, hoping to keep one step ahead of his accusers. He had recently added a skip and a set of roadworks to his other full stops, which included a car bonnet and a pond in Victoria Park. He was on first-name terms with most of the staff at A&E.

Searching through the rest of the desk drawers and the big built-in cupboard in the niche next to the fireplace yielded nothing obvious. Stationery, piles of meticulous accounts, a thick roll of old wall charts, the odd medical book and brochures for courses and workshops on anything from stress management to personal development and accountancy. Not that Jenny had ever been given enough time off to take any of them. Her struggles with the management committee about pay, her working conditions and improving the residents' lot had been long and fruitless. The Culverhouse Trust, which ran similar houses in London and Brighton, was a fossilized and bureaucratic organization which resisted change with zeal. Or as Jenny used to put it, was composed of a bunch of anal, tight-fisted bastards.

The kettle had started wailing on the stove a couple of minutes earlier and I let it scream, willing it to call forth Anne and Linda from wherever they had dug themselves in. When nothing seemed to happen I stuck my head out of the open door and yelled, 'Will someone get that, please!' to the house in general. If anyone, I had expected Anne to appear but it was Linda who after a short while unglued herself from her room and ventured out. She appeared soundlessly in the door frame, her eyes rimmed red, her mud-coloured hair scraped back into a ponytail held together by a black scrunchy. Despite the heat she wore jeans, heavy purple boots and a thick red Mickey Mouse sweater, which accentuated rather than disguised her skimpy frame. She kept her arms folded tightly inside it, no hands showing, hugging herself.

'Gordon gone?' she squeezed out.

'Yup, I'm gonna be looking after you lot from now on until the new housekeeper arrives,' I announced from behind the desk. 'Mine's a black coffee, no sugar.'

Linda blinked a couple of times and the ghost of a smile appeared around her eyes. Suddenly her hands shot out from her sleeves, she whirled around and ran down the stairs squeaking 'blacknosugarblacknosugarblacknosugar' as she went.

Perhaps Gordon had been right about his omelettes.

My search was going nowhere fast, and despite my determination to inject a livelier note into this decimated household a fluttering unease had taken hold of me. I took down the wall chart and spread it on the desk, trying to get a feeling of how the slow, inward-focused lives at Somerset, as everyone but the Culverhouse Trust function-aries called it, were punctuated and divided by the some-times eagerly awaited, sometimes dreaded visits of mental health workers.

Linda reappeared with a tray of coffees, mine, her own

and presumably Anne's. Before I could prevent her she set mine down on the wall chart, smack on the Friday of Jenny's murder. I swiftly picked it up and thanked her. Her dark eyes blinked twice before she turned and balanced her tray up the stairs. The coffee turned out, as I had known it would, to be a vile-smelling brown liquid, electric-coloured bubbles of badly rinsed-off Fairy Liquid floating on its surface. It would have been easy to pour it down a sink so as not to offend Linda but I had already decided to make myself drink it as a kind of penance for being so useless. The mug was a cheerful sunflower yellow. The print on it read I'M A MUG. Thanks, Linda. Going for all-out pollution I sat sipping the stuff and smoked a succession of Jenny's Camels, of which I'd found several unopened packets in a desk drawer. She had smoked thirty of these every day. Over the coming weeks I would find out just how heroic an undertaking that had been.

Gently I turned the office inside out again, checked every single phone book entry for a clue that anything out of the ordinary had been happening here. I dived into the cupboard for a third time, flicked through every book and brochure (just like the police had no doubt done before me) looking for concealed bits of paper, letters, scribbled notes, anything at all. I came up empty.

Next, I climbed the two flights of stairs into the attic where a large room with an en suite bathroom had been carved out for the housekeeper. The door was ajar so I pushed it open further. The room had been emptied of all but the furniture. There was white, impersonal bedding for the sleepover person who was due to start working today and that was all. Listlessly I opened a drawer here and there, turning up nothing but hairpins, rubber bands and dust. It had never occurred to me that Jenny's ageing parents, who had retired to a village somewhere near Marlborough, could already have been and gone, taking all their daughter's possessions with them. I had met them only once, very briefly; a quiet couple making polite conversation at a garden party, with all the committee members and residents mingling uneasily around the barbecue. Now I wondered whether it was appropriate or even at all helpful to contact them. At least they had been spared the painful experience of identifying Jenny's body. I had done it for them and fervently hoped they hadn't insisted on viewing their daughter's remains.

This had been a cheerful room once, with prints of those bright Expressionist paintings she had loved. There had often been flowers, bought for herself or picked in the garden, arranged in simple yellow vases that sparked off the deep cobalt of the walls. Those same walls now gave off a wintry chill which I knew lived purely in my mind, the attic being the hottest place in the house.

Next I tried Dave's room on the floor below. Here a similar transformation had taken place, except that all his belongings had been packed into cardboard boxes or slung into bin liners. All of them had little squares of paper taped to them, reading TO OXFAM. I untied one of the bags. It contained Dave's awkward, faded clothes. I was pretty certain they were on their way back to where they had come from.

Was this really what I should be doing right now? First things first. I preheated the oven to 180°C, plonked the fresh cod and smoked haddock into a roasting tin of milk and shoved that into the oven; next I set potatoes to boil and topped and tailed some French beans, grated the Gruyère and ran upstairs again.

Behind the office desk I choked my way through another Camel. The smoke seemed to help me think, in a coughing, spluttering kind of way. It was important to get my priorities straight or I might as well leave this thing to Needham and his slow but thorough style. By now I didn't think I could, for one simple reason: another murder might be on the menu. Jenny was dead. Dave was dead. If Dave had killed Jenny and afterwards thrown himself in the lock or died by accident, then it would all stop here. And if Gavin had killed one or both of them then I definitely wanted him. But if neither of those scenarios held true, if Dave had been pushed, then a third killing was the most likely thing to happen next. Whether he was guilty or innocent, I had to go after Gavin Backhaus.

Mrs Backhaus answered the phone just when I was about to hang up. I explained who I was. Could I come and speak to her in person?

Her voice came across as strained and harassed. 'We've told the police everything we could think of, Mr Honeysett, I really don't see what good it would do to go over it all again with you. It really is quite a strain on us and we just don't know anything that could help, I'm sure. This is the first day we've dared answer the phone again, the press have been pestering us so. And the police practically suggested that our son murdered that housekeeper and the other chap and we've rather had enough of it.'

'Did the police also suggest that Gavin's life might be in danger if he didn't commit the murders?'

There was a pause of several heartbeats before she answered. 'Mr Honeysett, to us our son has been dead for years. You can have no idea what it was like having him here. We have learned to live without him. Our lives have returned to a semblance of normality since they took him in at that place. Before, he was in and out of hospital and we dreaded his return every time. He never managed to live independently. So if you find my son – good. If you don't . . . I'm not sure I care. Please excuse me now.'

I heard Mrs Backhaus breathe for a second or two before she broke the connection.

Was I surprised? I had no access to Gavin's notes so had no way of knowing what exactly had occurred in the past or what he was like without heavy medication.

After I'd lifted out the fish I used the milk to make a white sauce, stirred in the cheese, sprinkled in capers and green peppercorns plus the flaked fish and poured the mix into an oven dish; piped the mashed potato over it and slid it under the grill. Then I dropped the beans into boiling water and gave the Chinese dinner gong a good workout.

Last Friday it had been Linda's equilibrium I had feared for most but it turned out that the events had worked their worst for Anne. Her medication had been upped and she didn't look good on it, her normally rosy cheeks pale and puffy, her eyes slow and dulled, her movements hesitant. The torrent of chat she normally sent forth was reduced to a painfully forced trickle. She was sweating in a lemon yellow cardigan, her normally carefully arranged hair hung tired and uncared-for. But she was unbowed and tried valiantly to talk through the balls of cotton wool the medication had left in her mouth.

'Nie pie. We din do it.'

'I know you didn't,' I said automatically, as if I was comforting a child, yet that was not a professional attitude. Anne and Linda had given each other an alibi, listening to a new Missy Elliot CD on two sets of headphones in Linda's room, something which normally wouldn't cut it with me. Yet I had played and replayed the frenzied attack on Jenny in my mind, with every person I could think of wielding the sharpening steel and all of them appeared equally unlikely. Despite their distress both Anne and Linda had been grilled by Needham in the presence of their social workers and a psychiatric nurse, and apparently Needham was satisfied with the answers he got. Sometimes even Mike had to fall back on his instincts.

'Is Gav dea?' she asked next.

'No,' I said without thinking.

'Where izzithn!?'

Anne was right, I didn't know anything for certain, I was just making polite, condescending conversation. 'I don't really know whether he's alive or dead. I'm hoping he just ran away. Perhaps he saw who did it and now he's hiding.' Without his medication. 'Have you ever seen Gavin when he hasn't taken his medication?'

Both Linda and Anne nodded vigorously with a mouthful of pie.

'What's he like when he's off it?'

Anne widened her eyes. 'Wy.'

'Why?'

She waved both arms in the air, a blob of mash taking flight from her fork. 'Wyyyy!'

'Oh, wild.'

'Mm,' Anne agreed. 'Soy.' She indicated the mash on the carpet.

'No sweat,' I said. We'd had worse.

At seven I handed Somerset over into the care of a young nursing assistant called Mel. Her straight, butter-coloured hair ended spectacularly somewhere around her tiny waist. She was wearing a long black tight-fitting dress and a tired expression. Uncharitably I thought she might enjoy the sleeping part of her job most. She tried to give the impression of being on the ball and ready for anything but when I offered her tea she dropped her bulging holdall on the floor, sat down heavily and gratefully on the nearest chair and turned pleading ultramarine eyes on me.

'Three sugars, please.'

I don't really care how much of the nasty stuff people shovel into their bloodstreams but my eyebrows must still have twitched because she added, 'Sorry, I know I'm the sugar queen, but I need the energy.'

Anne and Linda had retreated to their respective rooms after supper. Did I need to introduce them, I wanted to know when I joined her for a cuppa and a smoke at the dining table.

'I met them yesterday, and a Mr Hines? We'll be just fine. Actually this job is a godsend for me. Can I have one of those? I don't usually smoke but I just fancy one.'

97

'I don't usually smoke either.'

We sat and puffed and sipped.

'I've worked all day at the Min,' she continued.

'Min?'

'Mineral Hospital. Double shift. Then I did the shopping like a mad thing, cooked Joe's tea – Joe's my son – had some myself, told him what he's allowed to watch on telly tonight, not that he'll take a blind bit of notice, and then ran for the bus up here. He's old enough not to need a babysitter now, I hope, he's twelve. I still feel a bit guilty about it but he's got my mobile number, just in case. I'm also doing this course, an NVQ in nursing which I find really hard. There's tons of reading and I'm a bit dyslexic, which I didn't tell them though, I thought they might not take me. I brought all my books.' She indicated the holdall beside her. 'So I hope I can get some studying done during the night. I probably won't sleep much, I've got to pack Joe off to school first thing and rush straight back to the hospital for another shift. It's mad but I have to, Joe and I are broke again.' She shrugged her shoulders and held out her mug with a tired smile. 'Could I have another one?'

As far as I was concerned Mel could have all the tea and all the sugar in the world.

Chapter Five

Never stop painting. Never take a break, always keep working, no matter what, inspired or no. If it's rubbish paint over it, bin it, burn it, but keep going, that way you're already in gear when the real stuff starts happening. That's my advice. I wished I had taken it.

There were plenty of prepared canvases I could have used, I always keep a few hanging around in case I get a rush on and find I'm cramming too many ideas into one painting. But I hadn't lifted a brush in over a week and things had been fermenting. Like an overloaded bomber I needed a long runway for take-off, so I decided to start from scratch. Last night I'd put rabbit glue crystals to soak (painting is not for the squeamish). Now, while the evil-smelling stuff simmered slowly on the Primus stove, I slotted my stretcher together, solid kiln-dried pine, 80 inches by 72, my favourite size, cross-pieces fitting snugly like well-made furniture. With a flawless length of Belgian linen on the big work-table at the back of the studio I stretched and stapled, opposite sides then round and round until the tension was just right – not like a drum because the glue tightens it, yet not too soft since later it'll let go a bit. Outside, with my shirt off and the sun on my back, I fed rabbit glue to the canvas with a short-haired glue brush, a nice, moronic task I always enjoy. A bit like painting only with the brain pleasantly in neutral. In this heat the glue dried in record time, leaving a grey barrier on the linen to prevent the oil from rotting the canvas. Next came the first layer of white primer, applied with a thin, broad brush, quickly and evenly, not half as smelly as the glue. After a quick sanding the final coat went on to my canvas, a dazzling arena of white leaning against the weathered wood of the barn.

While it dried I lay on my back in the meadow, slurping black iced coffee, trying to concentrate on the images that had begun to pressure the painting side of my brain, but couldn't. I sat up again, looked around me. A blue tractor ground slowly along the undulating tarmac lane on the far side of the valley, its engine noise floating across in snatches. The wind barely moved in the trees behind the studio. Below, Mill House and its stream baked and sparkled in the sun. This was so bloody perfect. What evil spirit had moved me to introduce the murky world of detective work into this damn idyll? I could just survive on my paintings (and a couple of inspired investments I had made after a particularly successful London show a while back). The extra money Aqua brought in paid for our luxuries, yet right now it seemed an expensive kind of money. The real luxury was this, I thought, the choice to paint or lie on my back in the grass for just a little longer . . . I felt like ringing the Dufossees to tell them to use their brains and call in the police; to advise Mrs Turner to get up off her spreading behind and follow her own husband. Or possibly *ask* the sod what he was really up to. How difficult could that be?

Only Jenny's murder changed everything. I would stick with it. And after all, Aqua was my own invention and by now there were three of us. I wondered how Annis was getting on in Cornwall. There had been no phone calls, no messages. Surely no news was good news?

I worked like a wild thing, like some primeval swamp creature trying to fight its way out of a paint shop. The last week exploded across the pristine white of the canvas in a frenzy of slashes and splatters in greys and cool darks, biting cobalt greens and insane shadows. This was an aeon away from my carefully planned and joyful paintings, from Mediterranean light and calm, that restful imagery buyers like Al-Omari found spiritually soothing and uplifting. For a while I wasn't sure it was painting at all but I hardly stopped to look. The heat in the studio was tremendous, I sweated half-naked in the fug of stand oil, damar varnish and turps. Scraping off and painting in and through and over again I all but headbutted the thing into submission.

Only thirst and hunger finally made me stop the slaughter and I walked away from it without giving myself time to appraise the mess.

'Had a fight with your painter friend? No need to ask who came off worse.' Needham was sitting on my verandah, deep in the big wicker chair, his feet on another, blinking slowly and stretching luxuriously. Then he yawned and grinned sheepishly. Not a pretty sight. He was far too happy, too relaxed.

'If I didn't know any better I'd say you just woke up.'

'Well,' he shifted to a more upright position, still taking in my paint-spattered body, 'I might have closed my eyes for a bit. Almost wish I hadn't opened them now.'

'Give me half a sec for a shower and get yourself a drink from the kitchen,' I said, walking inside. 'Unless you've come to arrest me, in which case keep your hands off my fridge.' Not that I was really worried. If Mike ever decided to bring me in against my will he would send Deeks and a couple of constables and Deeks would have drawn a handgun from the stores. I did have a shotgun licence after all, and then there was that missing Webley .38. Even though Needham must have known by now I was more likely to attack them with a French stick. That's how hard I am.

When I got back to him, cleansed and cooled from my shower, with a peace offering of bread and olives, he was sucking on a bottle of Stella. I had armed myself with a couple myself.

'Spit it out, and I don't mean my Stella.'

'Matt Hilleker and Lisa Chapwin.'

'What about them?' I recognized both names, ex-residents of Somerset Lodge. Why bring them up now?

'What happened to them and where are they?'

'What do you want with them? Matt got thrown out for doing drugs on the premises and for nicking money from other residents. No idea what became of him. Lisa wasn't there long. Skin and bone, very jumpy and near catatonic. She went back into full-time care after deteriorating at Somerset. Neither have lived at Somerset for a couple of years now.'

'Then I don't think much of the cleaner,' Needham scoffed. 'We found both their prints at the house. Matt Hilleker's were all over the place. In the living room, dining room, on the fridge. Only one set of Lisa Chapwin's. Could have been old. Hilleker's were fresh.'

They had to be if they were on the fridge. Jenny kept it scrupulously clean. 'How come you had their prints on file?'

'Matt got pulled in for possession a while back. Chapwin girl for shoplifting.'

'So now you've got yourself . . .'

'. . . an intruder. We're trying to pick them up now.'

Lisa only lived there for a short while and never spoke to me, or anyone else, as far as I could make out, but Matt I remembered well. Then, he had been a gangly, desperately sloppy twenty-year-old with puppy eyes whom everyone instantly felt like mothering. It was the petty pilfering and occasional theft from other residents that got him thrown out. That and smoking so much grass in his room that he rendered himself near comatose. 'What kind of drugs was Matt doing when you picked him up?'

'Anything he could lay his hands on. He wasn't main-lining then but that was over a year ago. We let him off with a caution because he was booked into the RUH for rehab six weeks hence.'

'Did he show?'

'We'll find out shortly. He probably wandered in through the back door to pull a quick bit of thieving at a place he knew his way around, got surprised by Jenny and lashed out with the first weapon to hand. He's our best bet yet. Everyone else is either dead, missing or has an alibi. Including you.'

'I have? Everyone has? Do you mind running that past me in more detail? I'll get you another Stella,' I offered.

'Nah, I'm driving. But no, I don't mind. I'm convinced neither Anne nor Linda had anything to do with it just from interviewing them. We would have found some forensic evidence somewhere anyway and there just wasn't any. You of course had blood on your clothes, that was plain to see. But you were in transit at the most likely time of the murder. We checked.' He gave me a tired smile. 'Gordon Hines has no motive and anyway he's got an alibi.'

'Who is his alibi?'

'He ran a red light right in front of a traffic unit in central Bristol. They logged it as 1.08 p.m. and gave him a caution. You made the call at 1.40.'

'And the quiche was underdone when I walked in so Jenny was alive at around ten past when she put it in the oven,' I supplied.

'Even I worked that out and I've never cooked a quiche in my life. I checked the recipe. That leaves Dave, deceased, Gavin, in hiding, and Matt Hilleker as our best bets and that's what we're concentrating on. And when I say we I mean Avon and Somerset, not you and me. I'm only telling you all this to satisfy your curiosity so you don't get tempted to break our bargain.'

'We have a bargain?' I couldn't remember having made one with him.

Needham spat an olive stone at the barbecue and

missed. 'You keep out of this investigation and I won't arrest you for illegal firearms offences?'

Oh, that old bargain.

I needed to turn up bargains of quite a different order if I was to feed my Somerset charges on three quid each per day. How had Jenny done it? Shopping around town for the cheapest vegetables, the most economic cuts, the best offers, that's how. Where shopping was concerned, it only now dawned on me, I was a shove-it-in-the-trolley amateur. If I didn't change my habits pronto I might end up serving Spaghetti and Pesto three times a week. Fortunately both Anne and Linda seemed to be happy with cereal for breakfast. Perhaps there was something to be said for food that made such a noise in your head that you couldn't hear yourself think? But what did Jenny usually provide for lunch?

'Oh, she made soups, quiches and pies,' Gordon had said. 'She normally just left them out so people could help themselves.'

Now if life's too short to stuff a mushroom then I feel utterly justified in never going near pastry, unless it's filo and comes frozen. But soups? Just hand me the keys to your blender and watch me go . . .

Damn it all, the red mullet *was* the best-looking fish on the slab today, so I pounced on it. Once I had all the building blocks for supper I had wiped out three days' food money. Messrs Spag & Pesto were threatening to move in at Somerset Lodge.

I'd agonized so long over shopping that it was well past lunchtime when I burst through the doors with my bags. Through the kitchen window I could see Anne and Linda sunning themselves on the lawn. Or had they passed out from hunger? How long can a person survive on a handful of bran flakes, I wondered?

Nothing gets things done more swiftly than guilt.

I splashed boiling water over a pound of tomatoes and quickly grated a potato and red onion and sautéed them with crushed garlic; peeled, seeded and chopped the tomatoes and dropped them with oregano, celery and basil leaves, some seasoning and a pinch of sugar into the pan and let it simmer while I sorted the rest of the shopping into the fridge. Then all that remained to be done was blitz it in the blender and reheat it.

We slurped our tomato soup on the lawn and mopped it up with bits of bread torn from a baguette.

'Do you remember Matt Hilleker?' I asked Anne, who had been at Somerset for many years.

'Mm, nishe boy.' Anne's speech was still badly affected by her sedatives. 'Always shtone.'

'You haven't seen him lately, have you? Know where he hangs out?'

'Nn-n.' Anne wiped her bowl clean with a morsel of bread. 'Shme im shometie.'

'You smell him sometimes?' I was getting better at decrypting Anne's speech.

'Prolly imagine it. Da awfu perfum oi e wo.'

'No, you didn't imagine it.' Linda suddenly came to life. 'I've smelled perfume a couple of times. Patchouli oil, isn't it? Thought it had wafted in from the street.'

Now I remembered it too. Matt had doused his manky sweaters with the stuff instead of washing them. 'Do you remember when you last smelled it?'

Linda thought for a moment. 'Not long ago. But when exactly . . .'

Anne shrugged heavily. Her notion of time was so eroded that weeks, even years blended into each other. And she was aware of it. 'You thing es been he?'

'The police found fresh fingerprints in the house.'

All three of us looked towards the back door, usually wide open in this weather and hardly ever locked, except late at night. Anyone could walk through the parking bay into the garden and from there into the house. 'Better keep the door locked when I'm not here,' I said quietly.

Linda turned wide-open eyes at me without saying a word. She didn't need to. Two vulnerable women alone in a house where an unexplained murder had occurred – it was no one's favourite scenario. At least now that a sleep-over person had been found in the shape of Mel the Sugar Queen they could sleep a little easier. Or so I tried to tell myself, since fear feeds on silence and darkness. Only, Jenny had been beaten to death in what we like to call broad daylight.

Don't worry, I'll stay here and protect you, look after you, soothe your fears until Jenny's murderer is found. You can stop looking at me like that.

I fled inside before I made any such promises, under the pretext of preparing supper. In reality I sat down heavily behind Jenny's desk and rummaged around until I found one of her packs of Camels. I blew a thick cloud of smoke into the solid shaft of afternoon sunlight that burned through the open window, along with the light-hearted smells of summer. Broad daylight. Jenny's murder. Dave's death. Mr Turner's unexplained walkabouts. Gavin's disappearance. The Dufossee paintings. Somerset Lodge. My *own* painting, come to think of it. I sucked furiously on the cigarette. I had taken on too much. Why wasn't I getting any help? I had to kick Tim's behind a bit and insist that Annis get herself back to Bath pronto, otherwise the work-load would soon overwhelm me.

Annis appeared to have switched her mobile off. Fuming as I sat, listening to the ringing tone of Alison's phone, I imagined the two of them lying on a beach, probably with a bag of strawberries and a bottle of red, and it didn't improve my mood. Why did that damn technophobe not have an answering machine? Next I dialled Tim's number and drew a blank there as well. I tried him at home and left a grouchy message on his machine.

The thought of bright-eyed red mullet waiting downstairs on crushed ice perked me up again. I was working on the switch from harassed PI to caring housekeeper when I passed the little table in the hall where new mail landed and unwanted letters accumulated. I picked up the small pile. Some buff envelopes, probably full of forms, for Adrian, Dave and Gavin. There was one addressed to Jennifer Kickaldy, marked Private and Confidential. So I opened it.

Credit card bills can tell you a lot about people's lives, a fact most people don't take into account when they carelessly throw them out with the rubbish. (Going through people's dustbins is not my favourite part of the job but it's invariably rewarding.) Jenny's bill didn't reveal any dark secrets that would show the motive for her murder but it was remarkable for a couple of reasons. Just as I had suspected, Jenny had used her private funds to subsidize the meagre food rations at Somerset Lodge. One of the big supermarkets featured twice weekly on her bill. It didn't come as a great surprise, since I would soon be doing the same. The other feature was the fact that Jenny had kept using her card on the day after her own death. Now that was remarkable. Though whether I'd remark on it to Needham & Co. I hadn't decided yet.

Here was at least one possible explanation of how Gavin managed to keep himself alive out there without Jenny feeding him every day. In a sense she still was. The account was likely to be closed now, a fact which whoever had used it had probably anticipated. The amounts weren't colossal but someone had gone on a little spree on Saturday – supermarkets, off-licences and petrol stations around Bath. It also meant Gavin was not alone – he would have needed a female to act as Jenny for the transactions. A missing credit card was theoretically a motive for murder. Petrol stations had surveillance cameras and could link transaction times to their tapes, which they kept for weeks. But I wanted Needham to keep as open a mind as possible.

He would sooner or later investigate all of Jenny's accounts anyway, it was routine.

I descaled the mullet, then started on the salsa. Jenny's herb garden was nothing like the straggly, hanging-on-for-dear-life affair Annis and I kept near our kitchen door. The coriander, nicely shaded, was prolific, just what I was looking for. Five minutes later I had finely chopped a bunch of it, together with some red onions, a pound of ripe tomatoes and a couple of red chillies. I dressed the lot with lime juice and some extra virgin while the baby potatoes simmered away, then shoved the fish under the grill. We scoffed every bit of it with some rocket leaves outside under the overloaded walnut trees.

Halfway through the washing up I heard a mobile ring. It sounded like mine yet it also sounded far away. I checked my jacket pockets – no mobile. I was sure I had brought it. Now it was behind me. I opened the fridge: it was sitting in the salad crisper. Definite signs of a pre-occupied mind.

'I've got something I want you to see,' Tim got in before I could whine at him about feeling overworked.

'What is it?'

'I'm not sure but it's kinda interesting. Come over, I'm having a beer down my local.'

'Down his local' was an apt description. Tim lived in Northampton Street and the walk 'down the pub' involved descending a flight of stairs and turning in next door. I had congratulated him on his choice of location when I helped him move in, though I gathered the novelty had since worn off. As I drove over I realized that I hadn't been to his place since the move. Tim was using the pub as his reception room much as I used the Bathtub as my office.

I was so desperate for movement in any of our cases that I'd rushed across town like a wild thing. Tim was sitting at the bar, his glass conveniently empty. Tim always had good timing. I ordered drinks for both of us.

The place had been oldified with the standard fake

beams, replica brasses and books bought by the yard, all straight from Ye Olde English Pub Catalogue. A huge gaming machine flickered, whirred and gurgled in the vain hope of tempting the half-dozen or so drinkers entrenched at the bar. For extra privacy we settled into a niche with a neon-lit fish tank. I'd seen happier fish on my barbecue.

'So?'

'Got your pictures enlarged.' With a flourish Tim dropped an A4 envelope in front of me.

'You didn't bring me here for those, did you? I'd hoped for something more relevant to Aqua,' I complained ungratefully. 'I mean, thanks for doing them but as far as I can see we're stuck on every investigation we have on our books right now –'

'Shut up already and admire your pictures.'

Grumpily I pulled out the prints. 'Eh?'

'Exactly. The strip of negatives didn't match the prints of your house. Some sort of mix-up. Looks dramatic though, dunnit?' Tim's tanned face broke into a happy grin. He had finally dug up something to surprise me with.

There were four prints. The first one was a full frontal of Starfall House. Gillian had obviously followed my hint in her search for a Georgian villa and found the Dufossee residence. At the edge of the photograph the green BMW and the silver Mercedes were just visible. The next print showed the house with part of the gardens, shot from further to the left. Around the furthest corner, probably unnoticed by Gill at this moment, were two small figures, running towards her, hard to make out. The next print was more revealing. Closer up now, the figures had advanced on the camera. The man closest, in black chinos and T-shirt, pointed a menacing finger at the lens, his face flushed with anger. I had never seen him before. The shape running behind him, suit jacket flaring and no less intent to get his hands on the camera, I had no difficulty in placing – my patron of the arts and avid collector of Honeysett canvases, Al-Omari.

The last print was the most dramatic. A rear view out of a car, quite blurred with movement, it showed the silver Mercedes tearing out of the Starfall drive's gate. Gill had to have taken it over her shoulder while driving. A gutsy performance.

'Like them? Make any sense?'

'Not yet. I'm still on my first Stella though,' I said, taking a gulp in the hope it would reach my brain cells sometime soon. 'Well, the house is Starfall House . . .'

'I guessed that, I was there when you told her about it. But who are the uglies?'

'The het-up one with the short-cropped hair I've not seen before. But the other one I've met. He's one of the Saudis who bought my paintings.'

'What's he doing there, buying more paintings?'

'Good question. Last time I saw him he was acting all dignified and unflappable. Keeps strange company, judging by this picture.'

'Camera-shy art collector and psycho with bad taste in jewellery.'

'Has he?' I looked again. The het-up one sported a death-head ring on his middle finger. 'Indeed. And you're right, he looks about as stable as a pile of ball bearings. Judging by the last print they tore after her in the car, proper little chase it must've been too. Mercedes versus . . . what does she drive, a Punto? She was lucky to lose them.'

'Especially since she doesn't know the area. Could the Dufossee juniors be flogging off Daddy's collection, dressing it up as a burglary?'

I had already discounted that theory. 'Makes sense only if you can defraud the insurance company, in which case they wouldn't have called us, they'd have screamed for the police. The insurance company wouldn't pay up without a proper investigation and the police would surely prove it was an inside job. Dufossee senior might not have long to live anyway, so why not wait?'

110

'Who said he's on his way out?' Tim wanted to know. 'Virginia?'

'Both of them. You've got a point. We only have their word for it, he could be anywhere, fit and healthy. Or nowhere. Or dead. What am I saying? I'm getting paranoid now. But why contact us? It makes no sense if they're up to no good . . . Let's get back to the paintings a minute. The paintings at Starfall House are in a completely different bracket from the things he buys off Simon Paris Fine Art,' I thought out loud. 'And why would Al-Omari go and spend good dosh on my work if he's doing dodgy deals with Dufossee?'

'Don't know, but I'll buy you a beer if you stop alliterating.'

'Done deal.'

While Tim was at the bar having our pints refilled I went back to examining the prints. If this was TV there'd be this amazing hidden clue somewhere that would produce the eureka effect in part two and solve the whole case. Instead they raised more questions than they answered.

With a fresh Stella in front of me I lit a Camel and tried to puff my way to some sort of conclusion. 'So what have we got? Al-Omari, who's here just a few days to buy paintings, my paintings, just happens to know the Dufossees, our clients *re* art theft. When I met Leonard at Starfall House this Merc was parked smack in front of the house. No attempt at concealing it. Stands to reason Al-Omari or Nadeem, his sidekick, were there but didn't care to show themselves. And here endeth the lesson because I can't think of anything else.'

'Doesn't Leonard run a wine business?'

'Yes. Sulis Wines. It's a mail order company. Actually they sell all sorts of drinks.'

'Perhaps they're buying a few cases of wine to take home while they're at it? Since England is famed for its vineyards,' Tim added.

'Now that would be illegal. Drinking's a great no-no in

Saudiland.' Both of us took a hasty gulp of our beers at the mere thought of such a place.

'So a few cases of wine would fetch quite a price out there?' Tim said shrewdly.

I admitted Tim had a point. But if you wanted to smuggle alcohol to Saudi Arabia, would you buy the stuff in England? In Bath? 'Okay, I reckon it's time we paid Leonard another visit, only this time not at Starfall House. And without appointment.'

'His offices?' Tim came alive.

'His warehouse. Might find all sorts of things in a warehouse.'

Despite anything his name might suggest, Tim is not big on wood. We nipped to his little Georgian flat so he could tool up and I could clear my head with coffee while dusk deepened outside. Tim's style was techno minimal, which was just as well because the flat was truly tiny. The kitchen and sitting room were open plan by default since whoever had butchered this building hadn't left enough space for a dividing wall or a door to swing anywhere. The place was as close to unfurnished as a man could get whilst still having somewhere to park his bum – just a chrome and canvas sofa and a stone and glass coffee table. The rest was taken up by an overloaded computer desk and a flat TV screen twice the size of the windows. The whole place was spotlessly clean.

'Shall I make coffee?' I suggested doubtfully, looking round his kitchen. It had more gadgets than an aircraft carrier and I didn't recognize half of them.

'I'll do it,' he said quickly and fired up a black espresso machine in the corner.

'What do you do with all this stuff?' I asked, marvelling at the amount of wires trailing everywhere.

'Fully automatic breakfast, mate. Everything's run by my PC. When my alarm goes off the coffee-maker comes on, the egg-boiler starts making perfect five-minute eggs and by the time I get out of the shower the microwave has heated my croissant. Only way I make it to work, I'm crap in the morning. I'm crap in the evening as well, of course, but I usually manage to prime it all up before I pass out.'

While I slurped the best cappuccino I'd had outside Italy he busied himself next door and soon reappeared with a black holdall. 'Ready.'

The warehouse of Leonard's Sulis Wines business stood on the small, low-tech Locksbrook Trading Estate, just off the Lower Bristol Road. We drove the short way from Northampton Street in Tim's 007-worthy Audi TT. With a hum its dashboard lit up with twice as many dials and screens as it had when it left the assembly line. It looked every bit as bewildering as his kitchen and as far as I knew made perfect five-minute eggs as well.

The evening was mild, almost sullen in its stillness, as we squeezed out of the TT opposite a short Victorian terrace on Locksbrook Road. Identical rectangles of TV screens cast changing lights in most of the front rooms in near identical houses. We sauntered down the road for a first reconnaissance without Tim's giveaway of a black holdall. The trading estate proper began as we turned the corner. It had a charmingly ramshackle feel to it. Dimly lit, without a central gate to keep out undesirables like us and as far as I could see no CCTV to cover the general area. Apart from the car dealership at the front this was definitely downmarket. We found the soot-blackened Victorian warehouse of Sulis Wines between a foundry specializing in drainage casting and a coal merchant-cum-scrap dealer. The yard that fronted Leonard's unlit premises was protected by an imposing ten-foot metal gate, its effectiveness curiously cancelled out by being set into a five-foot wall of crumbling red brick topped with a couple of strands of rusted barbed wire. Even the coal merchant next door had better security. We were over the wall in seconds and landed cautiously among the clutter of carelessly stacked pallets and overflowing wheelie bins on the other side.

On this kind of caper I'm usually happy to follow Tim's lead. His criminal instincts seem to be honed to a finer pitch than mine. Tonight he came far better prepared than me too, dressed in tight-fitting clothes and dark trainers, while I thought I could hear the leather of my jacket and boots creak in the dank silence of the yard.

The large, navy blue double doors, high enough to admit a trailer-lorry, were securely barred and impressively padlocked. Tim didn't even give them fleeting consideration but immediately loped off along the narrow passage between the building and the brick wall that shielded us from the road. Beyond a blue plastic barrel and a high clump of weed growing from a crack in the worn concrete we found a battered metal door with blue flaking paint. There was no door handle, only a Yale lock. We were in the purple shadows thrown by the sodium lights on the other side of the street, quite safe from casual observers.

'How did you know there was a door here?' I whispered to Tim who was already attacking the lock with what looked like a pair of tiny flattened crochet needles and that rapturous middle-distance stare he gets when confronted with a closed door.

'A warehouse is a warehouse is a –' CLICK – 'warehouse.' We were in.

'How come the alarm didn't go off?' I wanted to know next, since I had seen the red and white alarm box high up at the front.

'The alarm's a fake, first thing I noticed. Which means Dufossee junior is either stupid or skint.' When the darkness leapt back from the acid blue beam of his powerful LED torch I could see we were in a narrow corridor with doors leading off it, one to the left, one at the end straight ahead. I added the weaker beam of my Mini Maglite to the illumination and we set off. Tim tried the first door. 'Office.'

114

We let our lights travel over the drab interior, grey filing cabinet, plastic-covered armchairs, littered desk. This was not what I had expected from a wine dealership. The place had all the desolate unloveliness of a minicab company's waiting room. There wasn't even a computer, only a cheap BT answerphone. Tim's torch beam probed into the furthest corner. 'Baby!' he whispered lovingly. He had picked out a tall safe with two gleaming dials and a highly polished handle. 'So that's what he spent his dosh on. That's a seriously posh money box, mate. Won't be easy,' he added gleefully.

'Let's have a look around first, perhaps we don't even have to go there.'

Tim's reluctance to turn his back on the challenge of a modern safe was palpable. I pulled open the door at the end of the corridor and we stepped into the dark cavern of the warehouse proper. I turned my torch here and there, illuminating precious little. It was musty and chilly in here but looked exactly as you'd expect. Most of the space was taken up by row after row of grey metal shelving units full of boxes. Thousands and thousands of them. There were also stacks of plastic crates, piled high against the wall opposite, teetering towers of pallets and a forklift truck parked on the litter-strewn floor.

'So it's a drinks warehouse,' I said disappointedly. I wasn't sure what I had hoped for instead but I felt badly deflated.

'You go and inspect,' Tim offered, 'I'll get the kit from the car and blow the door off the money box.'

'You're going to *blow* it?' I was nearly shouting.

'Figure of speech, mate, relax. I haven't blown a safe since, well, the first time really,' he said wistfully.

'What happened?'

'It blew smack through the wall and into a lift shaft. Lacked finesse, I thought.'

'I'm glad you see it that way. Okay, go ahead, and I'll do some wine sampling.'

As soon as he had slipped away, taking the strong beam of his torch with him, I realized the craziness of this undertaking. A Mini Maglite is fabulous for looking through a dark cupboard but not the kind of illumination you'd want for searching the inky vastness of a warehouse. The few near-blind skylights set impossibly high in the ceiling admitted hardly any light at all but would advertise my presence quite clearly if I switched on the lights. Starting down a narrow aisle between shelves at random I let the feeble beam travel along the wine crates without the slightest inclination to start a proper search. I poked a box of Australian Chardonnay which was heavy and unyielding and felt suspiciously as though it might be full of Australian Chardonnay. I turned down the next aisle and found much the same there. Wine from all corners of the world: France, Chile, South Africa. I rapped against a few more crates. If you wanted to hide something here you would hardly leave it within easy reach. A proper search would require a team of people and a couple of days. We had to pin our hopes on finding some clues in the office, especially the safe. I sauntered all the way to the back wall and turned down yet another identical-looking aisle.

A small noise, like the quiet opening of a door, made me stop in my tracks. 'Tim?' I pointed my light down the aisle and slowly advanced but the beam seemed to be swallowed up by the canyon of crates. A small rustling sound, perhaps a scrap of paper disturbed on the ground, perhaps a cockroach. In the next aisle. I killed the light. The result was complete blindness. No doubt my eyes would adjust again in a minute. It turned out I didn't have a minute. The first blow struck me across my left side and threw me against the nearest shelf where I crashed my face against something cold and unyielding that left a metallic taste in my mouth. My first thought was to switch the torch back on but my arm had gone numb and seemed completely useless. I wasn't even sure I still had the torch. I had just enough of my wits left to let myself tumble to the ground

116

away from my silent attacker who was unlikely to wait long for his second blow. I could sense rather than see a bulky shadow advance, and a split second later lights danced before my eyes as his weapon glanced off the side of my head and hit the ground, metal on skull on concrete, sending sparks across the floor and through my temporal lobe. Great circles of whirling colours filled my vision as lightning pain shot through my skull and down my spine. Whoever it was had to have fantastic night-vision, while I was worse than blind. I knew I was just crawling now, trying to find a space, a hole, anything to hide my head from the next blow which I instinctively knew would finish me off. Not a word had been exchanged but I could hear myself groaning, feeling unable to stop. The metallic taste in my mouth mingled acidly with that of blood and my head seemed to have become a dead weight filled with electric whirring sounds and burning lights. There was light now, I had a brief, blurred impression of a dirty spurt of blood on concrete, frantic movement, jumping shadows. I tried to shout but produced nothing but a spray of pink froth and a gurgling sound in my throat. The light advanced and added to the pain behind my eyes. For a brief moment I could see the black-clad legs and laced boots of my assailant. They suddenly disappeared into the air and the whirring light filled my entire vision. Then my brain tilted like a torpedoed freighter, rolled over and slid into the dark.

Chapter Six

Swept into brief snatches of consciousness on waves of nausea I had fractured impressions of being on the move, paralysed or restrained, in the dark, of being talked about ('Shit, he's puking again!') and later of being manhandled in a way that made me want to scream. Perhaps I did, it was hard to tell above the fierce electronic screech in the middle of my head.

When the lights did come on again they took a while to stop dancing nauseatingly across the little room. 'Hey, Honeysett, welcome back.'

I forced my eyes to focus on Annis's face and eventually succeeded but the effort tired me out and I soon closed them again. Some bastard yanked them open and shone a light down the tunnel to the pain factory in my brain.

'Shit, my head hurts,' I thought I said but it seemed to come out as a string of rasping sounds.

'Told you he'll be all right,' said Tim's unmistakable voice.

'He doesn't look it,' I heard Annis say.

'I'm Dr Martin – can you hear me, Mr Honeysett?'

I just grunted but it seemed to satisfy the man.

'You're lucky to be with us, Mr Honeysett. Please try and open your eyes again.'

He sounded pleasant so I tried. He was a tired-looking, clean-shaven guy who smiled at me as though I'd given him an unexpected present. Then he gave me an unexpected present. He jabbed a needle in my arm, shone the light back in my eyes and repeated, 'Very lucky.' Finally he gave me some water to drink. I guzzled down three glasses and he smiled again. Annis supported the glass for me, it seemed extraordinarily heavy in my hand. He asked all the usual questions to test the extent of my brain damage and warned Annis and Tim, 'You can't stay long, I'm afraid. Ten minutes at the most. He needs to rest.' Finally he left us alone.

The drink of water had unglued my tongue from the roof of my mouth. 'You didn't tell anyone we were in Leonard's warehouse when it happened, did you?'

''Course not. You were mugged waiting for me in Locksbrook Road, where I found you seconds after,' Tim primed me. 'That's what I told the PC but they're bound to want to talk to you too.'

'What really happened? Why am I alive?'

'Because I saved your arse in the nick of time.' Tim grinned from the foot of the bed.

'I guessed. Cheers, Tim. How?'

'Pointed the forklift truck down the aisle and made to run him over. He jumped out of the way though. Climbed the shelves like an orang-utan and scarpered.'

'Good effort. Did you run me over instead? Feels like it.'

'The doc was right, you were damn lucky.' Annis nodded gravely. She sat down on the side of the bed and nearly patted my head but fortunately thought better of it.

Strangely enough I didn't feel lucky. Quite apart from the fun and games going on inside my skull the feeling had returned to my left arm, which I wished it hadn't, and my whole left side protested every time I drew breath.

'A couple of hairline fractures to your ribs, nothing too dramatic, and you didn't break your arm either. It's your head they were worried about,' Annis said reassuringly.

'Don't worry, I'm in here somewhere,' I grumbled. 'Tim, did you get a good look at him?'

'Guy from the picture, with the bad jewellery. I don't think he's too fond of you.'

119

'He couldn't have known who I was in the dark, unless he saw us go over the wall and saw you coming out. Jesus, he never said a word, just laid into me like I was vermin to be exterminated.' In retrospect I found the silence of this guy's attack the most frightening thing about it. 'I don't suppose you had time to check out the safe, then?'

''Fraid not. I heaved you out of there and into the car and made tracks to A&E. Rang Annis on the car phone on the way there. You kept puking, I was afraid you'd choke on it.'

'How did you get here from Cornwall so quickly?' I asked Annis.

'I didn't really. Fortunately I'd got a bit bored out there and fixed up Alison's old Beetle. So I jumped into that but broke down halfway here, so it actually took me ages. She said I could keep the car, which I thought was nice of her.'

'Great, more junk. So you're saying I've been out for a whole day? Today is tomorrow? If you know what I mean.'

'Told you.' She focused the green beam of her eyes briefly on Tim. 'Sound as a bell. You groaned and rasped and snored a lot but wouldn't wake up. We were bloody worried but they said your brain scan showed up normal. Just some swelling.'

'Which surprised everyone,' Tim chipped in.

'Blimey.' I'd never lost a whole day. I'd been robbed after all. 'Right, help me get out of here.'

'You want to go home?' Annis said, outraged.

I thought about it for a moment but fell asleep in the middle of it.

Next morning, once the nurse had finished prodding me with an electronic thermometer and had taken her excessive cheerfulness to wherever she wanted to spread it next, I thought I was feeling much better. Until breakfast arrived. Fancy offering a man cornflakes when all he really needs is Nurofen on toast. There was also an offering of two types of brown water, which I politely declined, but I emptied a whole bottle of orange juice instead which just made me hungrier.

Having previous experience of discharging myself from the RUH with various body parts in questionable working order, I hurried to get dressed in the change of clothes a forward-thinking Annis had left for me. Arguments with nurses and doctors are won much more easily if you can show you can dress yourself like a grown-up. It took some doing though. I found I couldn't straighten my left arm or do a lot else with it for that matter and twisting my torso was out of the question. When I finally managed to struggle into my clothes I felt quite proud. I should have avoided the mirror in the bathroom though. My right ear had been painted orange for some reason and the area above it shaved around the place where the stitches had gone in. Combined with a three-day growth of beard it gave me a dubious, moth-eaten flair. The orange washed off, it was probably disinfectant.

I called Annis, then argued in turn with a nurse, her superior and a doctor, signed a waiver absolving them, the RUH and the entire National Health Service from all responsibility for the inevitable disaster that would befall me as soon as I quit the premises, then hobbled out with prescriptions for painkillers and anti-inflammatories. Annis had picked up my DS and was waiting when I stepped outside. It had rained overnight. The air smelled fresh and the sky was full of scurrying clouds. Our little heat wave had broken.

'Was that wise?' she asked as I slid behind the wheel. I raised my eyebrows, even though it pulled on my stitches. 'Okay, so you've had that conversation,' she concluded. 'Where are we going?'

'Breakfastland.'

*   *   *

121

Lovejoy's, named after Jonathan Gash's rogue antique dealer, is at the heart of the only surviving antiques centre in Bartlett Street. Service is minimal and grudging but nowhere else in the city can you have a full Edwardian breakfast with devils on horseback and enough toast to build a shed. I worked my way methodically across my plate while Annis nibbled distractedly on cinnamon toast.

'Did you have any more trouble in Cornwall?'

'No. No, not really.' Annis came alive again. 'I was just thinking about that. We didn't have any more visitors or anything like that. But something's happened with Alison, she's so different, and I couldn't get anything out of her. She's clammed up. We went out for walks, hung out on the beach, went to every decent restaurant in the area, but . . . It was as if she wanted to spend as little time as possible at the cottage. And she never touched her brushes once. I had the feeling she wanted someone with her but wanted to be alone at the same time. I was quite glad to leave in the end, but I worry. Perhaps I just caught it from her but I did feel uncomfortable down there.' She acted out a shudder for me. 'I was beginning to feel watched and caught myself looking over my shoulder more than once, especially in the dark. And that was with your gun in my pocket. Thanks for the loan by the way, it's back in your car now.'

'You think you should go back?'

'I would if I knew what it was all about but I can't go riding shotgun for her without her laying her cards on the table. I tried to push her but she told me to mind my own business. My business is here.' She shrugged. 'Aren't you going to eat your kidneys?'

'Don't even think about it, I'm leaving the best till last.'

'I used to do that. When I was a little girl, that is.'

'And now that you're all grown up what are your immediate plans?'

'Looks like you could do with a bodyguard, doesn't it? State you're in, a four-year-old could beat the crap out of you.'

'Can't they always?'

'Are you sure you want both your kidneys?'

'I was told you can survive with one,' I admitted reluctantly and surrendered my fork.

Puddles of milk, eggshells, lots of eggshells. Congealing mince meat, some brown stuff, a lot of black stuff. Vegetable peelings, slices of cheese curling and hardening. Burnt toast floating in the sink with an orange and some teabags. The freezer lid open, the contents defrosting, the hot tap running. Every saucepan used. An enthusiastic sprinkling of flour, a mangled tin of tomatoes, lying on its side, bleeding quietly into a tea towel. Chris Honeysett, Food Detective.

'See? Told you they could look after themselves,' Annis said triumphantly.

I had worried that Anne and Linda, institutionalized and unused to feeding themselves, had in my absence been reduced to living on cornflakes but the evidence pointed to some kind of cooking activity. The recipe was harder to guess at. Anne and Linda soon cleared up that mystery. 'I made pie,' Anne said, her speech completely cleared up. 'But it's not easy.'

'I made frozen spinach,' Linda said, pointing to the charcoaled pan by the sink. She frowned angrily at it. 'The spinach didn't work.'

'Must've been faulty.'

'So I made eggs.'

'Sounds yummy.' I introduced Annis who surveyed the kitchen with dispassionate interest. 'I'm sorry I couldn't be here, I had a little accident, needed some stitches. But I'm back now and I'll take over the kitchen again. After you've cleared it up, that is.'

While Anne and Linda set themselves to the unusual task of clearing up after themselves we withdrew to Jenny's office. The first drops of blustery rain hit the window pane and a pleasant twilight filled the little room. I sat behind the desk where the wall chart for June was still spread out, Annis pulled up a chair and planted her trainer-clad feet on another one.

'Were you and Jenny ever an item?' she asked out of the blue.

'No, never, why?' I lit a Camel, took a deep draught of smoke into my lungs and instantly regretted it. I tried to exhale quickly but the coughing overtook me halfway. I thought I could hear my ribs cracking. It felt like someone was beating me up all over again. 'Gahh.'

'Stupid mutt, put it out. I was just thinking, she had no boyfriend, did she?'

'No time,' I rasped out.

'Don't think you'll get sympathy from me. So no jilted ex, driven to murder, no crime of passion. What about the druggy bloke . . .'

'Matt Hilleker,' I supplied, breathing a little easier with the cigarette stubbed out. I desperately wanted one though.

'Could he have done it?'

'Needham's got his money on it. The Matt I remember couldn't have . . . wouldn't have done it, I'd like to think. But that's a fatuous thing to say, really. Everyone is capable of murder, given the right circumstances. Which includes motive. Drug money is a powerful motive. Drugs change everyone. Change everything.'

'What they don't change is Dave drowned in the lock with the murder weapon.'

'And Gavin missing.' Spotty, shy little Gavin. 'If they dig him up somewhere, and I mean literally, then Somerset Lodge is finished. You should have seen the fuss people kicked up when it was first established. Objections, complaints, petitions, the whole neighbourhood up in arms and united, trying to stop the Culverhouse Trust from setting it up here. The same had happened everywhere else they had tried, naturally.'

'Not in my back yard. Curtains twitch a lot in this street, I noticed when we got out of the car.' Annis groaned. 'Did you read the letters to the *Bath Chronicle*?'

I had studiously avoided looking at the local press. I shook my head vigorously. The whole room sloshed, slewed and went dark for a second before things zoomed back to normal. Sweat had risen from every pore in my body in an instant. Now I felt cold and queasy. I'd have to watch my head movements for a while.

'They were full of I-told-you-sos and wasn't it time they closed the place down.'

'House prices,' I got out, still trying to steady myself.

'Oh, they weren't coy about that either,' Annis concurred. 'Said it affected the value of their properties as well as endangering their children's safety and so forth.'

'Look out of the window,' I suggested. 'To your right? See the huge fence?'

'Hard to miss.'

'The neighbours put it up as soon as the Culverhouse Trust took over the house. It's probably mined on the other side. And they think they're the sane ones.'

'One in four,' she said cheerfully.

'You what?'

'One in four of the population needs psychiatric help at some stage in their life. Told you I read in bed. So I wish them all the best,' she said with a smile that could have frozen the rain on the window.

'So there we have it,' I speculated, 'Jenny and Dave were murdered by a first-time buyer trying to depress house prices in the area so they could get on the property ladder.'

'If Somerset Lodge folds house prices are sure to rise, though. First one to sell in the street after that might be our man. Case closed. Not that the houses round here are a first-time buyer's kind of property. Certainly not Somerset Lodge. With that huge extension, six bedrooms, study, the garden's massive . . . It's the biggest house in the street, a bit of an anomaly, really.'

'What would the price tag be, half a million?'

'No way, closer to a million. House prices in Bath are rising by close to twenty-five per cent a year right now.'

'At that rate you'd have to exterminate everyone in the street to depress the prices enough for the average mortgage holder.' I took a deep, satisfying breath. Despite the fact that both of us were hideously sober we had managed to slip back into the easy humour with which we usually discussed Aqua cases. I had turned a corner. Or perhaps Annis had gently pushed me around it.

'Right, let's go over this whole thing again,' she said now, 'there's bound to be something we've missed somewhere.'

And that's what we did. We took it step by step, making notes of every detail, discarding all speculation, just sticking to the facts. We laid out a time plan for the events and eliminated everyone with an alibi, without a motive and anyone too unlikely or wholly unconnected.

'Looks like it was you after all, I'll be making a citizen's arrest,' Annis concluded as the list dwindled.

After that we pored over the wall chart. The Friday of Jenny's murder had acquired an ominous but somehow appropriate halo of a stain where Linda had set down a mug of coffee the day I took charge of the house.

'What's ATD and ATG?' Annis wanted to know. I had wondered that before. It was noted in tiny capitals in Jenny's writing at the bottom of each rectangle for the Fridays, before and well after the fatal date.

'ATD . . . Anarchist Tea Dance?'

'ATG . . . Arachnophobic Transvestites Group?'

'It happens most Fridays, whatever it is,' she said, 'and we're missing out. Let's go backwards. Every acronym starts life in longhand. Perhaps we'll get lucky.'

She dived into the pile of rolled-up wall charts Jenny had kept. They'd been tied up so long each wanted to stay in its own tight little roll and soon the room looked like an ancient library, filled with scrolls.

'ATG, ATD, ATG . . . hey, we've lost ATG.' Annis peeled off more layers. 'ATD, ATD . . . gotcha! Art Therapy Dave!'

'The Silver Star will be awarded . . .'

'Sod that, I want the Annis Jordan Brains of Aqua T-shirt, my own office and my own gun.'

'You're on.' I was buzzing. This was the first, the tiniest thing we had uncovered that added anything to our knowledge of the affair. I had no idea what it meant but I felt something had shifted.

There was no entry in Jenny's black phone register under art therapy or even therapy. Out came the Yellow Pages. Nothing under 'Art' but the therapists were at home between 'Theme Parks' and 'Thermic Cutting'. It was a surprisingly short list and only two art therapists advertised their services. One practised at a 'centre for healing' in Bristol, the other from a private address in Bath: Kate Lythgoe, Dip. Hum. Psych., Abbey View.

'Widcombe again,' we said in unison. Abbey View starts not two hundred yards from the Kennet-and-Avon Canal.

Kate Lythgoe answered in a soft, neutral and non-threatening voice but went on the defensive as soon as I explained who I was. 'Client confidentiality, you must appreciate that, Mr Honeysett. I cannot reveal the identity of my clients or anything about them without their consent, and even then . . .'

How often had I used the very same words when Avon and Somerset's finest were trying to muscle in on one of my cases? I went for the blunt approach. 'The client in question was murdered and I need your help in finding his killer. You've no objections to that, I hope? You run classes on Fridays?'

'They're not classes, they're therapy sessions. But yes, between six thirty and eight thirty. You may come along afterwards if you want to talk, though I can't promise you anything.' She cut the line without formalities.

'Of course there's no such thing as Spaghetti Bolognese.'

'What?' Annis put the knife down, a neat mound of finely chopped onion on the board in front of her. 'Perhaps the guy hit you harder than we thought.'

'The dish is called Ragú Bolognese,' I said, undeterred, 'and is always served with tagliatelle. Spag Bol is strictly for the tourists. Italians never eat spaghetti with meat sauces.'

Annis smiled benignly with her head to one side. I wasn't fooled for a second. 'You've no idea how annoying you are, have you?'

'I just wanted to point –'

'Well, don't. I *liked* Spag Bol.'

'Okay, we'll have it with spaghetti.'

'Oh no. Too late now, I'd feel like a dumb tourist. I'm going to have a look through the things in Dave's room, if that's all right.' She whirled around, hair flying. 'Spaghetti with meat sauce – yuch, what a revolting idea!' I heard her happily skip upstairs.

When I was ready to add a slug of wine to the browning meat it just didn't smell right. It whiffed of patchouli oil. I was around the corner as fast as I could move to find a figure already running back along the corridor towards the open door to the garden. I made a grab for him but he twisted in my grip and managed to elbow me in the ribs, just where I didn't need it. Another one of those and I'd have to let him go.

'Annis! Now!' I croaked.

She couldn't possibly have heard that but came sailing down the banister, already alerted by the sounds of our undignified scrap. It was over in two seconds. Annis twisted his arms back and Matt stopped struggling.

'Ow, you're hurting me,' he blurted with the voice of a kid in a playground brawl.

'You really do need a bodyguard, Chris. What's that awful smell?'

'Patchouli? His trainers?'

'The other awful smell.'

'Oh shit.' I hurried back to the kitchen and whipped the smoking saucepan off the heat and into the sink. Behind me, Annis marched Matt into the kitchen. He'd gone quite limp, rubbing his arms and looking with his furtive pin-prick eyes from me to Annis and back, calculating his chances and coming up with nil. He decided to flounce against the freezer, arms crossed in front of his narrow chest. 'You've no fucking right,' he whined experimentally.

'Oh shut up, Matt,' I said, still poking the pan in the sink, feeling too tired for any of this.

'He's not happy,' Annis explained to him. He looked up at her, half furious, half curious, from under his fringe of thin, colourless hair. 'You've ruined his ragú. Makes him mad.'

I made the necessary introductions. 'Matt, meet Annis, Annis, kick Matt in the balls if he moves.' I needed more recovery time so I poured myself a glass of Valpolicella and chucked it down my bruised throat. Don't ever cook with cheap plonk, you never know when you might need to drink the stuff. 'Yuch. Right, living room.'

Matt slouched away in front of Annis, all thoughts of flight apparently shelved, and let himself be pushed on to the nearest sofa. I sat on the other one, tapping my foot on the place where Jenny's body had lain. Annis shut the door behind her and leant against it.

'Why did you do it?' I bellowed at him. He shrank back into the cushions. I took another swig from the bottle I had brought, trying to look mean and moody.

'Do what?'

'Why kill Jenny?'

His eyes widened and he sat bolt upright in an instant. 'I didn't, Chris, I didn't kill her. How can you say that? She was already dead. There.' He pointed with a trembling finger to the floor in front of me. He hadn't even tried to deny that he was at the scene that day. Then why come back?

'Bullshit. She caught you pilfering and you hit her with the sharpening steel.'

'She was already dead. She was lying there, with her face to the ground. I turned her over, didn't know if it was her. It was fucking awful, mate. She was all blue in the face and smashed up. It made me fucking sick.'

'Not too sick though. Not too fucking sick to rob her, for instance.'

'I never . . .' he started but floundered.

'You took Jenny's credit cards and went on a shopping spree. You were chucked out of Somerset Lodge for stealing and you've been coming back to pilfer it ever since. Cash, candlesticks . . .' I waved my hands as though I had a long list. 'And finally Jenny's cards.'

'It's not like she needed them any more,' he mumbled. 'Insurance pays for that kind of thing.' The universal bit of wisdom from the petty thief.

'You had financial advice about that, did you? Who's the girl who helped you use them?'

'You don't know her. We went halves.'

'Was she with you when you found Jenny?' A shake of the head. 'So what's all this thieving in aid of? What are you on now?'

'I'm clean, mate, I'm on a programme now.' A certain pride crept into his voice, on surer ground now.

'Methadone? How long?'

''Bout six weeks. NA meetings three times a week. Well, used to, anyway.'

'You stopped going to Narcotics Anonymous?'

'I don't have a choice, do I? They staked the bloody

place out, it's totally out of order. They want you to stay clean then they stop you from going to meetings, I mean, make up your minds or what?'

'You clocked a surveillance team outside?' I was ready to be impressed.

'A mate did. This van turns up, only no one gets out and the driver disappears in the back. Obvious,' he said with new-found bravado.

'So you're trying to go straight but turn up here, and God knows where else, and steal what you can? Oh, I get it. You still owe.'

'Too fucking right and they're scary bastards, you don't mess about with them. Only, however much I come up with, it's never enough, is it? They slap on interest too. Only the full whack will do. And if I don't find some every day . . .'

'. . . then you have to start selling your methadone.'

'I don't want to do that, Chris,' he said, meeting my eyes straight on for the first time. It wasn't a look of appeal but a timid kind of determination. I almost felt sorry for him. But sorry wouldn't get me anywhere.

'You've got a place of your own?'

Matt shrugged and snorted. 'I did rehab at Hill View for five weeks, after that they gave me a council place in Phoenix House.'

How kind of them. Phoenix House in Julian Road had everything a recovering drug addict needed, drug users, dealers and loan sharks. Perfect.

'Doesn't matter. I can't go back there. Either I'll get picked up for murder or get my knees bashed in for being late with the money. The door's been kicked in so many times there's hardly a thing left.'

'So where're you hiding out?'

He tapped the side of his nose, a gesture employed by people who think they're cleverer than they really are. 'I'm not telling you or you'll want to move in. It's got everything; water, it's cosy, it's even got food. No toilet but I'm not fussy. No one's gonna find me there. So I'm not about to tell you.'

'You seem to be labouring under the illusion that I'm not handing you over.'

He jumped up, looking from me to Annis who was still barring the door. 'You can't do it, Chris, I've done nothing, I didn't kill her. They're going to pin it on me, I know what they're like, they're never gonna believe me.'

'And why should I?'

'You have to!' he shouted and flopped back down on the sofa. 'You have to fucking believe me,' he said again, defeated.

I looked across at Annis who shrugged her shoulders. I did believe him. And perhaps Needham's investigation would clear him, but it would take a long time and I had better plans for him. I was just about to give them an airing when the doorbell chimed its electronic ding-dong. It was so rare an occasion I had forgotten what it sounded like. I slipped past Annis to the front door and put my eye to the spyhole. Through the distorting fisheye of the tiny lens Detective Superintendent Needham appeared to have piled the pounds back on since I last saw him. I retreated hastily to the sitting room.

'Cops,' I announced quietly. The word electrified Matt. 'Get upstairs, quickly and quietly.' The moment I was sure they were both out of earshot I wrenched the door open. 'Hey Mike, what can I do for you?'

'Move to Greenland.' He hefted past me into the hall. 'Thought I'd see how you are. We heard you got yourself clobbered.'

'The royal we?'

He ignored it. 'We sent a PC up to the RUH to get a statement but you'd discharged yourself. Glad to see you're well,' he said and gave me a manly and calculated slap on the arm. He even knew which side I'd been hurt and looked pointedly elsewhere while I winced.

'So they've got you on muggings now, have they?' I managed. 'You can come to the station and give your statement there, we don't have time to run after you. I was just passing, thought I might show my face. What's that awful smell?' He sniffed towards the kitchen. 'Not burning dindins while we speak, are you? Not that I care. But don't burn your fingers, Chris. If someone clobbers you that hard he must have good cause. Stands to reason you're messing with things I should know about.' Needham rattled his fingernails over the Chinese dinner gong.

'I got mugged.'

'Standing around in Locksbrook Road, as one does of an evening. Take much, did they? Did they get your magnifying glass, Sherlock?'

He really was in a foul mood and that could only mean one thing. 'So you haven't made any progress.'

He didn't meet my eye but scratched his nails in an angry move across the gong, making it sing. 'Junkies, crusties, squatters. The people who know where Hilleker and Chapwin might be don't talk to us, Chris. But I know I'm on the right track. We've staked out Matt and Lisa's flats, they both have council places, the Chapwin woman's right here in the bloody neighbourhood, just up the road in Odd Down. Amazing, isn't it? All you need to get a council flat is break the law or pump yourself full of recreational drugs.' He waved it away. 'Whatever.' I could feel even Needham was tired of that particular rant of his. 'Both of them have scarpered.'

'Must have clocked you,' I rubbed in. 'Doesn't mean they're involved. They've got enough reasons not to want to talk to your lot.'

'I know that. It doesn't help me, though.' Needham still wasn't meeting my eyes but appeared busy examining the photographs pinned to the wall. Still without turning he whipped out a couple of seven-by-five prints from inside his suit jacket and held them out to me. Mug shots of Matt

133

and Lisa. When I made no move to take them he rubbed them impatiently against each other between his thumb and index finger.

'We had a deal, remember?' I reminded him. 'Is this a *new* deal by any chance?'

'Just keep your eyes open for us,' he thundered. 'Take the damn pictures, Chris,' he added quietly, facing me squarely at last. 'And don't say anything cheap now. And don't phone it into Manvers Street.' He put his card on the rim of the gong. 'My mobile number is on the back.'

'Why did you do that? One minute you accuse me of killing Jenny then you hide me from them.'

'Because now you owe me,' I said with what I hoped was an evil grin. We had taken up our station in the kitchen again where I chucked together a salad to go with the dreaded Spag & Pesto I had settled for. 'Gavin is still missing and so is Lisa. Have you any idea where they might be?'

'I never met the Gavin guy. Lisa is still around, but she doesn't look too good on her medication. She had a bit of a rough deal, really; they sent her back to Hill View from here and when she got out of there she was shunted about a lot. She's got her own place now and goes everywhere on a moped so she doesn't have to stop and talk to anyone. Tried to ride it through Sainsbury's once. It nearly landed her back at Hill View. But no, I've no idea where either of them are.'

'Then get one.' If Needham could delegate then so could I. I fished one of my cards from my pocket and slapped it on the counter.

He ignored it. 'The crazy thing is I never really wanted to leave here. It's a good place. It's much harder out there by yourself. This is a good place, really.'

'Shouldn't have buggered it up then, you were warned often enough, as I recall.'

134

'I know, it was the money thing. It's so expensive here.'

'What do you mean "expensive"? It's a charity and everything's paid for by the Benefits Agency.'

'Shows what you know. Sure they pay benefits. Housing benefit and disability. Only the housing benefit never covers the rent they ask, which is pretty hefty. So that comes out of your money for a start. Then there's the food money, you've no choice, it's part of the package. At the end there's practically nothing left. It's a good place, I'm not knocking it and I wish I was back here. But I didn't see much charity going on.' He seemed to contemplate it for a moment. 'You think there's any chance . . . now that . . .' He trailed off. I was glad to see he was capable of embarrassment.

'Any chance of moving back in, now that there are a couple of vacancies?' I needed Matt to trawl the doorways of the city, check out the squats, chat to *Big Issue* sellers and the beggars pretending to play the penny whistle, but to make false promises would have been cruel. 'I'll ask but don't hold your breath. Drug addicts aren't their scene at all.'

'I'm clean now, I told you,' he said, injured.

'Then make sure you stay clean. You haven't had a birthday yet.'

'I know. They make a big deal at NA of someone who stays clean for a year. And every year after that. I like that about them.'

'Not them, Matt. Us. You're part of it now and you're in for life. When this blows over you can go back and have your birthday. I'll bake you a cake myself. First though, this needs sorting. The sooner we find Gavin and Lisa . . .' I furnished him with the mug shot of Lisa that Needham had left. A desperately thin face, a large nose over a pinched mouth, vacant eyes. Mug shots always had the effect of making the subject look guilty. Lisa's hair appeared to supply only the thinnest covering over her bony skull. Matt's own picture looked no more flattering. In fact it didn't look much like him at all, as he was quick to point out. 'If they're looking for the guy in this picture they'll never pick me up.' On the picture board was another snapshot of Gavin, this time with Jenny behind him, carrying a tray full of Christmas crackers. I watched his reactions closely. He seemed unperturbed. 'Haven't seen him. But I'll look. Honest.'

'My numbers are on my card. Now scram.'

Matt slunk away, uncharacteristically without trying to scrounge money off either of us.

Supper was running late. A tired but cheerful Mel arrived for her sleepover duties with her holdall of textbooks and I asked her to join us. She accepted. Spag & Pesto, a sure way to impress the girl. Why Matt hadn't tried to scrounge any money became patently clear when I went to sound the Chinese dinner gong. It had vanished.

Chapter Seven

I knew I would never feel this good again and refused to move a muscle. 'Any more beer left?'

Annis reached out and pulled another bottle of Stella from the sink, opened it with her teeth and handed it over. Mmh. I lifted it in a silent toast before drinking deeply. It was reasonably cold. 'How did *this* happen?' I asked at length.

'It didn't *happen*. As far as I remember I've never got into bed with anyone by accident.'

'This isn't a bed, it's a bathtub.'

'Same rules apply.' She went nearly cross-eyed examining her breasts riding proud of the soap bubbles. 'D'you think my breasts are too small?'

'Too small for what? I don't care what size they are as long as they're pointing at me.'

'That's very shelfish of you.'

'As in prawns and scallops?'

'As in ever so slightly shnuzzled.'

We were on our third refill of hot water and in serious danger of prunification. 'You haven't answered my question.' I really needed to know. Our unexpected, if slightly disabled lovemaking had unnerved me. It altered everything. It interrupted the careful dance we had been engaged in for so long. Annis had changed the music without consulting me. Mind you, I hadn't put up much of a fight when she walked naked into the bathroom and told me to 'shove up'.

'Because I don't want to spoil it by analysing it. We were bound to do it sooner or later and I thought this was a good moment.'

'It was an excellent moment,' I admitted.

'So leave it alone. You're already thinking about later, about tomorrow.'

'Could be.'

'Well don't, all right? If you're thinking about tomorrow that means the moment is already over.' She got up and stepped out of the tub, leaving my bruised and now half-shrivelled body in six inches of soapy water. 'In fact, forget all about it.' She struggled into her bathrobe without bothering to dry off. 'I did it because I felt like it, okay? And I'm glad I did.'

'And do you think you might ever feel like it again?' Sometimes I really can't help myself.

'Not if you keep going on about it, that's for sure.'

My room was in shadow but bright sunshine burned through the cracks of the four-leafed shutters like a medieval cross of fire. Never mind body-clocks, my stomach knew the instant I woke up that it was lunchtime and said so. The rest of me was quite content to just lie there. Judging from the burning sensation down the left side of my chest, anything but lying down would involve pain. My head felt better – though I hadn't tried moving it yet – but my side felt, if anything, worse. Had I not discharged myself I could still be lying snugly in hospital of course, having food brought to me at half-decent intervals, doing very little. Only in my experience no one lets you sleep in hospital after six in the morning. Now my bladder started taking sides with my stomach, which settled the argument. One piece of vitreous china being as good as the next I bypassed the toilet altogether and headed straight for the shower.

Upstairs I could hear the faint bleeping of my office

answerphone, always a source of vague guilt but impossible to face without coffee; downstairs a small sheaf of
letters on the little Moroccan table in the hall. A cheque
from a satisfied client, not before time either, and a couple
of bills which, together with the Inland Revenue, would
cancel out the cheque completely. Win some, lose some. All
doors were closed despite the heat so probably no Annis.
A quick peek into the yard confirmed it, her antique Land
Rover was gone. Which was just as well. I had fallen
unconscious soon after last night's triple bath-time and
needed some time to think about it properly. Either that or
forget all about it. Some hope. I stuck Nirvana on the
stereo to clear my head and investigated the breakfast
opportunities. Not only did it turn out that I was still
incapable of wielding a griddle pan without my left elbow
screaming abuse, there was also nothing in the fridge
worth frying. So better make it lunch. My stomach
growled all the way to the Bathtub.

'How's the Great Detective?' Clive said by way of hello.
'Stella?'

'Not so great and I haven't had breakfast yet, so no to
the Stella.'

'Never stopped you before.'

'You sound like my mother, it's most unbecoming. Give
me some lamb rissoles with lots of sweet chilli sauce,
orange juice and all the coffee you can carry.'

'And a Stella?'

'And a Stella. I hear alcohol is a great painkiller.'

Half an hour later I felt, if not positively, at least possibly
human. I took stock. The Existential Fear Factor had gone
down considerably (because I had too much to worry
about to worry about it), the General Decrepitude Index
was rather high (my ribs still ached when I moved too
quickly) and my Accumulated Guilt Quotient was rampant: I had to admit I was floundering in suppositions and
mere guesses. I was nowhere nearer finding Jenny's killer,
though I had all but eliminated one suspect (Matt); I had

139

searched a warehouse and found nothing (apart from intense hostility); I'd got laid in the bath by a woman half my age and then spoilt it by asking stupid questions; I hadn't set foot in my studio for days for fear of what I might find on the easel and the MOT on my DS had run out.

Enough to be getting on with.

Clive came to clear the plates away. 'Did you ever catch up with the lady you were supposed to meet in here?'

'I didn't. That's a good point though, perhaps it's time I did.'

'Then I'd do something about your hair first. Looks like you shared a hole with a vicious rodent.'

I turned out the pockets of my jeans. Not exactly marbles and bits of string but enough rubbish to make me feel lighter. Notes to myself (since my dictaphone was in Cornwall), letters, my Maglite, petrol receipts I was meant to file for my tax return, my Zippo, which I intend to buy flints for one day, and finally Gill's BBC business card: Gillian Pine, Location Finder. I dug out my mobile from where it had disappeared into the lining of my leather jacket and dialled. If she hadn't noticed the mix-up over the negatives I would start by suggesting a meeting. No use spooking people on the phone, they can simply hang up on you. *The number you have dialled has not been recognized.* I dialled more carefully but got the same result. Directory Enquiries furnished me with the number of Broadcasting House in London. After being shunted about for a bit they set me straight.

Not only did they have no Gillian Pine on their payroll, full, part-time, freelance or otherwise but, 'There is no such job description, really. Yes, production teams have so-called location finders but it isn't a job as such. We use agencies who have properties we can use on their books. And certainly no one goes out looking for picturesque locations in the vague hope of filming them one day, it's always very specific. We don't send people out with BBC

140

business cards knocking on people's doors. I think you've been conned, Mr Honeysett. I suggest you contact the police.'

I said I would and knew I wouldn't. Not yet, anyhow. So Gill was a fraud. What a shame, I had instantly taken to her vivacity, had enjoyed the elaborate stories of her adventures scouring the planet for the BBC. She had definitely travelled, only in a different capacity, it appeared. I wondered if she really had a young son at home, wherever home was, or if it was part of her cover story, making her seem more real. Only what was she after? If she had pretended to be from an agency she could have conned people out of a registration fee. But she didn't. There was a simple explanation – she was casing well-appointed houses for burglaries. The BBC is interested in our house, darling. Flattered home owners invited her inside, let her take photographs, showing off their possessions. Only at Starfall House she had run into our Saudi prince who banks with Sainsbury's and a man with dubious jewellery. And they hadn't liked that much. Since the negatives had found their way to me she had obviously got away from them. The way my ribcage felt that was just as well for her. I had little doubt about who had clobbered me. Yet instead of flooring the accelerator of her little Punto until Bath was a speck in her mirrors she had come here to keep our rendezvous at the Bathtub and leave the photographs for me. Perhaps she didn't scare easily. I thought of Matt, hopefully keeping his ear to the ground, of Lisa, staying away from her flat in Odd Down, of Gavin, alive or dead somewhere in the city, without medication. What had Anne said? *Wild*. Mr Turner, the estate agent who liked to walk by the canal, was out there too, and an irate art collector who hung around Starfall House where an armful of nudes had disappeared without a break-in. Virginia Dufossee, on behalf of her father, concerned lest the police might get involved, her black-eyed brother with his warehouse full of shadows and no burglar alarm. Had I left

141

anything out? Jenny's funeral was today, immediate family only. I toasted her memory, not the last and bloodied one I had of her but of the competent, dedicated, radiant and benevolent presence she had been on this planet.

I have never been overly fond of hospitals and certainly have no favourites. The Royal United however seemed to have a firm fan base in Bath. 'Hands Off Our RUH' was the headline in the *Bath Chronicle* today. Branded the worst hospital in the West, one of the few not to earn a single star, its management team was soon to be replaced, after it had emerged that waiting lists had been massaged and vast sums of money wasted. Yet the citizens of Bath fiercely defended their hospital, remembering only friendly nurses and dedicated doctors. And nurses and doctors, like private eyes and art therapists, are fiercely protective of their patients.

'I couldn't give out any information like that, certainly not to a private individual.' The psychiatric nurse had agreed to speak to me in the reception area of Hill View, the psychiatric wing of the RUH. He had not, however, agreed to tell me anything. He had an impressive, rock-like quality, standing perfectly still while he spoke, only his eyes intelligently mobile.

I tried for reassurance. 'I'm not after medical details. The fact that Mr Backhaus was a patient here is now public knowledge anyway. You are not protecting Gavin by refusing to talk to me. On the contrary, he is missing and the sooner we find him the sooner he'll get the help he needs. Gavin needs care. He's not getting it while he's in hiding.'

He looked straight into my eyes for half a minute, perhaps trying to gauge the level of my sincerity, then nodded. 'You're right, he did make a friend here. After he was moved from Balmoral, that's the lock-up ward, to Sandringham. Carol Hicks. They became quite inseparable. They never seemed to talk much. Gavin was very very quiet. But they did have a good rapport; sat together, went for walks in the grounds. Whether they stayed in touch or not I don't know.'

'Is Carol still here?'

'She's no longer a patient here.'

'Any idea where she went?'

He opened his arms wide. 'Even if I did . . .'

I thanked him for his help, went back to my car and rang Tim at work.

'I need an address for a Carol Hicks. Probably a council tenant.'

'Sure. Now?'

'Now.'

'Call you in a mo.' I felt restless so I started driving back towards town, even though it might turn out that I was going in the wrong direction. I was on Weston Road, passing the Approach Golf Course, when he called back with an address in Milsom Street. I hadn't known that anyone lived in Bath's main shopping street, I'd imagined all upper floors to have been converted to storage or office space. Apparently not. Carol's flat turned out to be one of three above an expensive-looking shoe shop a few doors down from the Loch Fyne Fish Restaurant. The door into the stairwell was propped open with a wooden wedge, the floor was damp as it had just been cleaned. On the second landing I knocked on a dark green impersonal door in a way I hoped sounded light-hearted, possibly even neigh-bourly. I could hear a slight noise, like a door being opened, on the other side yet it was another minute before I heard the clinking of a security chain and the opening of the door. Half a face appeared in the crack, level with mine. Carol was a tall woman, late twenties perhaps, and from what I could see at least half of her short-cropped hair was blonde and one of her eyes was blue. 'Yes?'

'Hi, are you Carol?'

'Says so on the door, last time I looked.'

143

'My name's Chris Honeysett. I'm a private investigator. Would you mind if I asked you a few questions?'

'Depends. What's it about?'

'Gavin Backhaus.'

'Gavin? Haven't seen him for ages.'

'Still, anything might be helpful. Could I come inside for a moment?'

She considered it for a moment. 'S'pose so.' She shut the door to unhook the chain, then stood back to let me into the narrow corridor. 'Straight through.'

The living room was tiny. A two-seater sofa under the window took up most of the space. To the left a door opened into a kitchen galley, next to it a shelf unit with a few books, a midi system and a portable TV. Most of the remaining floor space was taken up with sports gear, trainers, a hockey stick, racquets, a set of orange plastic-covered weights.

'You're into sports.'

'Used to be a lifeguard. Then I fell ill and had to give it up. Now I'm trying to get back into shape.' She indicated the sofa for me to sit on but remained standing herself. 'I heard about Gavin, the whole thing about the murders. Read it in the *Chron*. Do they think he did it? He didn't, I can tell you that for nothing.'

'You spoke to him?'

A shake of the head. 'As I said, I haven't seen him for ages.'

'Did you keep in touch after he left the hospital?'

'No, that was it. He went to Somerset and I got housed here. But I got to know him quite well at Hill View. Believe me, he'd never harm anyone. Especially not the house-keeper. He really liked her. Would you like a mug of tea? I was making some anyway, kettle's just boiled.' Without waiting for an answer she walked into the tiny kitchen, flicked the kettle back on. She had noticed her blunder but hoped I hadn't.

'Tea would be great. Do you mind if I use your bath-room?'

'Go ahead, it's the door on the right.'

The bathroom was directly opposite what had to be the bedroom door. I squeezed in, shut the door noisily. Only one toothbrush. Not stupid, then. As quietly as I could I opened the door again. The handle squeaked a little but I could hear the clinking of mugs from the kitchen. One step across the ridiculously narrow corridor. I tried the bedroom door. Opened it a few inches, enough to peer into its gloomy, curtained interior. The hockey stick caught me across the side of my knee, then Carol crashed her weight into me, knocking me off balance. 'Go, Gav, go, go!'

He'd been hiding behind the door and now shot past me, while Carol blocked my way, brandishing the hockey stick like she meant to use it.

'Gavin, I just want to talk!' I called after him but all I got in answer was the hammering of his feet down the stairs. I really didn't feel like another scrap and a dash after a bloke half my age, so just stood rubbing my knee. 'I only want to talk to him,' I tried to reassure Carol. She didn't even acknowledge I had spoken. She continued to bar my way in a goalkeeper stance, knees slightly bent, light on her trainer-shod feet, her eyes alert little pinpricks of suspicion. After a couple of minutes she suddenly stood aside, knowing she had given Gavin enough of a head start.

'I'm trying to help. I really just want to talk.'

No eye contact. Carol inclined her head towards the door. 'He doesn't talk well. You should know.'

'Is he getting his medication?'

'He's better off without it. And without you lot. I'd like you to go now, please.'

The door closed quietly behind me.

So Gavin was alive and had found himself a champion. If I'd had any sense at all and had contacted Needham he would now be in custody, being questioned. Instead I had sent him running, God knew where. Was I going to contact Needham now and tell him all about it? No, I'd had enough grief for one day. Now I'd try something easy for a change.

Back to the valley but out the other end, up and up towards Chippenham and Jake's place. Another small farm had bitten the dust up here and Jake had moved in a few years ago with the intention of breeding ponies and living quietly. It hadn't worked and so he had turned his hobby into a livelihood: repairing and restoring vintage cars. His business had turned into a goldmine but I have yet to see him without his overall and covering of black grease. By now he could easily afford to give the spanners a rest but he still worked on every car himself. Which is why I trusted him.

The concrete yard between the barns that now served as workshops was full of what looked like junk to me, spare parts, sad shells of once much-loved cars, some under tarpaulin, some sitting on blocks in the sunshine. A couple of short-legged dogs tore through the place like lightning and disappeared again. Jake swaggered out from the largest workshop, wiping his hand on a rag, his shaven head deeply tanned and shiny with sweat. 'You should have rung me first,' was his greeting.

'You'd have told me you were busy.'

'I'm telling you now.' He pointed behind him into the garage at a fabulous white Jaguar, the Inspector Morse type. 'Got to get this fine British motorcar up to show quality by tomorrow so I've got no time for your Frog rust bucket.'

'It's just my MOT's run out and the cops are keeping a beady eye out for me as it is.'

Jake disappeared inside and returned a minute later with a pad and stamp, which he put on the roof of the DS. He walked quickly once around my rust bucket, then reached in through the window and beeped the horn. He shrugged. 'There is nothing wrong with this vehicle.' He stamped and signed the certificate and held it out to me. 'But you have to come back up and have that welding done I mentioned last time or your arse'll hit tarmac soon. Fifty squidlets.'

'There's another little thing. Could you check out a couple of plates for me?' I handed him a piece of paper with the registration numbers of the Mercedes and BMW I had seen parked at Starfall House.

'Seventy, then.'

'I don't carry that much with me.'

'Then you'd better be carrying it when you collect these registrations, hadn't you?' He was already walking back into his workshop.

As I turned out of the yard and on to the track that would take me back to the road something made me feel queasy. Sweet chilli sauce for breakfast? The sunshine flickering through the hedge was altogether too bright today. I put on my shades. A belated hangover? I tried winding down the window, found it was down already. And I was sweating. My heart hammered as though I'd been running. On the narrow tarmac road I stopped to catch my breath. Then I saw it.

The landscape had a hole in it. I shut my eyes hard and opened them again. The hole had become a gash. It was getting bigger and travelled wherever I looked. Its edges flickered like lightning, inside a bright Technicolor movie was playing, things I couldn't quite make out, too fast to catch. I closed one eye, then the other, rubbed them hard. It made no difference but added some interesting swirls. The rent in my vision stayed, sweeping directly across the centre, from bottom left to top right. For a moment I considered going back to Jake's but couldn't see what good it would do. The man was busy. I needed to get out of the heat, out of the glare of the sun. More than anything I wanted to be at Mill House, shutting out the light. But could I drive? I pulled away carefully and found that by angling my head and moving it this way and that I could catch glimpses of the road ahead. All this movement made things worse, the edges of the gash started to curl and pulsate, threatening to obliterate my vision altogether. I slowed down even further, edged my way into the main road at walking speed, stayed as close to the verge as possible. Cars sped by, horns blaring. Fortunately the back roads swallowed me up again soon. I tootled along the narrow lanes, trying not to think of what was churning away in my stomach, my head out of the window, probing the way ahead with the fringes that remained of my vision, trying to ignore the home movies on show in the centre. Now a loud noise appeared behind me. I angled my head back. A beep from a horn. Great. Now I was holding up a tractor. Was I going that slowly? I pointed to the bonnet, hoping to give the impression I had engine trouble. The noise of the tractor's engine seemed to cut through my brain like an angle grinder. The infernal machine followed me all the way home, so it was probably being driven by one of my neighbours, only I couldn't make out which. Annis's Land Rover was in the yard. I made it into the house, up the stairs and into my bedroom where the shutters were still mercifully closed against the glare of summer. Shutting my eyes fast I lay still, very still, for what seemed like a very long time.

'I can't give you a diagnosis over the phone but it sounds to me like you experienced a migraine.' Some experience. My vision had cleared up gradually, my stomach had eventually stopped churning. I felt a bit wobbly still but otherwise okay.

'But I didn't feel any pain, apart from where my head hurts, if you know what I mean.'

'Then you're quite lucky. It's still a migraine, I'd say. It's not so uncommon to get visual disturbances only.

I received your notes from the hospital today. You had quite a nasty crack on the head which could easily be the cause. You really should have stayed in hospital. I suggest bed-rest for the next few days. And do call me if it happens again. In fact, let's make an appointment right now.'

And I thought GPs were overworked. 'I might be too busy for the next few days.'

'Bed-rest, Mr Honeysett . . .'

I checked my phone messages; Virginia Dufossee wanting to know why I hadn't contacted her yet. Could I ring her asap; Simon Paris telling me that naturally the cheque for my canvases had cleared, doubting Thomas that I was, and he in turn had stuck a cheque in the post for me. He had also made enquiries about the Dufossee paintings but drawn a blank. And that was it. No new clients. Small mercies.

'If I didn't think it indelicate I'd say you looked shite.' Annis was sitting at the kitchen table, dressed in her spattered painting gear, with a glass of red wine, stabbing a fork into a huge bowl of salad that seemed to have just about everything in it: salad leaves, cherry tomatoes, cucumber, spring onions, anchovies, feta cheese, parmesan shavings and tiny white ovoid things.

I joined her with a fork and speared one. 'What are these?'

'Quails' eggs.'

'Pathetic size.'

'I think they're fun.'

I popped one in my mouth. It was fun. 'Do you realize we spend most of our money on food, booze, and keeping a couple of thirty-year-old cars on the road?'

'And paint. We spend lots on paint.' She waggled her fork at me, then skewered more greenery and folded it into her mouth. Her perfect, sensuous, generous mouth, glistening now with wine and olive oil. She caught my stare. 'What?'

'Nothing.' I gently put my fork down. 'I gotta get some therapy.'

I drove slowly and carefully, enjoying the spectacular warmth of evening light on the Bath stone of every building I passed. Nothing like going half blind for a while to make you appreciate the simple joy of looking. At anything. I took the long way straight through the centre along George Street, people milling about on the high pavement outside the RSVP bar; down Milsom Street, tourists and locals window-shopping in the sticky evening air; across North Parade Bridge, the weir churning to the left, past the new Magistrates Courts and turned right into Pulteney Road to Widcombe. It was still early. I found a parking space near St Matthew's church and walked down to the towpath. Ducks were going about their lawful business on the pond behind the locks. Few people were about. Bits of police tape still flapped lifelessly in the quiet air near lock number ten. Never one for heights I approached it carefully and peered down into its noisy, shadowy depth. Though the lock was empty, water from upstream continuously squeezed through the bottom of the heavy doors, barred against the pressure of the canal. The cool and slimy wetness of the dark opening reminded me more than anything of an open grave after a spell of rain. A rusted ladder set into its concrete side led all the way down to the unquiet water level. I set one foot on it. A shudder ran down my body and I withdrew it. How desperate would you have to be to jump into that darkness or how easily pushed? Who would hear my short scream before I hit the water? Traffic was still strong on Pulteney Road nearby. The gardens and garages of Caroline Buildings backed on to the towpath here but would anyone hear my shout of surprise and dismay as I fell? I pulled back from the edge and lit the last of Jenny's Camels. Soon I would have to buy some myself and admit that I was

150

smoking again. It was only a short walk along the canal to Horseshoe Walk and Abbey View. A deceptive name more use to an estate agent than the residents. Standing in the street I could see the abbey quite clearly but I doubted the residents could from any of their windows. I was early, the therapy session couldn't have finished yet, but I was curious and decided to barge in if at all possible.

The house was not what I had expected, an ordinary terrace, indistinguishable from its neighbours. Lights were on behind drawn curtains. There was no sign to advertise art or therapy but the name under the bell was right, K. Lythgoe, Dip. Hum. Psych. The door yielded to light pressure, left on the latch, for latecomers perhaps, not early comers like me. Quiet voices, some laughter behind a door on the right off the near empty hall. I opened it quietly without knocking. The little room was crowded. A couple of kitchen tables had been pushed together in the centre, leaving just enough room for the seven people to squeeze past the chairs, plan chests and shelves full of art materials. The clients were clearing their things away. A woman in her fifties with steel grey hair and an apron over a flowery dress pushed wordlessly past me with jam jars of mud-coloured water on a tray, others were putting away drawings and sheets of painted paper. A man in his late forties, also wearing an apron over a blue shirt and red tie, was busy moistening a clay relief with a plant spray.

'You're a little early.' Kate Lythgoe, Dip. Hum. Psych., didn't look nearly as forbidding as she sounded on the phone. She wore a long white painting smock over faded jeans. In her early forties, with short, mud-coloured hair, she even managed a smile that enlivened the laughter lines behind her fashionably small glasses. 'I didn't hear a doorbell though,' she added.

'The door was ajar,' I lied. But I was distracted by the man moistening his clay sculpture. Now he pulled clingfilm over it. The therapist too was distracted. 'Careful you don't smudge it now; yes, of course you can take it home

151

with you; if you leave it on top I'll put it away when it's dry; goodnight, Ben; did you write your name on it, Gail? Won't be a minute,' she said to me. Spray-man looked up, our eyes met briefly. There was no sign of recognition in his. I broke eye contact casually, pretended he was just another face to me. The place emptied with goodbyes and a rustling of paper. Spray-man took his time, was the last to leave. 'Goodnight, Kate,' he said in an imploring voice, making middle-aged puppy eyes at her. 'Goodnight, John,' she answered with professional cool.

So when Mr Turner, our elusive estate agent, pretended to work late, showing houses to clients, he was really making clay sculptures at art therapy classes in Widcombe. There was no doubt in my mind that he had a monumental crush on his therapist. Which came first, his secret therapy sessions or his feelings for Kate Lythgoe, I couldn't judge, but either might go some way towards explaining the behaviour that had made his wife suspicious.

'I feel in need of a mug of tea, would you like some?' she offered when the door closed after him. The therapist suddenly looked tired, as though she had merely been holding herself together for the last session of the day. I needed something to wash down my evening dose of painkillers and anti-inflammatories and nodded, not feeling so hot myself. While she busied herself around the kettle and tea things on top of one of the plan chests I looked around. The walls were covered with mud-coloured paintings, stark cardboard constructions and some bright offerings in tissue paper and glue. My last painting, still festering unvisited on my easel, might have fitted in well. Silently I was handed a mug of weak tea, white specks of curdled milk floating on its surface, and silently invited to sit. She might not be a champion tea maker but she certainly knew how to avoid chi-chat. I squeezed my meal of pills out of their plastic strips and chased them down with a gulp of truly awful tea. She merely raised her eyebrows and inclined her head a fraction.

'Not for psychological reasons, I assure you. Painkillers. Had a little accident.'

'Everything has psychological reasons. Especially so-called accidents.'

'I can't see psychological reasons for this particular accident.' Unless of course it was the warped psyche of my attacker.

'With a different psychological make-up, behaviour pattern or attitude you might not have been in a position to get hurt in the first place.'

In other words, if I hadn't forced my way into a warehouse, if I was in the habit of leaving things to the police, if I hadn't lent my gun to Annis . . . I was beginning to see her point. Which for some reason annoyed me considerably. 'What if the accident is clearly someone else's fault?'

'It has nothing to do with fault or blame. It's the accident itself and what brings you to meet these circumstances that matter.' She shrugged: it didn't matter.

'But what if, for instance, someone suddenly threw a mug at you?' I proposed.

'Then I'd assume that I'd annoyed you just a little?' She smiled a tired smile. I smiled back. She really was quite good at this. A useless friend in a brawl perhaps, since like some Zen master she probably wouldn't be there in the first place. But otherwise quite good.

I repeated my reasons for coming to see her. 'I don't need any medical details. But both Gavin Backhaus and David Cocksley are murder suspects in the eyes of the police.' I didn't mention that so was I. 'And Dave is dead. You could help. Have the police interviewed you yet?'

'You're the only one to have contacted me.'

'So both Dave and Gavin were clients of yours?' A nod. 'And they came to therapy sessions together on Fridays?'

'They came on Fridays. But never together. Dave was quite upset, I think, that Gavin decided to come to the same sessions. Gavin lacks confidence. He was following him around like a puppy dog and Dave couldn't stand it. It interrupted his inner monologue, and he had come to depend on that to keep himself calm. He especially liked walking by himself. So they always arrived separately. Dave usually arrived here first.'

'So, should you be telling me all this?' I couldn't resist asking.

'As you pointed out, David Cocksley is dead.' She took a swig of tea and pulled a grimace. 'I make lousy tea.'

'I'm glad you said it first. Have you ever examined the deeper psychological reasons for making lousy tea?'

'Far too complex.' She waved it away with a weary hand. 'Years of therapy required.'

'Gavin and Dave did come to the therapy session on the Friday of the murder?'

'They did.'

'Did they seem different?'

'Yes, both of them were . . . no, that's not true. David was very agitated. He took up a lot of space, kept bumping into other clients and muttered a lot, but wouldn't really talk. He spilled a lot of paint and produced a big, nervous painting.'

'Of what?'

'It was abstract. Jagged forms, angry colours.'

'Do you have it here by any chance?'

'Gavin took it.'

My turn to raise my eyebrows.

'Gavin was also upset but it showed in a different way. They always arrived separately, a few minutes apart, but this time they arrived simultaneously. I had the impression that Gavin had been haranguing Dave outside or on the way here. They were both quite a handful that evening. Towards the end of the session David ran out. Gavin

154

grabbed both their paintings and ran after him. Some of my other clients got upset with the disruption. People like to have rituals, they come to rely on it. Another of my clients ran out too, because I had been forced to focus all my attention on those two and he felt neglected. So I brought the session to an early close.'

'You know of course that David died in the lock that evening, not far from here?' A slow nod. 'And you didn't feel you should contact the police?'

Another shrug. 'Clearing up a murder is being wise after the event.'

'You want to be wise before the event? Do you realize that whoever killed David might kill again?'

'It had occurred to me. And that's the only reason I'm talking to you.'

I'd had enough by then and made for the door. 'Just one more thing. Which one of your clients ran out after them?'

'I feel I shouldn't implicate anyone. I'm sure it had nothing to do with what happened later.' She gave me a tired look, cradling her mug. 'Very sure, in fact.'

'It wouldn't have been Mr Turner, then?'

She swallowed. I didn't wait around for any more. One Dip. Psych. swallow was enough for me.

I wasn't in the best of moods when I got back to the car. The migraine had unnerved me and lunchtime drinking at the Bathtub had rewarded me with a fuzzy headache behind my eyes which started up a jam session with the perpetual pain that seemed to sprout daily from the back of my head since the warehouse disaster. Hopefully the pills would soon dull both of them. This whole investigation was making me ill. I had to simplify things and what better way to do that than resolve one or other of my cases? Not that I really thought of Jenny's murder as a case, it was far too personal for that. Which is why Needham had warned me off it more than once. At least the

155

police were working on it, unlike the case of the missing Dufossee canvases, which had turned into a right nuisance. I had one more call to make before I'd confront the art-loving siblings: the trusted Mrs Ibbs. I checked my watch – it was an impolite hour to call on her, so I pencilled her in for the next morning. What else could I usefully do tonight? Try and get rid of my assorted aches in a long hot bath followed by . . .? Too bleak a prospect. I turned left into Claverton Street and switched right after the railway arch, crossed north of the river by way of Churchill Bridge. A couple of pints in the Waggon and Horses, Tim's quiet, unloved local, would do me just fine, with or without Tim. The DS zoomed smoothly around Queen Square with its drab obelisk, up Gay Street and past Mr Turner's estate agency into the Circus. The car moved as though revitalized by its dodgy MOT so I drove once around the centre green with its five, century-old plane trees just for the heck of it. Whatever welding it might need there was nothing wrong with the suspension. I flicked it effortlessly into Brock Street the second time it came around and whizzed past the sad green where St Andrew's church had fallen victim to the Luftwaffe, now just a triangle of ragged grass known locally as the *dog toilet*. I found a parking space smack in front of the Waggon and Horses in the shadow of Phoenix House and heaved my bruised carcass out of the car. A quick look inside the Waggon: no sign of my favourite boffin. Stepping back into the road and scrutinizing Tim's windows I detected a glimmer of light. I leant on his bell. It took him a whole age to come crackling over the squawk box.

'Yeah?'

'It's me.'

'All my friends are called "me",' he complained as he buzzed me in. He appeared at the door to his flat in nothing but boxer shorts, his woolly hair a tangled mess.

156

'You been asleep?'

'Bit of a session at lunchtime, had a kip.'

'Want to go back to bed? I just fancied a beer, that's all.'

'No, I'll come. Only give me a couple of minutes for a shower. Why don't you nip next door and start getting them in? I won't be long.'

I pulled out my mobile and keyed in Annis's number. 'Let's see if Annis wants to make it a threesome.' A phone rang beyond the half-open bedroom door. 'Yours?' Tim's face creased into a painful grimace.

Annis sidled through the opening, wearing even less than Tim, and leant against the door jamb. She folded her arms. I folded my mobile. 'Hi, Chris. Yeah, I'll make it a threesome.'

This was one of those situations that required the delicate diplomacy I pride myself on having developed in my later years. 'You're sleeping with both of us?!' I blurted out. She gave the slightest of shrugs.

'You're sleeping with Chris?' Tim's embarrassment had instantly evaporated.

'I only slept with him once.'

'You only slept with *me* once,' he complained.

Annis shrugged again and pushed herself off from the door jamb. 'If you two are going to make a big deal out of this I won't sleep with either of you again, okay?' She slipped back into the bedroom and after a short minute, during which Tim and I exchanged raised eyebrows and head-scratches, re-emerged in deck shoes, jeans and black vest. 'Coming?' she shot at Tim.

'Ehm, yeah, yeah.' I watched him jump into chinos and pull a fresh T-shirt over his head while Annis walked out, leaving the front door wide open. Tim stopped in front of me, still wriggling into his shoes. 'Correct me if I'm wrong, mate. Did we just agree to share . . . the favours of our esteemed colleague?'

'Looks like it, dunnit?'

'Bloody hell, Chris, do I need this drink . . .'

We sat by the aquarium again, the fish huddled near the sputtering pump, dying to the slow rhythm of a Cowboy Junkies tune. Annis had got in the Stellas, which seemed only fair. All three pints were still untouched.

'So what exactly are we drinking to?' I enquired.

'To . . . us?' Tim suggested, looking from me to Annis and back.

'There are conditions.' Both of us got a green flash from her eyes. 'First: no one knows. Number two: no comparing notes.' Tim and I looked at each other like a pair of nodding dogs in the back of a car, our pints lifted. But Annis hadn't picked hers up yet.

'Anything else?' I asked.

'Yeah. Three is company. Agreed?'

'Two's a crowd, I always said so.'

'I really need to drink this *now,*' Tim insisted.

After we'd drained our pints it was decided the next round was Annis's too. By majority vote.

Chapter Eight

It was midnight when the taxi dropped me off outside Mill House. As usual, I had to be the pilot for the last part of the journey along the country tracks. I was barely awake enough (or sober enough) to do it but I had no trouble picking up the driver's chagrin at finding himself in the back of beyond on a Friday night with next to no chance of picking up a return fare on the long haul back into town. He acknowledged my tip with a grunt and sped off, lights on full beam.

During our second round Annis had revealed her decision to go back to Cornwall to see Alison, this time unannounced. 'I have a bad feeling about it somehow. It's been constantly on my mind these past couple of days. I should've stuck it out, whatever Alison said. In fact I'm going now, I can still drive, I only had a pint and a half.' We didn't try to stop her. Annis's hunches usually paid off (unlike some of my own I could mention) but I did get her solemn promise to keep her mobile on *and* charged and to call me at the first opportunity. After she'd left, the evening had turned into a bit of a session, conversation on general bloody-hell-I-can't-believe-it lines. But no comparing notes.

There was only the battered Beetle in the starlit yard, so Annis had taken the Land Rover. Perhaps I could drive the heap into town tomorrow and hand it over to the first scrap merchant before it grew roots here like the rest of our junk collection. Somewhere in those sheds sat a 1950s

Norton, a quad bike, a diesel generator and at least six lawnmowers. None of them worked.

I fumbled for my keys by the front door. They had disappeared into the lining of my jacket and kept eluding my probing hands. Damn, this was difficult. To steady myself I rested my forehead against the cool surface of the door. It gave. Annis hadn't closed it properly. Handy. I reached up and flicked the light switch in the hall. Nothing happened. Not so handy. But I still had my Maglite, somewhere. Ah, that was better. Our unwanted mail lay strewn across the floor by the little Moroccan table. Perhaps this wasn't the moment to clear this up, though. Especially considering the mess I found in the living room. It only took me a nano-second to realize that this chaos wasn't due to Annis's hasty departure. Every drawer open, a small bookcase knocked over, CD cases strewn everywhere, broken glass underfoot. I crunched on tiptoe to my kitchen – it made Alison's look fastidious by comparison. Every jar seemed to have been smashed, their contents oozing everywhere and the whole mess caked in flour. It seemed more like vandalism than burglary. Or perhaps frustration? Back in the devastation of the sitting room I took in the fact that the stereo had been shifted but not unplugged. Even in my befuddled state I realized that this was no ordinary burglary. It was a search. Someone had taken a good look around for something specific. Who and what? Avon and Somerset would never have left such a mess, nor would they have searched the place without me while I was in town. The french window to the verandah was ajar. From the top of the meadow a flicker of light. They were still here and they were in the studio. Even though the alcohol had anaesthetized me well against my aches I was quite sure that fisticuffs with a burglar were out of the question. It would have to be persuasion. I unlocked the gun locker in the cupboard under the stairs and got out the twelve bore and my special cartridges.

My father had tried for a while to teach me to shoot, when I'd turned fifteen, after we'd quit the city and moved to Mill House. But not only did I feel uncomfortable with the big unwieldy weapon, I also had objections on vague moral grounds I'd never quite thought through then. It was enough that my father thought it was something I ought to master for me to deliberately make a mess of it. I was a lousy shot, closing both my eyes at the moment of firing. I winced at the noise. I complained. I hurt my shoulder. My father soon gave up. And I'm still a lousy shot.

It felt good to hold a licensed weapon, though, in case I actually had to use it. (The Webley is really just a deterrent and I've only ever fired it into the air.) I had made up some special cartridges for my up-and-over twelve bore for just this kind of emergency. I'd chucked away the shot and replaced it with rice, which can save you from a lengthy jail sentence if you intend to go blasting away at real-life walking-talking people. It can't kill anyone but I have it on good authority that it hurts like hell. (Arborio rice is best, of course, and highly appropriate for scaring Italians, but I found pudding rice does just as well.)

With a handful of the cartridges stuffed into my jacket pocket and the safety catch off I eased myself out of the verandah door. The moon had been around all afternoon but naturally now, when I needed a bit of illumination, there was no sign of it. I walked slowly up the rise, placing each foot carefully. My breathing seemed by far the loudest thing abroad. Too much booze, too many cigarettes, too much fear. The light still flickered in the studio, swaying shadows danced against the barn door. Only small sounds came from inside. For some reason my visitor didn't seem to throw things around here but worked more systematically, much like our friend at Alison's cottage. I made it to the front of the barn undetected, leant my back against it a few feet from the door, dizzy with suppressed breathing. I tried to calm myself. Breathe. Quick in, slow out. If

161

I guessed right my visitor would turn out to be a masked man armed with a machete. Since our last meeting, though, I had upgraded from a length of copper pipe to a loaded shotgun. No contest.

And then it all went, as they say, pear-shaped.

From the shadows of Mill House the dark shapes of two men appeared, advancing up the meadow towards me. Then, like some evil magic, a bright pinhole appeared in the meadow and swallowed them. The hole turned into a gash, slashed straight through my vision. I ducked down and angled my head away – the shapes reappeared in my peripheral vision. They didn't speed up so probably hadn't spotted me yet. Covering three men with one gun was an unattractive proposition at the best of times but you can't cover what you can't see. A strategic withdrawal then. There was still time to slip away and hide. Then my mobile rang.

It was good to know that Annis was keeping her promise to call me as soon as she got safely to Cornwall, only at this precise moment I felt positively ungrateful. I plunged my hand into my jacket pocket but the phone was hopelessly lost in the lining somewhere. The dark shapes sped up the hill and at the same time my original quarry stepped out of the barn door to my left, his eyes glistening in the starlight. He wasn't brandishing his machete. Even half blind I could make out the glint of the pistol in his hand. I levelled my shotgun at him.

'Shit!' He spoke for both of us and jumped back inside, firing a shot through the wooden wall at my back. The noise made the lights dance wildly in front of me. Splinters flew but he'd missed. Just. There was little point in trying to hide while my mobile chimed insanely away in my jacket. Straightening up I blasted blindly at the two men in the meadow and ran around the corner of the barn towards the shelter of the tree line behind it. Another shot rang out, thumped into the foliage ahead of me. As soon as I reached the trees I shrugged off my jacket and flung it as far away from me as possible into the dark. It stopped ringing instantly. Typical. In a sideways lope, always angled at the remains of my vision, I trampled through the undergrowth for ten seconds, then flung myself down behind a tree, panting. I could hear urgent voices from the direction of the studio but couldn't make out what was being said. Only now did it dawn on me that I had thrown away not only my sole way of calling for help but also the spare shotgun cartridges in my jacket. One barrel loaded with pudding rice was what I had left. Not much good against a real gun and pretty useless to a blind man. Where there wasn't total darkness the bright acid of overlit images flickered and twisted like burning celluloid. The doctor's advice about coping with another attack had been: complete darkness, lie down, relax. Well, two out of three wasn't bad. I closed my eyes and concentrated on listening. A few birds had been upset by the ruckus and complained to each other from the safety of their perches. If I held my breath I could even make out the rush of the mill stream far below. Nothing else, apart from the pounding of blood in my ears. What would they do next? What would I do in their position? They hadn't come here to kill me or they'd have jumped me in the house – I'd be dead by now. So all the blazing-gun nonsense was just a panic reaction to finding a bloke with a twelve bore on the prowl.

Still no sign of them. On all fours, as quietly as I could manage in the undergrowth of ferns, brambles and nettles, I inched forward towards the edge of the trees, aiming roughly for the place where my jacket should be. After a few more minutes of crawling, waiting, listening, I stood. A car engine started up somewhere, then total silence. They were gone. Knowing nothing of my handicap and the culinary nature of my ammunition the idea of entering the wood to flush me out must have looked pretty uninviting. Eventually I found my jacket. I reloaded the first barrel, just in case, and stepped into the meadow. It felt peaceful.

The gash in my vision had contracted into a small light-ning strike in the corner of my eye. My head was pound-ing but that was nothing new. For the first time since I got home I had time for any emotions other than fear and the first that surfaced was anger. This kind of thing was not supposed to happen. Mill House was my refuge, the only place I could run to and forget about the murkier things the Good People of Bath got up to. Of course Simon Paris, fearful of losing a sale, had kindly taken the Saudis directly to my doorstep. I had little doubt that it was Al-Omari and his retinue who had just paid me a visit, but I was shocked that guns had made an appearance. Guns are invariably bad news. In Britain only a certain type of crook uses guns: drug dealers, those defending their territ-ory against other crooks, and very rarely the loner holding up a pub or post office (nobody robs banks any more, it can't be done). And desperate people of course, who don't count the cost.

I didn't get paid enough for this nonsense. But I'd give it one more shot, so to speak, and if that didn't do it then I'd hand the whole shebang to Needham to sort out. And perhaps I'd take early retirement while I was at it.

Back at the house I found that the fuses had been ripped out. Even after I had restored the lights it took me a while to satisfy myself that I was really alone, poking the gun barrel into each room, closet and corner. Everywhere the same mess but nothing missing as far as I could see.

'But how could you tell in this mess?' Tim said, slurping coffee from his mug and indicating the scene in my office with a sweep of his free hand. 'I mean, even before they came and messed it up this was a bit of a tip, mate.'

I'd restored every room so far except my office, which is usually where my occasional cleaning frenzies peter out. It had taken me all morning but it had miraculously cleared my head, only not sufficiently to see the obvious. Tim wasn't so handicapped. 'So you think it was the Saudis? And the guy from Alison's cottage?'

'Pretty certain. But what on earth has Alison to do with it all? What are they after? They searched her studio, then my house and our studio.' I swivelled idly on my office chair, stirring the mess of papers on the floor with one foot.

'Looking for any evidence we might have found that they've been naughty Saudis?'

'In Alison's studio? Doesn't make sense. What's more, we didn't find any evidence, did we?' I was thinking of our disastrous trawl of the drinks warehouse.

'What about Gill's pictures?'

And of course Tim was right. Not that I had the foggiest notion where I had put them but even after going through every scrap of paper in my office, where I thought I might have dumped the prints, we found no sign of them. 'Hey, your office looks quite neat with everything in piles,' Tim said. 'All you need now is a skip to put it all in.'

'It's not me who needs a skip. *They'll* need a skip, a towtruck and an ambulance if I ever catch up with them.'

'Would you say you're a bit annoyed then?'

'Very astute. Wouldn't you be? I've been threatened with a machete, beaten senseless, burgled and shot at. And all since I've agreed to find the missing Dufossee canvases.' I didn't even count my lacerated behind, which was mending nicely, thank you.

'I still don't understand why they'd buy your paintings, for good money, too, and then get involved in art theft five minutes later.'

Five minutes later. 'They didn't,' I muttered to myself. 'Ay?'

'Five minutes later, you said. But they went to Simon Paris on the same day the canvases disappeared.'

'That's what I call busy.'

'Or organized.' I suddenly had an awful feeling about

this Saudi Arabian interest in my paintings. I swivelled round and switched on my computer. While it gurgled away sorting itself out I rang Simon Paris, a wonderfully organized man. 'When was the first time we sold to Al-Omari?' Simon took less than a minute to call up the information on his screen. 'And you have the list of paintings, naturally?' He had. 'Fax it to me, will you?' I hung up before he could bombard me with questions. Tim sat patiently while I went on to the Art Loss Register and trawled the relevant pages until I found what I had hoped was not there. But no doubt about it, four paintings had gone missing from a country house just over the border in Wiltshire on the day of the first sale. By the time the fax machine spat out Simon's neat list I felt quite ill. I rang Jake. 'Had any luck with those number plates?'

'What about my money?' was the prompt answer.

'It's on its way, Jake, this is urgent.'

'It's always urgent with you. You don't know how to relax.'

'There's truth in that, any suggestions?'

'Try winding up a private eye, always works for me.' He cackled. I hate it when he cackles. 'Hang on, I'll get it for you.' After an eternity he came back on the line. 'The Beemer belongs to a Leonard Dufossee, the Merc is rented, from Bath Exec. That do you?'

'Cheers, Jake, the cheque's in the post.'

'I don't want a bloody . . .'

I hung up and turned to Tim. 'Chuck me the phone book and make some more coffee, will you?'

He groaned but moved. 'The kitchen is miles from here,' he complained, going downstairs.

That was the idea. I had a delicate phone call to make and Tim was prone to fits of the giggles when I did impersonations. I called Bath Executive Cars. 'Detective Inspector Deeks, Bath CID. I'd like to run a check with you on a silver Mercedes 500S, registration number . . .' It works every time. I'm quite good at doing Deeks' voice too, I just pretend I'm falling asleep. The car was rented out to a Mr Al-Omari. The smug bastard had used his own name. And it was due back in three days, to be collected at Bristol airport. 'No, no offence has been committed, it's just a question of elimination. Thank you for your co-operation.'

That fluttering feeling returned. Was I doing the right thing? What exactly *was* I doing? Airport. I didn't like the sound of that and I still only had a vague idea of what was going on. I rang Alison's cottage and Annis's mobile, for the fifth time this morning, and again got no answer. Annis had promised to leave her mobile on and keep it charged . . . If ever there was a time to call Needham it had to be now. Hadn't it? How long would it take to bring the Superintendent up to speed . . . how would he react . . . would he commit resources to what was no more than a bad feeling in my gut, a bad taste in my mouth . . . how long would I be stuck in Manvers Street cop shop, unable to make a move?

Move. I clattered down the stairs and shouted for Tim. 'Scrap the coffee, we're moving.' I handed him the shotgun and a handful of cartridges.

'You know of course the police wear bullet-proof knickers for a job like this?' he asked as he loaded the gun. 'And they absolutely refuse to do this kind of job on their day off?' We walked out to his car. 'And they're practically immune from prosecution if anything goes wrong?' He put the shotgun on the tiny back seat and covered it with his raincoat. 'Not to mention the fact they're highly trained professionals?' He started the car and we moved off towards Bath. 'And they get a detailed briefing about what their role in the operation will be?'

'All right, here's what I want you to do. Anyone shoots at you, you shoot back.'

'Sounds reasonable. What if someone shoots at *you*?'

'Just don't join them, is all I ask.'

I picked up the DS at Northampton Street. From there,

167

Tim followed in his TT. Two black cars, two good guys, two guns. This felt better. If we got caught Needham would hang us from the nearest lamppost.

We accelerated at the turnoff for Starfall House, swung through the gate at speed and crunched side by side into the gravel, just as Leonard slammed shut the boot to his BMW. No sign of the Mercedes but Virginia's yellow Lotus and an old-fashioned red Fiesta were parked in the bay. Too wound up to think straight I got out of the car and walked towards Leonard. He'd acquired a new set of black eyes and wore a broad plaster over his left temple but it didn't impede his movements one bit: he was in his car, flooring the accelerator before I had time to grab him. Tim furiously lent on his horn. I had come between him and the BMW and he couldn't cut him off without running me over. No slouch, he threw his car into reverse and the TT and Beemer both slewed towards the road. By the time they reached the gate it had become a side by side race of chicken: there just wasn't enough space for two cars to go through the opening. At the last moment Tim threw his car into forward again, wheels spinning, while Leonard kept going. He missed by a few inches and hit the stone gatepost with that hideous sound only crumpling car metal seems to produce. The BMW pivoted, bucked and stalled.

Inside the car Leonard was holding his own balloon fiesta. He tried to struggle out from what appeared to be at least four airbags. He hadn't worn his seat belt and had slid forward during the impact and smashed his knees against the dashboard. I pulled him out by the passenger door. He had trouble standing up and slid to the ground, his back to the car, and rubbed his legs, groaning.

'Remember me, Dufossee? I was hired to find your Daddy's paintings.'

'Piss off, you're fired!' Petulant.

'It was your sister who hired me. Let's go and ask her.'

'You arseholes! You ruined my car and now I can't even stand up. Wankers!'

'Language,' Tim chipped in. Cradling the shotgun in his arms like an American Indian Chief he looked effortlessly menacing in a way I never seem to achieve.

Virginia had appeared at the porticoed front door, her arms folded, her look more of disgust than concern. She didn't move, just watched and waited. Leonard seemed to consider his options, holding his knees, grimacing with pain. He had no choice but to let me help him up. Leaning heavily on my shoulder he hopped the thirty yards or so to the house, from time to time checking out Tim's Indian Chief impressions. The battle of wounded knees. All over bar the shouting.

It was Virginia who did all the shouting. 'You stupid, stupid man! You bastard! You stupid, stupid shit! I don't want you back in the house, you can go and rot, I don't care what happens to you.' She was loud but not as loud as she could have been. There was a tiredness, an edge of resignation in her voice, and she didn't make any move to stop us as I helped Leonard inside. From the passage to the kitchen came the sound of broken glass being swept up. Perhaps Virginia had used some of the horrible lustre ware to back up an earlier argument. Best thing for it. I steered Leonard through the open door on the right, into the room with the baby grand, and dumped him on to a sofa where he crumpled into an unhappy heap. Virginia had followed us in. Dressed as she was in white silk top, slacks and delicate sandals she looked like a guardian angel who was ready to quit the job.

Tim shut the doors behind us and broke open the shotgun. 'Sorry about the armoury,' he apologized to her.

'I don't care if you stick it up his arse.' Leonard looked as though he minded very much. She lit a cigarette and sucked on it so hard, not a wisp of smoke re-emerged when she exhaled.

'So you know?' I suggested.

'All I know is that this shit of a little brother is *somehow* responsible for the lack of paintings on these walls. That's why I hired you in the first place, I always suspected it was him. But he swore blind he had nothing to do with it. I wanted to believe him, I guess. Shit.'

'Send them away, Ginny,' Leonard pleaded. 'They're going to make things worse. Perhaps I can work something out.'

'Shut up! I want those paintings back. Every one of them. And what do you do? You run. You've always been the same, you useless shit. Just like the time –'

'Wait a second,' I interrupted. I had the distinct feeling we didn't have time for a complete list of her sibling's shortcomings, especially if Leonard had tried to run off somewhere. 'What are you running from? Not us, you couldn't have known we'd rumbled you.'

Leonard looked at me, bit his lips and looked away again. He was very much the younger brother now, the only one sitting down, the grown-ups ranged around him.

Virginia exploded into the silence. 'I chucked him out, that's why. I threatened him with the police, told him I knew it was him. He didn't deny it but he didn't tell me how and who.'

'Or why?' I enquired.

'Because he fucked up again and this time Dad refused to bail him out. His latest business is in tatters, he owes huge sums, and naturally not just to the bank. Oh no, that would be far too straightforward for Leonard. He has to get into the deepest shit on offer.'

I turned to Leonard. 'Who are you running from? Creditors? Al-Omari?'

He looked up at me through his half-closed, swollen eyes. 'You've no idea what Al-Omari is like. And Eely's gone and flipped his lid. It all went to his head.'

'Tom Eels,' his sister supplied. 'My idiot brother took

him into the business. He's an ex-con and he's got psycho written all over him.'

'This Eely, he's got close-cropped hair, wears a death-head ring?'

'That's him,' she confirmed. 'Charming character.'

I sat down and faced Leonard across the coffee table, trying not to let my anger show. 'All we want is the paintings. I'm not interested in taking this to the police, that's for your sister to decide. But I want to get to those paintings before they leave the country.'

'Well, you can't,' he said bleakly. 'They left the country years ago.'

Without warning Virginia jumped on him like a leopard defending her cubs. Before we could pull her off she had landed several badly aimed blows all over his body. Her brother made no effort to defend himself other than to curl up into a ball in the corner of the sofa. I got the distinct feeling this was something he had learnt to do early in life.

It was a while before we could continue. I persuaded Virginia to organize coffee for everyone. After a few moments a kind-faced grey-haired woman in her late sixties appeared with delicate china cups of coffee on a lacquered oriental tray. Mrs Ibbs looked exactly how I'd imagined her. If I ever hired a housekeeper, she would have to look like this.

We were all sitting down now: Tim curious, Virginia fuming, Leonard biting his lips and digging his fingernails into his thumbs, not touching his cup. After my first exposure to Dufossee coffee I approached mine with caution but it turned out to be excellent. Mrs Ibbs, unlike her charges, knew the difference between coffee and chemical warfare.

Knowing that Al-Omari's hire car was due back so soon had made me jumpy but the news that the paintings were out of our reach had calmed me down again. 'How could they have left the country years ago?'

'The paintings that were stolen were fakes. The real ones

171

went a while ago,' Leonard said weakly. He didn't dare look at his sister, concentrating instead on his hands. 'No one ever noticed. Dad's eyesight's not what it was and Virginia knows nothing about art. And the fakes were very good, as long as you didn't look at the back of the canvases. It started with one, but Al-Omari wanted more and more. Once I was in, they wouldn't let me stop.'

'You wanted to stop?'

'I wanted out ages ago. But Eely wouldn't let me, for a start. He's mental, every bit as vicious as Al-Omari and Nadeem. They do this everywhere. Usually it's straightforward theft but I wouldn't let them. So we came up with the idea of replacing the originals with forgeries.' Virginia snorted with contempt. 'I thought I was going to inherit them anyway, Dad had been ill for so long . . . it was more like borrowing from myself, from the future.'

'Then why steal the fakes?' I wanted to know.

Virginia sighed. 'Because Dad hasn't got long and he suddenly decided to leave the paintings to the nation. It would all come out then, of course.'

'So they had to disappear or it would come out that I had been involved.' Leonard groaned. 'And they decided they wanted the fakes as well. Real art, fake art, it doesn't matter. It all sells in Arab countries, as long as they're figurative, preferably nudes since there's an injunction against depicting Allah's creation. They're selling to rich Muslims who really don't give a shit about the Koran. I mean, they've got zillions of oil dollars, they want all the trappings of wealth. And that includes paintings, Western art. It's just like the Nazis, they vilified modern art in public but kept the stuff they confiscated for themselves.'

'What about my paintings? Why buy those?' I thought I already knew but wanted to hear it confirmed.

'Yours? Wrapping paper. Your stuff goes over the top, then into a modern frame. It means they've got legit documentation for what they export. Same with all the others

172

they nick. They picked on you because you're prolific and they can get roughly the right sizes.'

They can be an incy bit larger, Simon had said. 'So why all the panic?'

'Because of you lot, of course. They got rattled and are taking their business elsewhere. Most of it comes from Italy anyway, only some collectors specialize in British art. But Eely really went apeshit. He's not all there, you know? He wants everything "cleaned up". He says he's never going back inside, so "no loose ends". And you and your lot seemed to turn up everywhere, here, the warehouse, the forger's cottage –'

'The forger's cottage? You mean Alison, Alison Flood?'

'That's her.'

Alison's new car, the new white goods. *I worked so hard to afford the cottage, you've no idea how hard.* No wonder she couldn't show us her latest work. 'So it was Eely who searched her studio when I was there. Why?'

'I told you, he's gone round the bend. He's convinced the woman made other copies. Or has kept some failed ones that could give the game away if she tried to flog them. Whatever. He wants everything destroyed, he's paranoid. He looked for copies in your place too. And the pictures that woman took when she turned up here. They followed her, trying to figure out how she fitted in. Eventually they saw her leave the photos at a restaurant. Then you arrived to pick them up. So they knew you were behind it. We assumed you'd long figured it all out.' This was not the time to set the record straight. I let Leonard run on. 'They got the photographs back from your place. But Eely thinks everyone's out to get him. Gave me these as a warning, in case I squeal.' He pointed at his bruised eyes. 'And now I've squealed,' he trailed off.

'Keep doing it. Where are the Saudis now?'

'I've no idea, honest. They never tell me where they hang out. They come to me. I think they've probably gone by now, at least I hope so. But it's Eely who scares me the most. I knew you were getting closer, close enough to get yourself clobbered by him. I'm sure he'd have killed you if this one hadn't turned up.' He jerked his head in Tim's direction. I certainly shared that conviction. 'He's completely out of order. I'm not going to hang around and wait for him to blow up in my face again.'

'Of course you're not, you're coming with us,' I said cheerfully.

He stared at me in genuine horror. 'What for? No way! If he sees me with you he'll go apeshit. He'll kill me.'

'Don't worry, we came well prepared.' Tim lovingly patted the stock of his shotgun in confirmation.

'It's that or the cops and protective custody.' I shrugged. 'It's all the same to me, matey. Take your pick. I've too many questions to ask and not enough time to sit around here.'

Tim and I stood. Leonard reluctantly unfolded himself and rose too. He looked like a man about to go for the long drop. I realized I would have to watch him like a hawk or he'd disappear at the first opportunity. In the hall, Virginia called me aside. She had recovered some of her brusque business manner, so I knew what was coming. 'Do you believe him? About the paintings being lost, I mean?'

'I do. He's right, I'm afraid.'

'No chance of retrieving them?'

'From Saudi Arabia? None at all. Even with Al-Omari in custody and a full confession we wouldn't get them back. We're not talking local criminals receiving stolen goods, here.' What we *were* talking about were very rich and powerful people in secretive and undemocratic societies, with a medieval justice system, where the rich are able to hide behind a thousand veils of influence and patronage while ordinary thieves have their hands chopped off. Only the religious police would show any interest in finding the paintings, and they would happily destroy them on the spot if they clapped eyes on them. 'For the sake of your insurance the police should be told now. Keep my name

174

out of it if you can. I must warn you, though, your insurer will only pay out if you're prepared to have your brother officially charged with the theft. I don't see how you could keep him out of it.'

She considered this for a moment. 'I feel I should leave that decision with my father. If it was up to me . . .' She opened her arms in a gesture of defeat, then held out one slender hand for me to shake. 'Thank you, Mr Honeysett. Please send me your bill.' I certainly would.

Tim followed my car as before. Next to me Leonard had sunk deep into the passenger seat trying to become invisible. It took another threat of delivering him straight to the police station to get Eely's address out of him, and it nearly wasn't enough. The little toad never realized how hard I had to fight the impulse to thump him. Everyone else already had. How had he managed to get himself involved with a character he feared and loathed so much? Debt, of course. Leonard had needed money to save his drinks business. With his father unwilling to bail out another failing business venture and the banks refusing point blank to extend his loans, he looked for alternatives. And stumbled on Mr Eels in a pub, freshly released from a stretch of two and a half for aggravated burglary; who boasted that it had all been worth it, since he had a tidy sum stashed away. Leonard in turn boasted to him about his brilliant mail order drinks business. No doubt at that time Leonard had felt superior to the uneducated young man, but that would change. Soon Eely's money disappeared without showing the promised returns. Eely became threatening and started making 'arrangements' to recoup his losses. Like delinquent children they began by stealing small items from Starfall House, uncatalogued silver and valuable china pieces which were never missed. Al-Omari arrived on the scene later. How did a small-time thug like Eely find a man of Al-Omari's calibre?

175

'We sold the stuff we nicked to an antiques dealer in Walcot Street who didn't ask questions. But when Eely mentioned there might be paintings and what they were he didn't think he could handle it by himself. He brought in Al-Omari and Nadeem. From then on we had no say in what happened.'

I knew only one antiques business in Walcot Street by name. 'Austin Antiques?'

Leonard was gratifyingly impressed. 'Jesus. Yes, it was. Skinny guy with a natty little beard. He takes a cut, of course. Everyone takes a bloody cut. And because I owed Eely and others, not to mention the bank, one painting made no impression on my situation. But now I was in, don't you see? They wouldn't have let me pull out if I'd wanted to. So we started borrowing them in pairs. The woman in Cornwall was good. She'd only need the originals for a weekend, then continue from a series of photographs, all digitally mapped, colour matched and what not. She knows her stuff, all the techniques and colours those painters used. Then we'd swap them over when they were dry.'

Considering the amount of money I had made from providing the 'wrapping paper' for the stolen paintings, the profits had to be astronomical. It was the oldest law of economics: supply and demand regulate price. Anywhere in the world a painting is worth whatever someone is prepared to pay for it. In Saudi Arabia of course the demand for a near unobtainable commodity like figurative art, especially nudes, meant prices well beyond anything Western collectors, even obsessive collectors, were prepared to pay. And so churches and palazzos in Italy, monasteries in Greece, country houses in England and Scotland kept on emptying. It was part of the constant flow of desirable goods around the planet: plundered icons from Russia and the Balkans going west, stolen luxury cars from Britain and mainland Europe going east; paintings from British collections disappearing to the Middle

East along with the four-wheel drives that vanish from the supermarket car parks; badly safeguarded artefacts from Italy going to the four corners of the earth and Asia's cultural heritage being dismantled for general distribution. The carnage goes beyond mere theft; sometimes whole monasteries are torched to mask the disappearance of a couple of artefacts. Even the pious community of Mount Athos had its fair share of suspicious fires . . . Did I mention I hate art thieves?

What rankled even more than having my own paintings abused to smuggle stolen masterpieces, even fake masterpieces, out of the country was the fact that I was powerless to bring the originals back. Fortunately I had never deluded myself about my chances of recovering them.

We parked behind the Holburne Museum, which at this moment had more Gainsboroughs on show than you could shake a stick at. All safe and snug, of course.

Tim carried the shotgun, wrapped into his raincoat. He looked desperately suspicious to me but the sunbathers on the grass and the families at the tables around the minute tea house were magnificently self-absorbed. As ever, the tea house had more visitors than the museum it belonged to. No one gave our little procession a second glance.

It took all of Tim's diplomatic skills to charm Leonard out of my car ('I have your sister's express permission to stick this gun up your arse, remember?'). We kept him firmly sandwiched until we arrived at Eely's basement flat on the west end of Darlington Street, opposite the little church of St Mary the Virgin.

'What car does he drive?' I asked.

'He uses the van from the business. White box van. Says *Sulis Wines* on all sides. He usually parks around the corner, in Edward Street.'

Tim loped off to check while we waited out of the line of sight from the basement windows. 'What kind of gun does he have?' I wanted to know next.

'A little silver thing. First I thought he was trying to fool me with a cigarette lighter but it's real. 4.5 mm.'

There were more lethal guns on the streets but at point blank range calibre becomes an academic issue – a hole in the head is a hole in the head. And I needed a hole in the head like . . . well, I just didn't.

'No sign of any van,' Tim reported when he reappeared from the Great Pulteney Street corner. 'Doesn't mean a thing, mind, he could have parked elsewhere.'

It was near impossible to descend quietly on the cast iron steps down to his front door, though the ceaseless stream of traffic on the nearby roundabout helped to mask the metallic clang of our descent. The little courtyard was littered with oozing bin liners and empty wine boxes. It appeared Eely was drinking his share of the company stocks. Nicotine yellow net curtains, encrusted with squashed flies, covered the two small windows. The opaque glass set into the scuffed front door revealed no movement. I bent down to peer through the letter box and hoped not to see a silver glint when I pushed the flap. If he was in and prepared for us . . .

Eely had aptly demonstrated his willingness to use his gun in my studio. But we had to go through with this. We had nothing on the guy apart from Leonard's testimony, and right now he didn't look up to much, staring at the door as if his doom lay on the other side. As well it might.

Gingerly I pushed the pock-marked metal flap. It was shadowy inside yet I could clearly make out that the hall was empty. I let Tim do the business. When the lock clicked open he unsheathed his gun and poked it into the widening crack. I cocked my revolver and pushed the unhappy Leonard in front of me. He had gone rigid and shuffled with tiny steps like a man with his shoelaces tied together. I deposited him against the wall. Both Leonard and the wall felt damp to the touch. We all stood still, listening to the ticking silence. Two doors led off the narrow hall, both were open. Tim and I sought each other's eyes, nodded a silent agreement, then got it wrong and tried to storm through the same door together.

'More Laurel and Hardy than . . .'

'Cagney and Lacey?'

'As long as I can be Lacey.'

'After you, Mary Beth.' We quickly established that the place was empty. Surely no one could live with a stench like this anyway. It went some way beyond dampness. There was the whiff of garbage decomposing in the moist heat as well as the base note of festering drains and stagnant dishwater in the clogged-up sink in the tiny kitchen-diner. Dining had consisted of takeaways – Indian, Chinese and pizza – and the mouldy remains of a couple of weeks' culinary debasement were scattered over the floor, sofa and coffee table. Beer cans and wine bottles were strewn everywhere, along with curled-up girly magazines and empty fag packets. Apart from the detritus this room appeared empty, no sound system, no TV, not a scrap of personal belongings. The bedroom was empty too, apart from a bedstead, its uncovered mattress sporting uninviting stains of dubious origin. Everywhere the debris of departure: scraps of paper, a broken biro crushed on the floor, the odd crusty sock, a clapped-out pair of trainers. The windowless toilet and shower room made me shiver. It had stains and encrustations, one bar of cracked pink soap and not much else.

'Looks like our friend quit his lodgings. Any ideas?'

Leonard looked relieved, shook his head. Tim hollered from the kitchen-diner. 'Chris, over here. How do you like this?'

I didn't. Blu-tacked to the wall under a stopped kitchen clock were three colour prints. The topmost showed Annis and myself entering the Bartlett Street Antiques Centre. It had to have been taken the day I discharged myself from hospital. It was a snapshot, probably taken with a cheap camera and from some distance. The second was of Tim walking towards his TT in a car park. 'That's up at the uni,' he confirmed. The last print was of Alison. Unlike the others this was taken from quite close up. Alison looked at the camera, one hand controlling a wayward strand of dark hair. An uncertain smile. The background was blurred. Had Eely taken this picture or did he steal it? All the prints and the surrounding wall were punctured by many small holes. The print of Alison was pinned by a dart piercing her forehead. He'd been using all of us for target practice.

'The guy's been following us around.'

'I don't think he's a fan, though.' Tim tickled the plastic plumage of the dart.

Eely had flipped. No loose ends, Leonard had said.

'Leonard?' I looked for him in the hall. The front door was ajar. I raced up the iron stairs and searched the horizons – no sign of the little shit. Only now did it occur to me that I didn't know where he lived, not that I thought he would go there unless he'd somehow managed to keep the place secret from his unstable partner. At this moment I couldn't have cared less. He had outlived his usefulness. Whether his family decided to shop him or not was immaterial now. I would drop him in it at the first opportunity. After all, he'd never been my client, had he?

As far as Eely was concerned, Alison had probably outlived her usefulness too. Or was that all of us? I keyed in Annis's number and got nothing. Alison's phone at the cottage rang but no one picked it up.

'I can't raise Annis or Alison. I don't like it. Eely might go down there. I think he might have tried to kill her once before, by running her off the road,' I told Tim on the way back to the Holburne. I was nearly running now. I'd handled this whole affair badly, right from the beginning. I should have made Eely my priority from the moment I escaped from the warehouse. 'I'm going down there. Now.'

'Am I coming?'

'No, I want you here. Find Al-Omari and Nadeem. If you do, call Needham and bring him up to speed. Tell him they're armed, that'll get him going like a bullet train. Tell him anything you like. Try all the hotels in and around Bath, the guest houses, B&Bs . . .'

'That could take forever. Why don't we let them get to the airport, have Needham pick them up there?'

'We haven't got anything on them apart from illegal firearms offences. The paintings could well be shipped separately and they're not likely to take guns on to the plane. They must have picked them up over here and they'll leave them here. No, we've got to get to them while they're still tooled up so Needham can hold them. Unless Leonard makes a full statement. And I just lost him.' I'd suddenly remembered what I'd needed Leonard for.

We had reached our cars behind the museum. 'Let me have the shotgun back.' Tim was only too glad to relinquish it, he's never been keen on guns. 'You can start with the Carfax down the road in Great Pulteney Street. It's the only dry hotel in Bath.'

'You mean dry as in teetotal? Weird.'

'I know, it's shocking. But it might appeal to Muslim clientele, so it's worth your first shot. One other thing. If you get time, get on to the Land Registry and find out who actually owns Somerset Lodge. The Culverhouse Trust only rents it, I want to know who from. And speaking of Somerset Lodge, you'll have to cook them a meal tonight, I'll never make it back in time.' I peeled the key off my key ring and shoved it into his reluctant hand.

'You have got to be kidding! I can't cook, I just throw stuff on barbies.'

I was already nosing the DS out of the wrought-iron gate. 'They'll love it,' I called back to him. 'Only make sure you get some rabbit food for them as well.' The look he gave me made me glad I had disarmed him first.

As soon as I joined the traffic on Darlington Street my own problems drove poor Tim from my mind. If I tootled down A-roads all the way to Tredannik it would take me the best part of the day. It would have to be the motorway and even that would spit me back on to minor roads at Exeter. I'd been all right on the road since my panic attack on the M5 but I hadn't driven on a motorway since. What if my panic returned? What if I froze behind the wheel again and ended up with shredded nerves on the hard shoulder, without Annis to take over from me? Slowing only for built-up areas I pushed the car as fast as it would go along the A368, heading for the M5. Chew Valley and Blagdon Lake flew by. I took none of it in but pushed on south on the A38. I would join the M5 at Junction 22. *Junction*. The word alone brought beads of sweat to my forehead. This was all wrong. As long as I went by minor roads I would definitely make it and only definitely would do. I dug around for my mobile. Driving and talking on my mobile at the same time? There were limits. I stopped at an old-fashioned corner shop in a one-eyed village called Rooks Bridge and called Needham on his mobile.

'Mike, this is Chris.'

'What's up, Honeysett? I hope this is about Matt Hilleker and Lisa Chapwin.' So neither of them had been picked up. I wasn't sure any more that this was a good thing.

'I'm working on that, promise. This is something else. I need a favour.'

'Favour? Go to hell, Honeysett, I haven't arrested you, what more favours do you want?'

'Only doing my duty as a responsible citizen, Mike. You wouldn't want me to keep quiet about someone running around with an illegal firearm, now, would you?'

'You've got some nerve.'

'You told me not to keep anything from you and I'm delivering: Tom Eels, six-one, shaved head, wears gothic jewellery. He's driving around in a white box-van in Cornwall or en route there. I don't have the registration but it's a company van, Sulis Wines. Registered to a Leonard

Dufossee double S double E. He carries a 4.5 mm pistol and he's got previous for aggravated burglary. Dangerous headcase. You got all that?'

'I'm all ears, Honeypott.'

'Don't start that again. He's probably on his way to a cottage on the headland south-west of Tredannik. A hamlet in Cornwall. The nearest cop shop should be Mousehole. The house belongs to an Alison Flood. She's in danger from Eels. Can you send someone round to make sure she's okay? I'm on my way there but it'll take me hours yet.'

There was a pause, then I heard Needham reel off instructions in the background. It seemed to go on forever. 'On one condition,' he came back.

Condition? Since when did the police barter for their services? What next, call-out charges? 'Anything, Mike, just name it.'

'Your gun. I want that bloody gun handed in.'

'You've got it.' I broke the connection. The words not, bloody and likely sprang to mind.

To keep me going on the road I stocked up on Camels and some unfeasibly green and bullet-proof apples. I was feeling a little less frantic now. Needham would send a patrol car to Alison's cottage. If that was too late then I was too late too. If they got there before Eely they would warn them that trouble was on the way. Annis would know what to do – get the hell out of there and not stop for anything.

Back in the car I pulled out my tattered road atlas. My hands were trembling as I flicked through it. Smoking furiously to steady my nerves I found the relevant section. The blue ribbon of the M5 slithered like an evil snake across the map, poised to inject its deadly venom of fear. I snapped the atlas shut. And made a decision that would change everything. I took the slower route.

Chapter Nine

I'm used to the left-hand drive, of course. It gives you the edge in right-hand bends but that's about all the advantage you get while driving in Britain. Overtaking on winding, narrow roads without a co-driver can be a heart-in-the-mouth trial and error operation. Error I couldn't afford. Time and time again I surged up behind the type of driver who only drives at one standard issue speed and never seems to change gear. Whether a village with 30 mph restriction or the open road makes no difference, they drive at 39 mph. Why? Are they asleep? Listening to *The Archers*? Got cramp? It's one of the dark unsolved mysteries of the British countryside.

Come on Pilgrim. Even The Pixies couldn't drown out the voice in my head. The voice in my head hurled abuse. At comatose drivers who'd never worked out what all those pedals were for; at people who build roads not wide enough for passing; at the pathetic Leonard, the psychotic Eely. But most of all at myself.

It was getting late. I was getting closer though, if the landmarks were anything to go by: a field of elegant windmills, a memory of Jamaica Inn and at last St Michael's Mount, now a mere fantasy, dramatically lit in the dusk. I whizzed through Penzance, crowded with tourists perusing the menus outside restaurants, and took the coastal route towards Mousehole, which would be even more crowded at this time of year. Nearly there. A few miles to Tredannik now. Soon. Soon.

There are many creative ways of losing time but one method beats all others in terms of its sheer stupidity. It's known as the Dodgy MOT. It could be corroded leads, a fading of your brakes, a fatal loss of oil or a tired gasket that gives up on you as you hurry along. Only for dramatic effect nothing beats the sudden disappearance of the floor under your feet. After thirty-two years, as predicted by Jake and without further warning, the bottom fell out of the DS and my arse hit tarmac. One minute I was straightening the car after a sharp bend, the next I was staring at the underside of the dashboard surrounded by multi-coloured sparks and the hideous sound of metal scraping on tarmac. I worked the pedals, hanging like a chimpanzee from the steering wheel, and wrestled the wreck to a stop without hitting anything. Of all the stupid . . . humiliating . . . frightening . . . infuriating . . . and of all the times. Half strangled by my old-fashioned seat belt I keeled out of the door on to the verge of the lane and stared with disbelief into the place where my seat should have been. Not only the floor but one of the spars under the door had given way. Below the pedals was nothing but air. If I'd been driving on the motorway . . . This looked pretty terminal, at least until Jake got on to it. I hadn't so much broken down as broken through. Of course I had a breakdown service (more important than wheels with a DS) but all they would do would be to cart it away and laugh a lot, perhaps not even in that order. As one might expect, there was suddenly no traffic on the road. I had passed Mousehole ten minutes ago and was now in glorious landscape, somewhere, if only I could see any of it over the high hedges.

The boot was full of the usual junk, including a forgotten bag of spuds, nicely sprouted. A bright red tow rope, the car jack and wheel brace looked more promising however. Half of the floor under my seat was still attached to the rest of the bodywork. I levered and yanked the twisted metal up, losing great bits of it in rusty flakes, then wedged the wheel brace and jack handle under what was left of the frame of my seat. It kind of held up but was too precarious like that. So the seat belt became just that, a belt to keep the seat in position, and the tow rope braced the whole ensemble in a triangle from the passenger seat to the hand grip between the doors and back. It looked feasible. Gingerly I tried my weight on the wonky platform and jumped off instantly. It would never hold my weight. It didn't work.

Twenty-five miles per hour. I think that's the highest speed I can recommend when driving a left-hand drive DS21 from the passenger seat. It was clearly insane but my innate ability not to think straight in times of crisis helped a lot. Shifting gear was the worst operation, having to stretch my left foot into the far corner where the fading daylight appeared below the clutch pedal, which is why I bansheed along in a protesting second gear. Fortunately the only thing I met was a boy on a scooter who never gave me a second glance.

The sun had long set and a light, wind-driven spray of rain was falling by the time I reached the gate across the track that led to Alison's hideaway. Hideaway was how I had come to think of it now, a faker's cottage, far from prying eyes. I still found it hard to believe but in retrospect everything seemed to make sense: Alison's jumpiness, her reticence about her recent work, the fine, handmade paints she used. The gate was closed but not locked and only wanted to open outwards, so I laboriously backed up, swung the rickety gate open and drove up the track. The swivelling headlamps of the DS picked out the yard. The junk in it had not been cleared but rationalized into one massive pile in a corner furthest from the house. There was plenty of space for me to park this time and no other cars. It looked as though Annis and Alison had been warned by the police and cleared out. There was some residual light in the sky along the edges of the rain clouds that drifted in from the sea but the cottage lay in darkness and there was no sound apart from the wind, which was picking up steadily. Annis and Alison safely away from here had been my favourite scenario, but one that hadn't taken into account a broken-down DS. I would have to somehow make it back to Mousehole and find a B&B for the night or sleep in the car. Just in case, I checked that my mobile was switched on. Why hadn't the silly girls rung me? Perhaps they'd left a message at the door? Unlikely, since they couldn't have known I was on my way. Unless somehow the police had remembered to pass that message on.

There was no note. Distractedly I tried the door. It was unlocked. My heart sank. This was too unlikely. I'd heard there were still places in Britain where people left their doors unlocked. Not here, not under the circumstances. Not today. Or had their departure been that hasty? There was one other possibility I could think of: Annis and Alison had hidden their cars and were lying in ambush for Eely, perhaps even with police inside. It never ceases to astound me how you can get things half right and still be so completely wrong.

I stepped into the stone-flagged hall and closed the door behind me to shut out the distraction of the wind and rain. Inside, the air was warm and a little sticky. I stood very still. The first opening on my left was the open kitchen door. Apart from the humming of the fridge a low, steady hissing sound came from there, along with the tiniest amount of light. I slid quietly along the wall and went inside. On the cooker at the far end a saucepan sat over a burning gas ring. In the blue light of the gas flame I could make out that no steam was rising from the pan, nor was there any smell of burning. Reluctantly I approached the cooker. The eerie blue and yellow of the gaslight and the soundless, steam-free pan spread an evil aura in the sticky room. In the beam from my Maglite I could see the content. The pan was full to the brim with quietly seething oil. I turned off the gas, glad the hissing sound had ceased. A boiling chip pan in an empty cottage was not a good sign.

How empty was empty? I felt a strange reluctance to switch on the lights or call out. I crept along to the living room and let the torch beam travel over the furniture: sofa, armchairs, coffee table and tiny secretaire. There was nothing untoward here, no sign of a struggle, no mess even. I checked the glass door to the conservatory. It was locked. The pane of glass Eely had cut during the break-in had been replaced with a rectangle of hardboard. Everything in the studio seemed as it had been. There was no painting on the easel. That left the upper floor to investigate. By the foot of the stairs was the small table with the telephone. My dictaphone was still sitting next to it. I rewound the tape, which took less than a second, then pressed Play. A short moment of hissing. Someone blowing on the microphone, then Alison's voice. 'Testing testing testing. Hi Chris, how'ya doing? You're missing a bloody good session.' Clinking of glasses. Then Annis's voice. 'You sure are. Hey Chris, remember what we said now, no comparing notes.' Laughter, then the recording clicked off. There was nothing else. I pocketed the machine and started upstairs. On my previous visit I had only made it as far as the bathroom. In contrast to the downstairs it was a complete mess. Crumpled towels everywhere, shampoo and conditioner bottles on the floor, a jar of talcum powder exploded over the toilet seat. The shower curtain hung half torn off its rail. I bent down and felt the towels. They were damp. Touching them made me shudder: bathroom scenes traditionally have a bad ending. I backed out of the tiny room into the corridor. There were two closed doors. I opened the one to the left. A cramped little bedroom. I felt for the light switch on the wall and clicked it on. A neatly made-up bed took up most of the space. On the rug by the bedside table I recognized Annis's leather travel bag. It was open. Clothes, her sketchbook and camera. On the bedside table lay a fat paperback, *The Oxford Handbook of Criminology.* So Annis really did read in bed.

I opened the remaining door and flicked on the light which illuminated my nightmare. Annis and Alison were lying on top of the bed, their naked flesh pale against the blue bed sheet. Both were cuffed by one hand high on the wrought-iron bedstead so that their bodies were twisted up awkwardly. Their eyes were closed. Neither of them moved. They looked asleep, only nobody could sleep in a position like that. There was a strange smell in the room, something I didn't quite recognize. It reminded me vaguely of the dentist's. Despair rose from the floorboards like a paralysing miasma, rooting me to the spot.

When at last I regained the power to move I flung myself at Annis in a rage. Perhaps I was screaming, perhaps not. I clawed at her legs, her cold torso, her dry, open mouth. How dare you! How dare you be dead! Then the light seemed to change. In the tiny moment I had left I realized that I had lost. In that split second all my mistakes stacked up in my mind like lead ballast. Then there was a crack and everything stopped. Freeze-framed. My vision broke into two, like a torn photograph. The bodies on the bed faded into black and white, then slipped away into darkness.

The first thing I heard was a moan. It was my own. I was on the move. On the move inside a car crusher, perhaps.

'God, how can a skinny piece of shit like you be so fucking heavy?' I had never heard Eely's voice but recognized it instantly. It went with everything I knew about him, vicious, arrogant, wired. And of course quite mad. It took every drop of adrenalin in my body to force my eyes open. I was travelling on the ground, I was being dragged, feet first, on some kind of tarpaulin. Eely's shape was outlined against the dark, wet sky, puffing with exertion, dragging me in spurts of two or three feet at a time. I tried to shout my fury at him but produced nothing but a gurgling roar.

'Good to hear you're still with us. I don't want you to croak before I get to the edge. This has gotta look right, you know? And it *will* look right. That's why I hit you with a rock, see? It won't look out of place when they do your autopsy. *If* they ever find your body, that is. Jumped off the cliff in despair. All your injuries will look just right. You see? I'm a bit of an artist myself.' A short laugh. Then hard breathing as we moved again. He had reached the end of the yard where two worn steps led up to the hundred feet or so of scrubby grass between the conservatory and the edge of the cliff-drop. He stopped to catch his breath. There was a broken saddle stone to my left. I managed to fling my arm out to grab hold of it. It seemed to give out electric currents of pain and fear.

'Oh yeah, I might have stepped on your hands back there. I'm really very thorough. Upsadaisy.' He yanked the tarp. I bumped up the stairs, then level again. When I tried to struggle up, tried to kick, none of my limbs would obey me. My legs trembled and shook in burning, involuntary spasms.

'You remind me of a dissected frog. Still twitching. Don't make me hit you again, now, it might spoil it. I do think of everything. I'm thinking much clearer than I ever have. It's all perfect. The two girls were a great help, they were in the shower together when I walked in. Perfecto. The tall one kicked up a bit of a fuss but didn't argue with my gun in the end. I gave them some knock-out drops when you turned up because I didn't want to gag them, that leaves marks. In case they don't get all burned up properly. So the way I see it pan out . . . hang on a sec, there's a bump here, better go round it.' He pulled to the left and we changed direction. 'Way I see it, some kinky, lesbo sex games went wrong here. The keys to the cuffs dropped on the floor, whoops. And with the chip pan going full-blast downstairs it's only a matter of time before it all goes up. Whoosh.

I switched it on again, see. I'll be doing three painters in one day, that's gotta be a record, don't you think? Mind you, I've seen the shit you guys paint and I reckon I'm doing the world a fucking favour. That Alison girl's not so bad, but you? What were you thinking, man? I've seen toddlers do better. I can't believe people buy this shit. We used it as wrapping paper!' There came the crash of shattering glass. 'Whoa, it started! Kitchen window blew out. I rigged that up well, put lots of cereal boxes round the stove. Well, it's time to get a move on. I love a good fire but I reckon . . . soon you'll be able to . . . see it from miles away, so I'm splitting, my man. And you're going . . . sailing, so you'll miss it too. Right . . . another couple of yards. I hope you're ready for this, made your peace and all that.' He heaved with greater urgency now and reached the edge in two steady pulls. The sound of the sea below competed with the noises in my head and the sound of rushing air as the burning cottage greedily sucked in oxygen. There was a glow to the left of my field of vision. I couldn't see the house from my position on the ground.

'Up you come.' I could smell his boozy breath as he swapped sides and began to lift me by the shoulders for the last push. My head lolled back, it was too heavy to control. Two painfully piercing lights appeared behind me, upside down from my vantage point, then the surge of a revved engine. 'Fuck. Fuck it!' Eely shouted right by my ear. He gave me another long push. I could feel my legs falling away over the edge. 'Aah, fuck.' He dropped me. 'Fuck off! Fuck off!' We were caught in blinding light now as Tim's TT came crashing towards us. Eely was sharply silhouetted against the approaching headlights. He raised his pistol and stood his ground, legs spread wide. There was the crack of a shot, then the car pivoted on the slippery grass. A loud thud, as the side of the car connected with Eely's body, then he sailed past me into space. The rear lights of the car stopped not two feet from my head. Since I couldn't move, all I could see now was a muddy rear wheel. It was the nicest rear wheel I'd ever laid eyes on.

It seemed an age before I saw or heard anything else. When I did it was the blinding light of a torch in front of my face and Tim's voice.

'So you're alive. Thought I was too late. Thought he was disposing of a body. You look pretty shit, mate. Again. Well, if ever a hunch has paid off, this has to be it. Sorry I couldn't be here earlier, I stopped in the village for directions. Where are the girls?' Tim shone the torch in his own face so I could admire my saviour. I managed to fling my left arm out again. 'Inside? Shit shit shit.' He was gone in a flash. The next thing I heard was the crashing of glass. A lot of crashing, a lot of glass. Tim was sensibly smashing his way into the cottage through the conservatory, away from the source of the fire, which had to be fierce by now. I willed him to get inside before the fire blocked his way, to get them out in time. Two unconscious women, cuffed to a metal bedstead in a burning house . . . The keys! The keys were somewhere on the floor, Eely had said. If I could move a little, could speak even . . . Things in my head were getting fuzzier. The noise of the fire was getting louder, a roaring sound, like a turbo-prop plane coming in to land, shifting pitch up and down, with the odd bang and crash thrown in. Very fuzzy now. Suddenly, after what seemed like no time at all, the light came dancing back.

'They're out.' Tim's voice, sandpapered by the smoke. 'I know you worry about little details like that so I thought you'd like to know. They're puking a lot and won't have to shave their legs for a month but they're out. Ambulance is on the way. So are the cops, of course. Do you want anything?'

All I could squeeze out was another groan. Did I want anything? Not really. The girls were alive, I was alive, well, kind of, and Eely had finally and literally gone over the edge. For the moment, I had everything I wanted. Well, if anyone were to offer, I could perhaps manage a tiny shot of morphine . . .

Morphine, the alkaloid narcotic principle of opium, really is a wonderful product, and entirely natural, being extracted from the beautiful poppy. Together with codeine, its younger cousin, it used to bring regular relief from suffering to millions. Queen Victoria was very fond of it and never left home without a decent supply. Then a few smack heads ruined it for all of us, so now the chemist will fob you off with inferior products, just to keep the real thing out of their hands. My advice: always insist on the genuine article.

This time I didn't even have to ask. There was a price attached to that level of care, though: they kept me in. I got poked, prodded, scanned, was put on 'nil by mouth' until the test results were in (in case they had to operate, which they didn't), then I got realigned, reset and plastered (with plaster), since Eely had apparently worn heavy boots: four of my fingers were broken, index and middle finger on each hand. In the beginning I mercifully drifted in and out of sleep and diligently filled several kidney-shaped dishes with vomit whilst awake, which apparently is the polite thing to do when you are severely concussed. Since I hadn't taken my first Eely-induced concussion seriously they practically nailed me to the bed, kept all visitors away and deflected all my questions, except to say that everything was *fine*, my friends were *fine*, and everything else was going to happen not now but *soon*. Rest rest rest. At first I was past caring, which meant it took me three days to realize I was at the West Cornwall Hospital in Penzance, not the Royal United in Bath. My headaches were richly textured and multi-layered, like a de Kooning painting recreated in razor wire and shoved into my brain via the eye-sockets.

My thumbs had escaped the enthusiastic attention of the

plasterers, which meant that at least I could feed myself, after a fashion, if the stuff they gave me was indeed food. I didn't get restless until the second week, when there was no more nausea, light flashes or dizzy spells and, unbelievably, the razor wire had rusted away inside my head. After that, every moment became torturous and so mind-numbingly boring that I started to look forward to feeding times like a demented puppy. This time, however, I sat the thing out. I knew I'd had a narrow escape. Perhaps one day even the nightmares would stop.

I arrived back at Mill House on a bleak Monday evening nine days after the fire. It was the first week of July. Summer had been cancelled and the sky concreted over without my permission. I'd made my own slow way home, by cab and train and cab again, and was thoroughly drained. Yet even in the chilled rain that blustered through the valley, standing back here in my own potholed yard was blissful. The house, the lively voice of the mill stream, the sagging outbuildings, the overflowing water barrel, even the puddle I stepped into straight from the taxi, felt like paradise regained. Side by side in the yard, a dirty white Beetle, a muddy Land Rover and an immaculate black TT kept each other company.

Annis, Tim and Alison had a welcoming fire going in the living room. They took turns hugging me gently, having been told I might remain fragile for some time. Earlier I had elicited grudging medical permission for a limited consumption of alcohol, so I gratefully accepted a bottle of cool Stella.

We had all talked over the phone before but couldn't help going over the whole thing again.

'Advanced school of motoring, mate,' was how Tim shrugged off my admiration for the handbrake manoeuvre that sent Mr Eels flying over the cliff and saved my life.

'Running him down worked at the warehouse, I didn't see why it couldn't again.'

'He shot at you. Did he hit anything?'

'Nope. Didn't even hit the car. The police found the spent slug in the side of the old fridge by the cottage. Which was just as well, since it backs up my story that I lost control of the car when he aimed his gun at me.'

'And Eely?'

'They eventually found what was left of him. Naturally I didn't tell them that I *tried* to hit him. It was an accident.' He looked around the room for consent. We did our nodding dog impressions. There would be an inquiry anyway but this way the question of manslaughter, justifiable or not, would hopefully never be raised.

I turned to Alison. 'The cottage?'

'Three walls and a pile of very smelly rubble. All that oil paint and turps went up like petrol.' I had been amazed that Tim had found the keys to their cuffs in time, until I remembered that he could probably open handcuffs with no more than a hard stare. Alison didn't seem unduly distressed by the affair. She'd lost some hair in the fire and had it cut very short, quite spiky on top. It suited her new energy. Having watched her inheritance burn down along with her studio and all her paintings seemed to have energized her, as if a heavy burden had disappeared from her life. 'I might be homeless and without a painting to my name but I still have some money left. And eventually, I hope, the insurance will pay out.' All evidence of her involvement with the art theft had disappeared. Not to mention the delightful Mr Eels.

'You'll go on painting?'

'Of course.'

I had to ask. 'Faking?'

She tilted her head and jangled a long silver earring, one of Annis's, with her fingers. 'I must admit I enjoyed doing it. At first. It was an incredible challenge. But . . . no. No more forgeries. It's time to get back to my own work.'

'How did you get involved with those guys in the first place? How did they find you?'

'Austin Antiques again, of course. I'd also inherited a watercolour, which I thought might be by Constable. Just a study of clouds, you know the kind of thing. Turned out I was right. Aldriges of Bath had it authenticated and put it into auction for me. Austin bought it, we got talking. I mentioned that I was a painter and over a glass of wine, perhaps too many glasses of wine, he asked if I would, you know, do similar stuff for him. He'd pay good money. It didn't really seem so . . . criminal then, more of a game. So I agreed. Constable's always been a favourite of mine. I'd made a close study of his methods when I was at college, so I found it fairly easy. Austin laid his hands on the right kind of paper and I did watercolours "in the manner of". No signatures or anything. It would never have stood up to much scrutiny but Austin still found his buyers. Mostly Japanese and American tourists. He never sold them as Constables but let the punters think they'd discovered them amongst his junk. Together with the real study he'd bought I made enough money in two years to buy my brother's half of the cottage. I stopped doing them after that, the medium started to bore me anyway. But then of course he asked me about doing these oil paintings. They weren't really fakes, since I always used modern canvas. If you took them off the wall and looked at the back you'd see they were copies straight away, only no one was supposed to do that. Of course I knew he was using them in some bloody scam, the way those guys turned up with the originals in the back of a van late at night . . .' Alison squirmed like a little girl in her armchair. 'I know it sounds bloody naïve now but I thought it would be . . . an adventure.'

And so it had turned out. 'They say you know you're having an adventure when you begin to wish you were back home in bed,' I offered.

'Yeah, but not chained up to it,' Annis asserted flatly.

'Oh, I don't know . . .' Tim started.

Annis fiercely cut him off. 'Shut up about it, Bigfoot.' The humiliation she had felt at being overpowered by Eely had turned into an icy anger that even the man's death couldn't temper. 'You've no idea what he was *like*.'

'True,' he admitted. 'I never got to talk to Mr Eels before I killed him.' He raised his Stella bottle in a silent toast.

'He told us the only reason he didn't rape us was so he wouldn't leave any trace.' Annis stared motionless into the fire. 'But he did . . .'

'Let's just say he was a complete *wanker*,' Alison said pointedly.

'Thank you, Al, exactly the word I was looking for. Eeeyuch! Enough of that.' Life flooded back into her eyes. 'Chuck a blanket or something in front of the hearth, we'll eat on the floor by the fire.'

When plates and cutlery were in place she lifted the lid on the big fire-blackened casserole and the aroma of cinnamon-spiced lamb filled the room.

'I had this tagine in Agadir once –' was as far as I got.

'Of course you did, you boring old fart. It was 1971 and a ticket to Morocco was two-and-six with Bakelite Airways.' She nodded a long-suffering see-what-I-mean to Alison. Annis had recovered her form.

'So when Eely searched your studio he was looking for what?' I asked instead.

'Further copies, I guess.' Alison shrugged.

'Did you ever make any?'

'Sure. They'd told me not to, of course, but I thought, sod them, there might be a market for that. I never left them in the studio, though, since it was clear they were a paranoid bunch. I clamped them under the beds. Quite safe. Until they burned.'

'So it was Eels who tried to run you off the road, the week before Annis and I turned up?'

'I bloody hope so.' Alison stopped dead for a moment, her fork hovering over a morsel of lamb on her plate.

197

'Can't think who else I might have pissed off . . . Well, not enough to nudge me over a cliff, anyway.'

The lamb was better than anything I remembered having eaten in Morocco, only I found it difficult to start that strand of conversation again without a broadside from Annis. So I just joined in with the general mms and ahs and nodded vigorously at Tim's evaluation of the dish as 'fab'.

Since my plaster casts made me exempt from washing up I kept Tim company by the sink while the girls got stuck into a new bottle of wine next door. Alison demonstrated once more her prodigious talent for putting the stuff away. Tim and I were glad she didn't drink Stella. Privately, I was looking forward to the day when I'd be able to get a bottle open without asking for help. Tim had just furnished me with a fresh one.

'One thing, though. You never explained how come you turned up at Alison's in the first place. I'd left you finding the Saudis in Bath.'

He gave me a sideways look. 'I told you all this on the phone. But you were probably still groggy from your Class A drugs, mate. I did find the Saudis. Or rather where they'd been staying. At the Francis Hotel in Queen Square.'

'How quaint.'

'Indeed. Only they'd checked out that morning and taken a cab to Bristol airport. Looks like they opted for early departure.'

'So . . .?'

'So I had a beer, got a weird feeling, which I don't usually get when I drink beer, you understand. So I bought the girls at Somerset Lodge a takeaway and followed you down. Simple as that.'

'Cheers, Tim. And while we're here . . . I don't think I ever really thanked you for saving my life.'

He tried hard to suppress a grin. 'Annis was right, you really do need looking after.'

She could talk. I went down to the cottage to rescue *her*. 'I think we all need looking after, sometimes. And you do it very well, Tim. You saved all of us. I'm not sure how to repay a debt like that, unless you'd care to put yourself in mortal danger while I'm around. And haven't got these.' I held up my heavy paws. 'And am armed to the teeth, naturally.'

'Well, there is one thing you could do. Urgently.'

'Name it.'

'Just get better, will you?'

Was I that bad? 'At what?'

'No, just get better, get the hands sorted and go back to normal.' He gave me a pained smile. 'Annis won't sleep with me while she's not sleeping with you. Something about not wanting to unbalance the emotional geometry of our relationships.' He flicked some lemon-scented lather against the dark window, shook his woolly head slowly. 'This is so typically Annis. She's got it all planned out, including her own rules for shagging the both of us. How come we never got a say in any of this?'

I thought that was blindingly obvious. 'She's non-negotiable. Perhaps that's part of the attraction.'

'Perhaps. I still can't believe we're in this ménage à trois.'

'But are we? Isn't a ménage à trois when you're all sleeping with each other? Or at least in the same bed. Or is that a love triangle?'

'I was always crap at geometry,' Tim said gloomily.

Just then the girls slid into the kitchen, Annis pushing Alison in front of her. Both were armed with full glasses of ruby-red wine.

I know when I'm being set up. They didn't want to rush me but didn't want to wait another day either. So they counted the Stellas I'd drunk and considered me now sufficiently mellow to pop the one question no one had touched on yet.

I didn't even let them ask it. 'On the condition that you buy your own wine and pay your share of the bills.'

Alison's eyes widened a fraction, then she shot an uncertain smile at Annis, who merely said, 'Told you,' and walked out again.

'Thanks, Chris. It won't be forever, just until I get myself going again. You'll hardly know I'm here.'

I doubted that very much.

There were other things none of us had mentioned yet.

Ousted by Alison from his usual bed in the spare room under the roof, Tim was snoring under a well-worn blanket on the sofa nearest the fire, which had burnt down to a quiet glow now. My old-fashioned alarm clock tick-tocked noisily beside him on the floor. He had to be up long before us painters to get to work at Bath Uni in the morning. I stuck a yellow post-it note on his forehead, reminding him that I still needed to know who owned Somerset Lodge. Jenny's killer was still out there.

As I was about to enter my room, not looking forward to the two-finger exercise in undressing, Annis stuck her head round her door. 'Want any help?' she whispered.

And why not. In my room she proceeded to gently but methodically render me naked, then added the pyjamas she'd been wearing to the pile of clothes on the floor and slid into bed with me. 'Now make love to me,' she asked matter-of-factly. So I did. Look, no hands.

Chapter Ten

If nothing else, the weather improved. The unseasonable heat, combined with the later downpours, had encouraged a profusion of all things green in the valley. The meadow behind the house had got out of hand again. Now, five of my neighbour's black-faced sheep were employed in cropping it back into shape, moving lazily away from me whenever I approached.

Mine was a restless convalescence. Finding lumps of heavy plaster at the end of my wrists each morning seemed to me a greater hardship than finding no hands at all. The blasted things had to be kept reasonably clean and, what was worse, dry, which meant I was barred from even the most basic kitchen activities. I'd often admired people who paint with their feet or mouth but somehow sensed my heart wouldn't be in it. So I avoided the kitchen as well as the studio, where Alison had now installed herself. Together with Annis she made countless expeditions to every art shop in the area to replace her lost materials and ordered armfuls from specialists in London and Cornwall. Their combined enthusiasm at Alison's new start left me more restless than ever.

Since I couldn't find my thinking cap I put on my grumpy hat instead, ordered in Stella in tins, which I didn't like but could open with my broken paws. I took to ghosting about the place, kicking at stones in the yard and the rusting junk in the outbuildings like a grounded teenager. All Aqua business was on hold (we weren't accepting any new business at the moment, was the message), not that anything of particular interest was offered, for which I was grateful. One morning a letter arrived from the Culverhouse Trust, thanking me for my help in looking after Somerset Lodge during 'difficult times'. They had made 'alternative arrangements' now and wished me a speedy recovery. Enclosed was a cheque for my troubles. I hadn't expected any remuneration, but couldn't resist a swift calculation (on my calculator, I can't count past ten). It revealed that my troubles worked out roughly at the staggering rate of £3.50 per hour. Jenny's assessment of the Trust's committee as tight-fisted had been kind. I got Annis to return the cheque in official Aqua stationery.

Virginia Dufossee's letter did nothing to cheer me up either. The note that accompanied her cheque (rather more painful to sign than the Trust's, I imagined) reiterated her hope that the matter would now be resolved *discreetly*. Perhaps she had a point. Car wrecks, shootings, fires and sudden death wasn't exactly what I'd promised when I took on the case. Not a single line about art theft had reached the press, locally or nationally, so I could only assume the Dufossees were writing the paintings off as a dead loss. Money, I gratefully noted, wasn't everything to everyone at Starfall House.

July had settled into the familiar routine of sunshine and showers by the time I got my hands back. Or rather what was left of them. I certainly didn't recognize the bleached, withered and unbending sticks that trembled where my fingers had been. They felt as useless as they'd been when still encased in lumps of plaster and I reckoned the firm handshake of a toddler would bring me to my knees. Plenty of moisturizer, I was informed by the nurse, and gentle exercises would soon restore them. I was furnished with a small, squidgy rubber ball with which to exercise my withered hands and sent on my way.

As soon as I could grab on to anything with confidence I walked into the studio, whipped the huge monstrosity from my easel and flung it out of the door. Therapeutic it might have been, a painting it would never be. Without looking up from her own work Annis said quietly, 'Thank the gods for that.' I plonked a ready-stretched canvas in its place and breathed a sigh of relief: one blank canvas is worth a hundred bad paintings. Before I got far into contemplating what could possibly replace the nightmare vision I had just expelled, reality broke in with a hiss of air-brakes and a blast on a car horn. Jake was backing his filthy transporter into the yard, with my gleaming black DS on the back. It was only the realization that Superintendent Needham's grey saloon was right behind him that stopped me from skipping down the meadow like a little boy. Needham and Jake were already laughing at something, at my expense, no doubt, when I got there.

'One French antique patched up for another round of abuse,' Jake commented when the car was standing on terra firma in the yard.

I couldn't restrain myself from lovingly running my hand across the elegant curve of its roof.

'How touching. He's going to kiss it next.' Needham sighed impatiently. Jake just shrugged his square shoulders: he'd come across car-nutters worse even than me. He intoned an unbelieving 'Yeah yeah yeah' when I promised prompt cash payment for his miracle work and left us standing in a blue cloud of exhaust as he thundered back into the countryside.

Needham looked around him with one hand in his pocket and squinted into a sudden shaft of sunlight. He wasn't wearing his jacket and carried nothing more sinister than his old-fashioned lump of a mobile, yet I didn't get the impression that he was here to socialize. So I came straight to the point: 'Coffee, Mike?'

He considered it and appeared to lighten up. 'I don't suppose you've got any decaf here?'

'Not a chance, Mike.'

'In that case, yes please.' He even followed me into the

203

kitchen and watched me make it, sniffing the beans I poured into the mill. Had he lost even more weight or was that an optical illusion? Whatever, the poor sod had been given doctor's orders. Naturally the doc never told him to get a less stressful job, just to make sure he wasn't enjoying his coffee while he got stressed out.

'Drop of milk, two sweeteners,' he begged next.

'Sorry, only real poisons in this kitchen.' I pushed the sugar bowl across.

'Ah well,' he beamed, 'it'll have to do.' And shovelled in as much sugar as he could possibly balance on a couple of teaspoons. Once lowered into a wicker chair on the verandah he groaned as he took his first sip. Forbidden pleasures.

'Glad to see you looking so well,' he opened procedures. 'You had a bit of a torrid time in Cornwall, we hear.'

'Only because some incompetent clown in a noddy car convinced himself the cottage was safe and empty without even bothering to check it out.'

'Eels had driven all the cars to a lay-by up the road,' Needham explained smilingly. 'The cottage was dark, securely locked and there was no answer.' He hadn't made superintendent by apologizing for his mistakes.

'I told you the man was armed and dangerous and you sent the village plod round there. Which makes me think that perhaps you didn't pass on the entire message?'

He tried to put on his inscrutable face but gave up on it halfway through the process. 'Well . . .'

I knew what he wasn't saying. You can get a bad reputation for overreacting by sending armed response units on wild goose chases, which Mike had obviously thought this was. It wasn't even his force and they didn't come cheap etc. etc. It had been his call and, as it turned out, a bad one.

'We're talking triple murder here, had it not been for Tim Bigwood turning up.'

'A most fortuitous RTA, I must say.'

'More like a CTA. Cliff Top Accident.'

'Quite.'

I had called Needham on his mobile that day, which naturally wasn't monitored. So he could pretend never to have heard that Eely was armed and dangerous and Tim's driving stunt would go down as a Road Traffic Accident. Horse trading was over.

'So what else can I do for you?'

'Another one of these would be great.' He held out his empty mug. 'And you can go back to spying on wayward husbands and finding mispers. I still can't believe you even thought of getting those paintings back without us. And of course you buggered it up, by all accounts. Do yourself a favour and stick to what you're good at. Like making coffee.'

Needham knew how to hit a raw nerve. The paintings *were* lost. I *had* buggered it up. No one had told Needham though that the paintings were fakes in the first place. Which of course was good news for Alison.

'What about Jenny?' I insisted.

'Oh, of course, you've been convalescing. The post-mortem on David Cocksley was finally done. The coroner's verdict was death by misadventure which, as you know, covers a lot of sins, including suicide.' He padded after me into the kitchen to watch me brew up another caffeine hit for him. 'There've been no sightings of Gavin. He might still turn up of course. Or more likely his body.'

Had I forgotten to mention I'd found and lost Gavin at his friend's place in Milsom Street? Must've.

'Dave Cocksley killed Jenny Kickaldy in a moment of diminished responsibility and jumped into the lock. We found Jenny's blood on his clothing. Not much, but hey. When he became lucid, realized what he had done, he jumped into the lock, still carrying the murder weapon. *Voilà.*'

'You're kidding, right?'

'Not one bit.' Needham didn't even look embarrassed. 'What about Matt and the Chapwin girl? Your intruder scenario? Did you find them? Did you interview them?'

Needham simply shrugged, never taking his eyes off the all-important cafetière.

'You're burying the case,' I said, deflated. 'I knew you would eventually.'

'I'm doing no such thing. The case will be reopened if new evidence comes to light. But none will, take my word for it. Matt Hilleker went back there for some easy thieving but not to kill the housekeeper. And forensics decided the Lisa Chapwin print was ancient. She did a runner from her place but so what? According to her social worker she goes walkabout frequently. She's unstable. She's entitled to behave idiotically. It means nothing. We've got a suicide and a murder weapon. End of story. Meanwhile I've got plenty on my desk to be getting on with, believe me. We've got a missing boy, possible abduction, and a bloke who forces his way into cars and sexually assaults the women drivers. And you know what Bath is like. A girl gets raped in Henrietta Park in broad daylight and ten dog walkers file past without seeing a damn thing. But someone claps their hand at a seagull crapping on his car and our switchboard gets jammed.'

I shoved another coffee at him which he started sipping quickly, sensing that our chat was rapidly coming to an end.

'You wouldn't know by any chance who the Culverhouse Trust found as a replacement for Jenny?' I asked. 'They sent me a letter, saying they had made alternative arrangements.'

Needham smiled unprettily. 'You really have been out of the loop. Yeah, they made alternative arrangements all right. They closed Somerset Lodge down. And none too soon, if you ask me.'

I was stunned. I shouldn't have been but I was. 'And the residents?'

'How should I know, Chris? Presumably they found them somewhere else to stay. Does it matter? Right! I'm off. Thanks for the coffee.'

I followed him out of the yard. The sun had burned away most of the cloud. A fine summer's day.

'Oh, I nearly forgot.' Needham wheeled round and gave me a hard look. 'But not quite. Your gun. Hand it over.' He wriggled a crooked finger at me: *give*.

'Didn't I tell you? That's at the bottom of the sea. It went over the cliff in the mêlée in Cornwall.'

He gave me a long stare, his face twelve inches from mine. I tried hard to look sincere. What I could never figure out was how serious Needham was about my gun.

'Did it fuck,' he finally concluded. But he had other fish to fry today. I opened his car door for him.

'If I don't hear from you for a while, Chris,' he said from behind the steering wheel, 'I really won't complain.' He nearly ran over my foot as he floored the gas.

What had Annis said? Blokey competition? Somehow I was left feeling that most of this round had gone to Needham. I consoled myself with the fact that it wasn't me who was driving back to canteen food and plastic cups of decaf.

It was a gorgeous July day, and if I got my skates on I'd still catch the fishmonger at Twerton Market. I slid behind the wheel of the DS with a sigh of satisfaction. At least I had managed to hang on to my revolver. I bent down to pat it in its secret holder under the dashboard. It wasn't there. I stuck my head under it – the space where it should have been was empty. There was a scrabbling moment of panic until I took hold of my senses and opened the glove box. There it was, black and heavy in its holder, wrapped in a note from Jake: *Did no one ever tell you that welding and bullets don't mix?!!* Followed by a few interesting invectives I'd never seen written down before. Also in the glove box was the pack of Camels I'd bought that day on my way to

Cornwall. I opened it: someone had smoked all but two of them. I congratulated myself: I hadn't smoked a single cigarette since that day. I returned the Webley to its secret hiding place under the dash and drove gingerly up the rutted track, listening for any complaints from the car. There were none. As I turned on to the single-track road that bisects the valley I had to slam on the brakes to avoid colliding with a step-through moped driven in a wobbly fashion past the entrance to the turn-off. The rider appeared to consist of two balls, the helmet and his massive body. He was either fat or wrapped in twelve layers of protective gear. The way he rode the thing, he'd need all the protection he could get. Before I realized it I had reached into the glove box and lit a Camel to recover from the shock. It was bliss. Then I drove carefully into Bath and up into Twerton.

Twerton is perhaps the most uninspiring corner of Bath, never visited by tourists, but it does have two attractions: a football ground, if you're that way inclined, and smack next to that a weekly market, if you're me. At Twerton Market you can carry away a cut-price crate of over-ripe bananas or a cheap box of mushrooms; cunningly repackaged cheeses hovering around their sell-by date, or three-year-old cuts of beef, hastily defrosted, that just have to go today for a fiver. But I was here for the fishmonger. The freshest fish in Bath, bright-eyed and slick, and at half the price paid anywhere in a city centre crippled by business rates. While middle class shoppers in the supermarkets buy sea bass as an occasional luxury the working class denizens of Twerton happily eat it every week. Who said there's no justice in this world?

It was the lobster that looked good today, mottled Prussian blue and so lively I was glad their giant claws were firmly secured with thick rubber bands. From the fruit and veg stalls I grabbed the makings of a salad, sent Tim a text to let him know supper for four was on tonight and tootled back to the valley, with a Tricky CD blaring through the rolled-down windows.

Annis and Alison were still busy in the studio, Alison slow and thoughtful, Annis on a roll. I swallowed my envy and made for the kitchen. First I shoved the lobsters into the freezer. Apparently it makes them so drowsy they don't notice you're boiling up a big vat of water for their final plunge. With the water rolling in the pan I dropped the sleepy crustaceans into it and while they sang themselves to death got the blender working. One egg, a clove of garlic, a squeeze of lemon juice, mustard, salt and pepper. I then whacked it up to full speed and drizzled in olive oil until the glugging sound told me it was done. Three-minute mayonnaise. No mystery there.

The sun was riding low by the time we clinked glasses and bottles on the verandah. The girls, hair still damp from their shower (how they squeezed into the tiny space together didn't bear thinking about – for long) pounced on the lobsters like a couple of starved seals. Tim, pale and tired from too much neon light and computer screens, picked more hesitantly at his in how-d'you-eat-this-stuff fashion and spattered his immediate surroundings with garlic mayonnaise. When he was happily covered in gunk he fished a piece of paper from his jeans pocket, unfolded it greasily and presented it to me. 'Stuff you wanted to know. Somerset Lodge? You were right, the Culverhouse Trust only rented it. It was owned by that Hines bloke. And he just sold it. He made a bundle.'

I looked at the figure at the bottom of the sheet, next to a mayonnaisy thumb print, and gave a low whistle. Even I could have retired on that kind of dosh.

'Ah, but there's more. I looked up the Culverhouse Trust on the net. They don't have a website but there were plenty of mentions. They used to run three other houses like Somerset, two in London, one in Brighton. The ones in London closed down. Financial mishandlings, "bad record keeping". The Trust lost their charity status because they paid themselves too much money out of the charitable pot. And Gordon Hines got an honourable mention, too. In the late nineties there'd been an allegation of abuse. Sexual abuse, I presume, of a resident in the Brighton house. No witnesses came forward and the case never even went as far as the police. But Hines was banned from the Brighton house and posted sideways.'

'To Bath, where he owned the premises,' I said flatly. I was stunned. To me, Gordon had always appeared as the more acceptable face of the rather stuck-up Culverhouse lot, whom I had only once met in force. And their main motivation had seemed a vague Christian morality, with an amateurish belief in do-goodism and civic duty, so greed and sex hadn't instantly sprung to mind.

Annis laid a hand on my arm. 'Wouldn't Jenny have known if any abuse had happened at Somerset?'

'I'd have thought she'd have been the first person a resident would have talked to. If they talked,' I confirmed.

'And what would Jenny have done?'

'Jenny was incredibly protective about her charges, she'd have raised hell . . .' I said, my mind already elsewhere. Would Jenny have told me about it? Probably not, given the confidentiality issues. She had seemed stressed and tired on the day before her death. I tried to remember exactly what she had said to me. 'A bit of bother. Quite a lot of bother, actually.' But she appeared to think that everything would be resolved at the committee meeting, which had been scheduled for Saturday . . .

'Would she have gone through Social Services? Or alerted the committee? Or gone straight to the police?' Annis wondered. I was thinking along the same lines. Jenny would have done whatever *she* thought was in the best interest of the resident in question.

'We'll see,' I said and went for my mobile.

Needham answered after only two rings. 'Didn't I say I wouldn't mind if I *didn't* hear from you for a while?'

210

I ignored him. 'Are you aware of any allegations of abuse happening at Somerset Lodge? Ever?'

'Don't you think I would have mentioned that?' he said. His voice had a tired, impatient edge. 'What are you on about now? Who was abused by whom? If you know anything, spit it out now, Honeysett.'

'I don't know a thing, that's why I asked,' I said, cut the connection and switched the mobile off. A minute later the phone rang, high up in my attic office. We ignored it.

'You should tell him,' Annis said. 'If Gordon abused a resident at Somerset and Jenny confronted him . . .'

'A perfect motive for murder,' I agreed. 'In fact the first real motive anyone has found.'

'So . . .' Annis widened her eyes at me.

'So we've got nothing on him. Needham wants the murder case buried and we have an unsubstantiated allegation of abuse Tim picked up on the internet. Something that did or didn't happen years ago in a different town. If it did happen and the Culverhouse lot swept it under the carpet then there's every chance they've got rid of that carpet by now.'

'Is Hines straight?'

'He was married, his wife died a while back, that's all I know. Doesn't mean a thing.' Anne, Linda, Dave, Gavin. And Adrian, forever in and out of plaster. Of all of them only Linda and Gavin seemed likely victims of abuse, but that was pure conjecture. I remembered Linda, buried deeply inside her Mickey Mouse sweater as though it could afford some protection from the world, and shuddered. Gavin ran from the house and from me. And Dave? Did he kill himself after all? And the sharpening steel in the lock . . . 'Damn it, I'm going straight round to Gordon's!' I said and stood up.

'And warn him? Siddown, Honeysett,' Tim said firmly. 'Siddown, drink beer. We'll think of something better.'

Reluctantly I sat down again. I took another look at the printout Tim had given me and angrily threw the greasy

211

sheet amongst the shell fragments on the table. 'How come a professional cat burglar like you . . .'

'Ex-cat burglar, please,' he interrupted.

'. . . leaves greasy fingerprints on everything he touches?'

He produced a superior smile, a smear of garlic mayonnaise round his nose and mouth. ''Cause I've got nothing to fear. I'm clean.'

We talked and talked, with Alison fast asleep in her wicker chair. The important thing was not to spook Gordon. He had recently made an awful lot of money from the sale of Somerset Lodge, which meant that if he wanted to disappear he could do it easily and in style. I needed to contact him under a harmless pretext and get him to a place where I held all the cards, i.e. a tape recorder and a witness. With Somerset closed, that could only mean Mill House.

Chapter Eleven

The morning, or what was left of it when I staggered out of the shower, looked uncomplicated. Not 'cloudy but brightening up later', not 'sunshine and showers', not 'some sunshine but with a cool easterly breeze'. The morning was simple: hot, still, without a cloud in the sky. It made me think of long Mediterranean, take-it-all-for-granted summers. I thought I could hear cicadas in the meadow. Perhaps not.

Annis was sitting next to me at my desk.

'You realize of course he's got an alibi?' I felt a sudden twinge of doubt.

'Alibi shmalibi,' Annis offered. 'Dial!'

Gordon seemed unfazed by my call. 'What can I do for you, Chris?' No questions about the state of my health, no small talk.

'You remember the photo board Jenny made? It hung in the hall at Somerset Lodge.'

'I remember it.'

'There were pictures on it of our last Christmas together. If they're around somewhere, do you think I could have some of them? I don't have any pictures of Jenny at all.'

'I have them here somewhere, in a box, with some other stuff from the house. I'd be happy to let you have them. Pick them up any time at my place.'

'Thanks, Gordon. The other reason I rang . . . we've got a barbecue here, next Tuesday, in the evening. Just a few of us. I wondered if you'd like to join us. You could bring the

213

prints with you then.' Gordon and I had never socialized before. I held my breath.

'Well, we've certainly got the weather for it, if it holds. And your cooking is supposed to be nearly as good as poor Jenny's was. So yes, delighted. What time Tuesday?'

'Make it seven, bring what you want to drink.'

'Sounds a fair deal. See you then, Chris.'

I hung up carefully. 'Did I sound convincing? I was terribly nervous.'

'You sounded fine. Natural,' Annis assured me. 'So what's next? If we want to dig up dirt on Gordon we'll have to go back a long time, speak to people in Brighton, talk to Anne and Linda.'

'That might be difficult.' I had made a couple of phone calls already this morning. Following the closure of Somerset Lodge, Linda had been taken in by her parents. Social Services had refused to furnish me with an address. Anne had reacted so badly to the break-up of the house, she was back in a closed ward at Hill View, heavily sedated, her mouth full of cotton wool. And if the Culverhouse Trust had anything to hide then they would hardly welcome me in Brighton with open arms. 'Jenny's murder is the priority here. And if the police couldn't find anything then they've missed something. Sooo . . . I'll just have to go over the whole thing, from square one. Like a proper little detective.'

'What, like house-to-house?'

'Like house-to-bloody-house.'

I got into the car and got straight out again. A medium oven, Gas Mark 5. And I was wearing a suit, shirt and tie. It helps when you intend to knock on doors. Any uniform will get you attention, a boiler suit works well, but suit and tie is more my style. I let the interior of the DS cool down for a few minutes before I drove to Poet's Corner.

I'd intended to park in the bay at Somerset Lodge but it

214

was blocked by two big yellow skips, brimful with rolled-up carpets and builders' debris. A dust-powdered, shirtless bloke emptied a bucket of rubble into one as I pulled up.

'Refurbishing,' he told me, once he had switched off the diskman he had clipped to his belt. 'New owners. Used to be a private loony bin. The one where that woman was murdered. I sure as hell wouldn't have bought it, far too creepy if you ask me.' He didn't know the new owners. 'Married couple with kids.' He shrugged his shoulders as though families were a somehow strange, unknowable species.

I cruised around for a parking space, found one in nearby Kipling Avenue and walked back to Somerset. Being at the end of the street I estimated that only four houses directly overlooked the entrance to the garden, where I presumed the murderer had entered. Five, if I counted Somerset's direct neighbour, where I would be sure to call. I started bang opposite; an immaculate lilac door, sentinelled by potted bay trees clipped into perfect spheres. I hated them already, so I worked on my smile as well as the over-polished brass knocker. I needn't have bothered. The bloke who eventually opened the door was in his mid-twenties, wore yellow marigolds and said he was the cleaner. The lady of the house was out at a luncheon engagement. 'Nah, I only started work here a couple of weeks ago,' he said when I asked about the day of the murder. 'Might jack it in soon, though, they're incredibly fussy.'

I looked at his feet. He was wearing nylon shoe covers over his trainers like a lab technician in a germ-free zone. We wished each other luck.

There was no answer at all at the next number, so I moved on. A well-worn front door this time, a nicely neglected front garden with an equal proportion of flowers and weeds and a green recycling crate crammed full of empty wine bottles. All of it red and from Chile. How

215

much can you tell about the inhabitants from the front of their houses? Nothing of significance, in my experience.

I knocked, waited, knocked again. The door was yanked wide open by a man in his sixties, with wild hair and specs. 'Oh, come in, come in, I could do with a hand. Through here, in the kitchen.' He never even asked who I was. 'Shut the door behind you,' he ordered once I was in his big, sit-down kitchen. 'Here, you take this.' He handed me a broom. I really wasn't dressed for this. The back door to his semi-wild garden was open. I looked at the floor. It appeared to be clean. 'I'll get up on the chair and you wave the broom at it,' he instructed next.

I've played strange games in the past but this one was a new one. Never mind, I'd wave a broom at his chair if it made him happy.

'Sorry about this. I don't know what you want but whatever it is, first help me get the damn bird out.' Ah. I looked up. A young starling glared at us from the top of some kitchen units on the right. 'I've tried to get him out for the last half-hour, I'm trying to stop him from bashing his stupid head in against the window pane. The window doesn't fully open. And does he get the message? Brains the size of peas!'

I waved the broom as instructed while he shooed. The starling took off, headed straight for the window, changed direction at the last moment and landed on the old boiler in the corner.

'Right. Now you stand on the chair and look big. I'll shoo him over. You make sure he doesn't get back on to the units. That might do it.' He circled the kitchen table, which was covered in score sheets and breakfast debris, and scared the bird into flight again. A frantic flutter of wings as it came shooting towards me. I defended the wall units and shouted, 'Out!' He hooked a sharp left and flew out the door.

'See? Much easier with two people. Thanks for that. I'm Roy. Who are you?'

216

I told him.

'Private detective, eh? Never met one before. Drink?' He opened the fridge. Every inch of it was crammed with cans of Guinness. A liquid diet? Then I realized he had two fridges. Very civilized. Unless, of course, the other one was also full of Guinness. 'I don't drink much else,' he explained. He handed me a can and a glass with the harp logo on it. We took them outside and sat on a couple of rickety folding chairs on his weed-infested lawn. The Guinness was ice cold. Not bad. I asked about the day of Jenny's murder.

'Yeah, I remember it, but I didn't know a thing about it until later, when the street was full of police cars. I was in the sub-basement, practising. I'm a session musician, drummer. And it's well soundproofed down there, so I wouldn't hear a damn thing anyway. As it turns out I wasn't actually in at the time of the murder. Around twelve the leccy went off. First I thought a fuse had blown but it hadn't. Some council morons in Shakespeare Avenue round the corner had dug through a cable or something. Cut off the whole neighbourhood. I didn't fancy drumming by candlelight and without a backing track so I drove into town. Came back after two. It was all over by then, apparently.'

'Did you know Jenny Kickaldy?' I asked.

'To say hello to, that's all. I liked her. Don't know why, really, she never said much.' Probably couldn't get a word in, I thought. But Jenny was like that: people took to her instantly, all she had to say was 'Hi.'

We eventually drifted away from the murder on to other topics. Roy was a retired engineer-turned-jazz musician, which explained the fading legend on his black T-shirt: *The Jazz Bar, Syracuse, Greece.* I found myself apologizing for knowing nothing about jazz.

He shrugged and chuckled easily. 'It's not obligatory, you know.'

I liked Roy and his Guinness. He offered me another can

but I knew I wouldn't get out of there for another hour if I accepted. I was enjoying myself too much. I promised to swing by the Farmhouse on Lansdown Road sometime, where he played jazz with friends every other Friday. I would, too.

Outside I looked back at Roy's front door and his crate of empty wine bottles. Perhaps he had a friend who drank as much wine as he put away Guinness. If so, it was just as well they drank red. There wasn't much space in Roy's fridge. Then I looked across towards Somerset Lodge. The same half-naked builder was leaning against the skip. He lifted a can of Sprite in a silent toast. From somewhere in the back of my brain I received the *stupid warning*, the vague feeling I get when I'm missing something glaringly obvious. There was no point in forcing it, though. It would come to me sooner or later.

I had left the house next to Somerset Lodge to last. I knew I wouldn't enjoy this conversation. This was the abode of Mr and Mrs Fairbrother, the couple who had erected an eight-foot metal fence between their property and Somerset. They had also led the campaign against it opening in the first place. Annis had dug out some old news clippings of an interview with the two. Scary stuff.

A preposterously long-winded chime brought first a yappy dog, then Mrs Fairbrother to the door. She was immaculately groomed, about fifty, and wore an expensively understated cream silk dress with an antique gold brooch above her left breast. I explained what I wanted and showed her my business card. The tiny dog, a short-haired, ugly thing, yapped so hard its front legs left the ground with each bark.

'Well, I'm not sure. I already told the police all I know. Which is nothing, really.'

'Perhaps I'll be asking different questions,' I suggested hopefully.

'That may be, Mr . . .' she consulted the card, 'Honeysett, but I'll still know very little. Oh all right, five minutes,' she relented. 'I thought the whole thing was dead and buried, if you'll excuse the expression.' I decided I wouldn't. She led me into a small reception room at the front, an off-the-peg Louis XIV reproduction nightmare. The dog still yapped incessantly but was never told to shut up. 'That place should never have been allowed to open here in the first place. In a residential area right next to us. Without proper consultation. Well, they've seen the light now, haven't they? But it took a murder before they came to their senses. We knew something dreadful would happen there. Eight years. For eight years we lived in fear. Who'll compensate us for that?'

I made a sympathetic noise which was misunderstood by yappy thing, who started growling at me. Did she remember anything unusual about the day, prior to the arrival of the police?

Well, there was the power cut. Did I know about the power cut? 'Incompetents. I rang the electricity board immediately and they were most unhelpful. They had no idea how long it would take to reconnect. My husband likes to fish,' she added enigmatically, her brow furrowed with anguish. 'And bring his catch home. The hunter-gatherer instinct of the male, I suppose. There's enough fish in the freezer for a year of Fridays. I was hoping the power would stay off long enough to spoil it, but it didn't. It came on again exactly an hour later.'

The *stupid warning* had paid off. The penny dropped as noisily as a fridge freezer into an empty skip. 'Precisely when did it go off?'

'At noon. I know because I had just turned on the telly to watch *Bargain Hunt*, the antiques show. That's when it went. I forgot to turn the telly off and when the power came back it started up with the one o'clock news, gave me quite a start that. Not nearly enough to spoil the trout,' she added with a sad little shake of her head. She consulted her delicate wristwatch and rose, so did I. Yappy thing went into another barking frenzy. 'I'm afraid that's all the time I can give you. Would you care to take some home with you?'

'You mean . . .'

'Yes, fish. You'd be doing me a favour,' she said invitingly.

'Actually, I'm not that keen on fish,' I lied easily. 'Perhaps you could get a cat,' I suggested as I slipped out of the front door.

I lost the tie and flung the jacket on the back seat of the car. My dropping penny and Roy's Guinness had given me quite an appetite. If I hurried, Clive's kitchen at the Bathtub might still be open for business.

When I got there every table was taken and more people arrived at the same time as myself, looking for a late lunch. I hovered for a moment until I spotted two elderly ladies fussing over change for a tip. I practically slipped under them as they vacated their chairs in a cloud of flowery perfume. I rearranged the remains of their meal into a carryable pile and put on my hungry face.

'You look marginally better than the last time I saw you.' Clive had come to collect the empty dishes himself.

'Cheers, Clive,' I said, then realized he meant the scratch I'd got the *first* time I got clobbered by Eely. That seemed a lifetime ago now. I had no intention of telling him about my latest mishaps and thus delaying the arrival of my meal. 'Thai fishcakes?'

'Sold out.'

'Lamb rissoles?'

'Ditto.'

'Venison sausages?'

'Wrong season.'

'Then whaddayagot?'

'Everything else. Try the grilled sardines. Fresh from Cornwall.'

'My favourite place. And a Stella.'

Clive shook his head gravely. 'We don't keep it any more.'

'You what!?' My universe began to tilt. 'What brought that on?'

'It's euro-piss, that's what. You've been drinking it for so long you no longer notice it actually tastes of nothing. I'll bring you a real beer. You won't complain, I can practically guarantee it.' He vanished towards the kitchen.

I lit my last Camel to bridge the gap. What exactly did Stella taste like? Strange, hard as I tried, I simply couldn't remember. Had I been affected by too many bumps on the head? I searched my brain for the memory of other tastes. Sardines taste fishy and oily and of the sea. Venison? Darkly satisfying and foresty. Roast pork? Moist and crackly and crying for mustard. No problems there. But Stella . . .?

Clive presented me with a tall, thin-stemmed glass and a bottle of beer as though he was serving a hundred-year-old brandy. The bottle was green and huge and beaded with condensation. 'Pilsener Urquell.' He poured me a frothy glass of the stuff with a practised flourish, then crossed his arms in front of him and waited. I sniffed it. Clive sighed and rolled his eyes. I took a brave gulp. It was cool, sharp and mellow at the same time. It had a clean taste of hops and reminded me of hot afternoons in the mountains.

Clive didn't even wait for my verdict. 'Told ya. Food's on its way.'

The sardines weren't half bad either.

Afternoon was slipping into early evening as I cruised aimlessly along the inane one-way systems of the city, round and round the Guildhall, Orange Grove, up narrow Broad Street, reputedly the most polluted stretch of road in the West. The Western World, that is. I let the traffic flow carry me along while I kept an eye on the pavements, alleys and doorways. My patience had finally run out with Matt, who was supposed to be looking for Gavin and Lisa for me. If I was to have a decent showdown with Gordon Hines on Tuesday then I needed all the ammunition I could get. I'd already checked on Matt's flat in Phoenix House and had found nothing but a kicked-in door and a girl with dreadlocks and other encrustations, who'd never even heard of him. So it stood to reason that he was still on the street, or at his fabulous hideaway: shelter, food, water but no toilet, he'd said. No one was going to find him there . . . I just couldn't work it out. No *stupid warning* either. I was racking my brains about the curious combination but got thrown by the lack of a toilet in the arrangement every time. A food warehouse? Surely they'd have to have a bog? The cellar of a restaurant? A secret chamber in the covered market? My speculations became more fantastic by the minute.

I cruised through the park, down Royal Avenue, past the public tennis courts and was filtering back into the flow of traffic around Queen Square when I decided that it was a pointless exercise. The chances of spotting him like this had to be minimal. I took a perfunctory trip down Milsom Street. I would have to talk to a lot of street people, *Big Issue* sellers, street traders, in other words, foot slog. But not today, thank you. I swung left and right again, into Walcot Street, where I joined the slow procession of drivers trying to leave the city behind. I was crawling along at 3 mph, something the DS doesn't enjoy, when I drew up to another thorn in my side: Austin Antiques.

I hadn't decided what to do about Mr Austin yet. It was tricky. He was obviously right at the heart of the art racket Leonard Dufossee had got involved in and should be taken down a peg or two, yet at the same time I wanted to keep Alison out of trouble. Then the matter decided itself. As I drew level with Austin's shop I spotted Fishers, his silent partner, outside discussing some item in the window with a youngish couple who nodded and shook their heads in unison. The man who didn't know anything about antiques. Must be a fast learner. It was an opportunity too good to miss, since we didn't have an address for Fishers and the phone book had been less than useless. I caused even more road chaos by forcing my way across into Walcot Gate and abandoning the car in front of the chapel. By the time I hurried back down the road the couple had finished their business and were walking towards me. I nearly ignored them, then changed my mind and stopped.

'I just saw you at the antiques shop, having a chat with Mr Fishers . . .' I started.

'Fishers? That was Mr Austin, the owner. I don't know any Mr Fishers,' he said. The young woman on his arm made to pull him away. Mum probably told her never to talk to strangers. I quickly explained that I had some antiques to be valued. Could they recommend their expertise? They thought they could, having bought several pieces of small furniture from Austin. And they were sure the man they'd just talked to was Mr Austin? They gave me another suspicious look, said they were, and pushed off, convinced they had escaped the clutches of a prize nutter.

I called Mill House on my mobile. After an age and a half Annis answered.

'Is Alison around?' I asked.

'She's in the kitchen, hang on.'

'Just ask her what Austin looks like.'

'Hey Ali,' Annis shouted, 'Chris wants to know what Austin looks like.' A pause. 'Tall, skinny, naff little beard, ear glued to a mobile. That do you?'

I said it did.

'Of course under no circumstances tell me what you're up to,' Annis warned.

'I'm not sure myself. You remember Mr Fishers, Austin's partner, asking us to check him out?'

'Ages ago. Tim installed pinholes and all that?'

'S'right. Only it looks like Fishers and Austin are the same person. In other words . . .'

'Austin used Aqua to check how safe his set-up in

Walcot Street really was and concocted a cover story to make it look quite harmless.'

'No secret is safe in a town like Bath. He should have brought someone in from Bristol, the lazy sod.'

'Are you going after him? I had wondered when you'd get around to that.'

I hesitated for a moment, realizing that I didn't have a plan at all. 'I thought I might just hang around a bit.'

'Spoken like a true professional,' she said and hung up.

I'd never heard of an antiques dealer who went in for late night opening, or one who started work before ten thirty for that matter, so I didn't expect to wait long for Austin to leave. And I was right. After just twenty minutes or so of loitering inside the front entrance of the Bell I saw Austin/Fishers lock up shop. He glanced up and down the road still choked with traffic, and set off on foot towards the London Road roundabout, carrying a light grey jacket over his arm. He stopped briefly to key in a number on his mobile, then clamped it to his ear and walked on.

It was one of those awkward decisions you always have to make when you do surveillance by yourself. Do you go for your car and risk losing the target or do you follow on foot until your target hops into a car, leaving you behind?

Walking at some distance behind him I made the right decision for once: at Walcot Gate I just stood and followed him with my eyes. Only thirty-odd yards ahead he pointed a key at a massive silver Lexus, which sprang to life with a flash of its indicators and that annoying 'euch'-sound car designers seem to love. I legged it down to my car, which didn't say 'euch' or anything else when I yanked the door open. A hectic three-point turn later I pointed the nose of the DS into the traffic. I was in luck. Austin's car was facing downhill and as yet no one had let him do his intended U-turn. I bullied myself into the middle of the road, waved my arm out of the window and was rewarded with a slot in the procession. Then I personally flashed my lights at Austin to let him into the queue inching up towards the London Road. He acknowledged my supposed kindness without a flicker of recognition.

I really have to get one of those boring, nondescript, forgettable cars, a Ford something or Vauxhall other, to follow people around in. Tim had been pestering me for a big van with spyholes for cameras, chemical toilet and fridge (naturally), where he can keep banks of electronic gizmos and pretend he's working for MI5. I was warming to the idea.

Meanwhile I tried to look bored or keep my head down, pretending to look for things in my glove box. Austin set his indicators left, which meant the Paragon. We both squeezed around the sharp turn. Traffic going east was practically stationary and stacked ten cars high up Guinea Lane. I hung back a bit, a bit too much as it turned out – Austin just caught the lights as he turned up into Lansdown and I had to run a very red light to a chorus of angry horns. So much for staying inconspicuous. But now I had somehow acquired a minibus in front of me, which was fine until it stopped and I had to make myself skinny and squeeze past in the middle of the road. I was not making friends here either.

Along Julian Road I let his car slip ahead, then put the pedal down as he turned into St James Street. We were in Tim's neighbourhood now. Austin exited St James Square at the top right as I entered it, and turned left again. He was parking his car outside a black-fronted garage on the left by the time I turned into Park Street Mews, so I drove past without looking and turned right on to the steep hill of Park Street itself. Two solid rows of cars parked on either side and a dead end to boot. I simply abandoned the car right there, blocking the entire road, and walked back down to peer around the corner. Austin had just shut the boot of the car, which closed with a luxurious clonk. Cradling a small cardboard box in the crook of his left arm he opened one half of the wooden garage door and disappeared inside. I watched a light click on, then off again. Austin reappeared minus the box, locked the garage, then got back in the car. He laboriously shunted back and forth until the Lexus was no more than five inches or so from the garage door, making it impossible to open. Lastly he fixed a bright yellow steering lock and got out. Another 'euch' as he abandoned the car and walked up towards me. If he didn't spot me now he had to be visually impaired – the DS in the middle of the road and nowhere to go for me. For a split second I considered pretending to wait to be let into the first door I came to but changed my mind and simply ducked behind a car. Across the street a bloke with shopping bags gave me a curious look but kindly decided it was none of his business.

As it turned out, ducking behind the car had been a good decision: the front door I'd so nearly pretended to wait in front of turned out to be the one Austin unlocked and disappeared into.

I groaned. This wasn't surveillance, it was Cowboys and Indians. There was no telling whether I'd got away with it until later. And what was I finding out here? That he had expensive-looking, olive green wallpaper and a small chandelier in his front room and a lot of period furniture, as you'd expect from an antiques dealer, even a crooked one. I ducked down deeper as Austin came to the curtainless windows to start fiddling with the wooden shutters. Just then a young bloke in a tracksuit walked up to the car I was hiding behind and coughed. I looked up. He jangled his car keys at me. 'Do you mind?' Austin was still by the window. Feeling like a complete prat I waddled on my haunches like an elderly duck until I'd gained the shelter of the next car along. The bloke never took his eyes off me while he got in, started his engine and reversed down the hill. I made some quacking noises and flapped my elbows at him but it failed to cheer me up. Until I realized what I had learned about Mr Austin-Fishers, which was: he liked to park his seriously expensive, executive hearse on the street, in front of his garage. Which made me hope that perhaps whatever was inside it was worth more than his spanking new Lexus.

'He parks his car so as to block access to his garage at night. We stake him out and wait until he goes out at night in his car. Then we raid the place.'

It was lunchtime the next day and Tim and I were popping moules marinière into our mouths in a lazy rhythm, at the window table in the Bathtub. We were on our second round of Urquells.

'Bollocks to that, mate.' Tim threatened to tweak my nose with a pair of empty mussel shells. 'He'll pick up a Chinese takeaway and be back in five minutes, and then what? No, we'll *make* him go out.'

'What, throw a brick through his shop window and call the police? He'd have to come out then.'

'Show some finesse, will you? We'll send him a couple of complimentary tickets to some hideously expensive do, where turning up in a Lexus is de rigueur, with a Bath City Council letter accompanying it, saying stuff about valued members of the local business community blah blah, opportunity for exchange of ideas with like-minded upstanding etc. etc. I'll run it up on my computer, no sweat. He'll go. I've done it loads of times. If they leave in evening dress you know you can clean them out at their leisure. Leave it to me. But it'll cost ya.'

Tim was right, on both counts. It cost Aqua a small fortune but on Saturday night, from Tim's TT, parked earlier near the Approach Golf Course in Park Place, we could just see Austin gently guide a familiar-looking blonde, in a sparkly blue dress and delicate heels, to his car. It was Gill, my very own BBC location finder. I was only mildly surprised.

Perhaps it was inevitable they'd eventually join forces so they didn't have to fight each other over which houses to rip off.

Austin, in full evening dress himself, pulled the car into the middle of the road, then did the gentlemanly kerfuffle with the doors before driving off to their literary dinner at Stour Head, courtesy of Aqua.

'Wait five minutes, in case he's forgotten his handkerchief.' Tim was supremely calm about the whole thing while I chain smoked out of the window. I suppose the fact that he's never been caught makes him feel invulnerable. I myself wasn't so sure. If the police did turn up we could (perhaps, eventually) explain that we were on the side of the angels, but only just. And only after an awfully uncomfortable wait in the bowels of Manvers Street station. 'Right, let's do it,' he said after a few more minutes. 'I'll walk up, you get the Land Rover.' I had filched Annis's wreck for the occasion, so we could simply load up and drive off.

By the time I had manoeuvred the brute in front of the garage Tim had the lock open. We slipped in and closed the door behind us. 'Lights or torches?' I asked in the darkness.

'Oh, lights, lights. Nothing's more suspicious than torchlight. Here.' He had found the switch and a strip light flickered on.

Austin's garage was an Aladdin's cave, only I suspect the fairy-tale robbers were probably less neat. Unlike Austin's shop, which cultivated clutter to encourage punters to explore the place, everything here was tidily stacked for maximum use of space. The right-hand wall held a grey metal shelf unit. It was packed with plastic storage crates in bright primary colours. Against the left wall leant a number of wooden packing cases, three deep. The rest of the space was stacked from floor to ceiling with small pieces of furniture, oriental cabinets, bubble-wrapped bronzes, large silver pieces, and a carelessly deposited Chinese dinner gong which looked suspiciously familiar.

Tim pulled forward a few of the plastic containers. 'Fine china, silver cutlery, more plates and stuff. Can't tell if it's honest or swag, of course. Do we really have to photograph everything? We'd have to move fast.'

'We might not have to. Give me a hand with these crates.' Each one of the nine crates against the wall had a felt-tipped destination scrawled on the narrow side on top: several said *Oman*, two *Dubai* and one said *Moscow*. I knew crated-up paintings when I saw them, having helped the gallery assistant at Simon Paris to pack my own for sending in the past. These crates were high class, screws, no nails at all. Tim produced a stubby little screwdriver, I made do with my pocket knife. We had the first one open in a minute. 'Welcome back,' I said. It was one of the paintings I had sold to Al-Omari and friends. So they hadn't left the country yet. Perhaps Al-Omari and Nadeem never bothered with that side of the operation, just flew in and out of the country and waited for their deliveries. It made sense. Why get your hands dirtier than you have to? I flipped the painting over. The canvas on the back was different from the one I normally used. I made short work of a row of staples and once I'd peeled back a corner of my painting one of Alison's forgeries peeked out, a Sickert. Damn, she was good. 'Wait,' I said to Tim who'd already pounced on the next crate. 'I remember the sizes of Alison's forgeries.' I counted off the seven crates. 'But these two don't fit, they're too large. Open those.' We took the canvases out completely this time. My own work stared back at me in the acid light from the neon tube overhead. This time we ripped off all the staples to completely reveal paintings underneath. Both were nudes, both done in black, fluid, unmistakable brush strokes. And both were signed by a bloke called Picasso. Never my favourite painter but still worth a bob or two.

'Did Ali do these?' Tim asked.

'Nope, they're the real thing. Look at the back. They've pasted modern canvas over the back of the original to match it up with what should be the back of my painting. Like a Picasso sandwich.'

'They worth much?'

'House in the country and a couple of cars.'

'I always fancied that, are we taking them?' Even knowing my feelings on the subject, Tim was only half joking, running his fingers lovingly over the famous signature.

'Not a chance, mate. We're taking the forgeries, my canvases and the Chinese dinner gong. Let's move.'

A deeply entwined couple walking by never gave us a single glance and we pretended not to notice that they had their tongues down each other's throats. We loaded up, locked up and drove off in less than three minutes. I parked up beside Tim's TT. 'Can you get on-line from here?'

'Sure.' Tim slid into the passenger side and started up his laptop and car phone.

'Art Loss Register, late Picasso, nudes,' I told him. They came up instantly, stolen four weeks ago from a private collection in Cheltenham.

I rang Manvers Street nick even before we set off for the valley. I refused to give my name but tried to inject some urgency into the sergeant. 'You have to get there tonight, soon, before the paintings are moved.'

'Okay, we'll send someone round.' He hesitated. 'This is Sergeant Hayes, by the way,' said the vaguely familiar voice. 'Is that you, Honeysett?'

'Certainly not,' I said, peeved, and cut the connection.

Monday's edition of the *Bath Chronicle* lay becrumbed and sauce-spattered amongst the leftovers from our lunch on the verandah table. ART THIEVES LAST SUPPER, the headline proclaimed ungrammatically. Avon and Somerset Constabulary, following an underworld tip-off (underworld? how dare they) arrested, in the early hours of Sunday morning etc. We had all read it several times already, not for the sketchy information the overblown article contained but for the satisfied glow it produced around the table. Austin and Gillian Pine had been picked up on their return from their literary feast after the police raided the garage. It appeared most of the items inside had been nicked from somewhere or another. Most of them, I knew, would never find their way home, being uncatalogued, uninsured, unregistered or unmarked. The Picassos at least would be reunited with their owner and that alone made it all worthwhile for me.

'Personally I wouldn't piss on a Picasso if it was on fire,' was Alison's pronouncement on the value of the man's oeuvre. 'I'd certainly hate to have to fake one,' she added.

'Your forging days are over, right?' I said sharply.

She looked me straight in the eye. 'Right.'

'Talking of forgeries,' Annis said quickly, 'what's gonna happen to the ones you liberated from Austin's garage? Do we give them back to the Dufossees?'

'I doubt they'd like a reminder of what they've lost on their walls,' I suggested.

'I don't see why it matters,' Tim said cheerfully. 'If Alison's fakes are as good as you say they should look identical. If you like the picture you like the picture. Who cares who painted it?'

Being shouted down by three overexcited painters all at once was a new experience for Tim. Of course it mattered! Originality! Provenance! Authenticity! We nearly drowned the poor soul in indignant jargon but he remained unimpressed. 'Get a grip, guys. They're nice, but they're only pictures, you know?' he said sensibly. By the end of the discussion Tim had talked himself into a small collection of faked twentieth-century masterpieces, and very nice they look on his walls too.

* * *

I had mooched around town for most of Sunday afternoon in the hope of catching up with Matt but didn't get a whiff of him. Now, after having helped Tim hang his new collection, I was on the same disheartening mission, trudging through the airless and oppressive fug of a town praying for a thunderstorm. I acquired another armful of this week's *Big Issue* and met with the same undisguised suspicion and hostility when showing the pictures around, no matter how many cans of Special Brew I doled out. No one admitted to having seen either Gavin or Matt and I was beginning to believe it. Gavin had most likely left town after I traced him at his friend's place in Milsom Street. I know I would have. Matt was different, though. He thought he'd found a perfect hide-out in the city and so far it seemed to work for him. In fact it was working rather too well for him. As far as Jenny's murder was concerned he was in the clear and there was no reason not to go back to Narcotics Anonymous now and invest in his drug-free life. I had checked. He hadn't been back. The longer he stayed out there the more vulnerable he would become. But my search had a more selfish reason too; I needed to quiz him about Gordon and I very much wanted to talk to the other ex-resident who was still around, Lisa Chapwin. I'd tried her flat several times without success. Matt had told me no one would recognize her from the photo Needham had furnished me with, so I needed Matt for that, too.

I let myself drift around town, sniffed around the backs of restaurants and cafés and peered into basements and courtyards. It was a pathetic way of searching for someone who was actively hiding. Most houses in Bath have basements and even sub-basements, and I was conscious of the fact that most of the pavements I trudged across were really the roofs of vaults, thousands of them, capable of hiding a million secrets.

I sauntered up the Royal Avenue which bisects the east side of Victoria Park. I had found a free parking space alongside the tennis courts there. Even though I longed to exchange this stuffiness for the coolness and comforts of the valley I made myself walk on past the DS. The lawns were crowded with groups of tourists, their coaches parked along the Avenue. Several football games were in progress below the ha-ha and children buzzed around the ice-cream van like wasps around a pot of jam.

For lack of a better idea I headed towards the west side of the park and the botanical gardens, more for the idea of the cooling stream than any hope of finding Matt hiding there. I was passing the bandstand where a group of Japanese tourists were taking turns having their picture taken when I saw him. For all of two seconds. He was crossing the Royal Avenue, right to left, just beyond the obelisk, then I lost sight of him behind some trees. I ran, shedding my collection of *Big Issues* as I went, just managing not to get run over by a bloke on an out-of-control motorized skateboard and an open-top double-decker as I crossed Marlborough Lane. By the time I reached the obelisk a lot of big lunches and too many Camels were catching up with me. I'd only sprinted a couple of hundred yards but my lungs were screaming and my head was pounding as though I'd just climbed Mont Blanc. I had to stop. And rest my hands on my knees. And wheeze a lot. Heroically I resisted the temptation to make rash resolutions concerning big lunches and as soon as I got my breath back I lit a defiant Camel and enjoyed a little coughing fit.

I walked on a few more yards past the arch, beyond which the Royal Avenue joined its own loop, and scanned the pavement ahead. There was no sign of Matt. Just then an old boy with a baseball cap and a brightly polished spade across his shoulder appeared to materialize from the bushes on the left, a few yards ahead. I found a narrow alley leading straight down towards the Upper Bristol Road. After a few yards I just knew I had found Matt's secret abode: on either side of a low chain-link fence stretched what looked like hundreds of allotments, and every one of them appeared to have that favourite of kids' hiding places, a shed.

There were few people about, and those oblivious to or unafraid of the threatening storm clouds rolling in from the south didn't seem concerned about me wandering among the plots. Pretending to show an interest in the profusion of beans, peas, carrots and spuds, I passed close enough to each shed to check for signs that someone had made a permanent home of one. I exchanged the odd nod with people looking up from digging or weeding. If Matt was hiding out here he'd hardly advertise the fact so I didn't stop to ask questions.

The place was a warren. If originally it had had a discernible layout it was now difficult to see where one plot ended and the next one started, and even though I began my search at the top of the gentle slope it was impossible to get an overview of the place. The huts, fruit cages and dwarf trees, the rows of bamboo canes, clumps of sunflowers, compost heaps and trained bean plants had me walking around in circles, unsure if I'd seen this or that particular plot before.

I'd come to another dead end against a dry stone wall and the thick undergrowth beneath the trees at the northern boundary. Too lazy to retrace my steps I squeezed sideways past a sprawling compost heap and a thicket of rampant Jerusalem artichokes and stepped right into Matt's home from home.

'Thought you'd never make it.' Supremely relaxed, he sat with his arms folded and his legs stretched out in front of him on a low, roughly made bench in front of a broad shed. I looked around me. The space was completely enclosed with massive redcurrant bushes, rows of Jerusalem artichokes and beans. The shed itself was half built into the hedge at the top and so overgrown with bindweed it had become part of the rampant growth all around us.

'You seem unsurprised,' I said, surprised.

'I saw you traipsing round and round for the last twenty minutes,' he said with a satisfied smile. 'I thought you'd miss it altogether, but just in case I put the kettle on. Cuppa?'

Incredulous, I followed Matt to the door of the large hut. It wasn't the set-up which surprised me, however. It was Matt. The inside of the six-by-eight hut was scrupulously clean and obsessively tidy. In one corner a narrow mattress on some pallets served as a bed, with an upturned orange crate as a bedside table. A dented kettle burbled on a camping stove, which sat on a home-made table. Matt released a couple of mugs from hooks screwed into the front of a shelf running above it. A plexiglass window filtered foliage-green light into the place. No, Matt himself was by far the greater surprise. He was no longer the jumpy, weedy and pasty ex-user I had been looking for. His movements had lost their impatient jerkiness, his skin was tanned, his eyes clear. He fixed me with them now.

'Milk?' He produced a plastic bottle from where it had been floating in a cooling bucket of water under the table. He was enjoying himself immensely, I could tell.

There wasn't a breath of wind. The first rumble of thunder rolled over as we settled on the bench outside, with our mugs sitting on yet another upturned box.

'Nice place,' I said appreciatively. 'How'd you find it?'

'Didn't have to, mate. It's my Uncle Stew's but he's waiting for a hip replacement and can't make it out here now. He used to bring me here when I was a kid.'

'And you've been working his allotment?' I could see the calluses on his hands and the black soil that stained his nails.

'Every day. It's not just this bit.' He indicated the enclosed space. 'It runs all the way down to that water trough. My neighbour says it could feed a family of four. Well, it certainly feeds me.'

'I'm impressed.'

'Good. It helped me stay clean, too.'

'I can see that.'

'Shame you found me. I knew it couldn't last. Do the Pigs know where I am yet?'

'The Pigs, as you so charmingly put it, aren't interested. Case closed,' I tried to reassure him.

'Who did it then?' he said without a hint of interest.

'They pinned it on Dave.'

'You're not convinced, I can tell.'

I grunted my assent. 'While you were at Somerset, did Gordon Hines ever . . . do anything weird to any of you? Did he ever make advances towards you or anyone else?'

'You mean sex?'

'I mean sex. Did you ever get the impression that he was getting overly close to anyone?'

Matt shrugged. 'Old Gordon and his prayer book. I don't know, mate. He never tried anything on with me, that's for sure. But I think Lisa found him quite creepy.'

'Did she mention anything?'

'Just an impression I got. Lisa didn't really speak then. Hardly came out of her room, hardly ate. She'd come downstairs at mealtimes, because it was the rules, swallowed a couple of mouthfuls and went back to hide in her room.'

Matt was right, of course. She was the invisible resident. She was there for less than six months, during which time I saw her perhaps two or three times, which is why I hardly remembered her. 'So you never got any inkling Gordon might have interfered with her?'

Matt raised an ironic eyebrow. 'I was stoned 24/7 those days. I didn't have any inklings full stop. Mind you, I wouldn't recommend that anyone try and interfere with her now.'

'Explain?' I invited.

'For a start she's ten stone heavier. Okay, I'm probably exaggerating, but she's massive now. The kind of medication she's on can do that to you. She packs quite a wallop, too, I can tell you.' He swung a fist out in illustration.

'So you did find her.'

'Lisa found me. She's not well. Babbles religious stuff, from the Bible or somewhere, I'm no expert; the days of the locust? Valley of the shadows? Stuff like that. She hit me last time I ran into her, didn't see her coming. She's got a moped now to get around on. She just suddenly appeared in front of me, helmet on and all that. Started haranguing me about nothing. By the time I'd figured out who she was she'd already thumped me. Angry girl,' he concluded.

'Where was that?'

'Outside Green Park station. After she thumped me for no reason she got on her moped, one of those 50 cc ones, and rode off into town.'

The clouds had turned from leaden grey to verdigris and the heavens opened with a lightning flash and an instantaneous peal of thunder overhead. We took our mugs inside and watched the deluge through the open door.

'What about Gavin? Any sign?'

'Nothing, mate. I reckon he's done a proper runner. That's what I call decent rain,' he added. 'Saves me a lot of watering. We've needed this.' He nodded sagely at the heavy raindrops bouncing on the hard-baked earth.

'You've turned into a proper gardener, then.'

'You're not wrong.' He turned away from the door to face me. 'I'm thinking of doing just that. Horticultural college and all that. Perhaps you'll see me on telly one day, the new Alan Titchmarsh. He only had one O-level, did you know that? I've got five GCSEs.'

'I think that's an excellent idea, Matt. But this . . .' I encompassed the interior of the hut with a sweep of my arm, 'it's cosy but it's not a solution.'

'D'you think I don't know that? It's not meant to be permanent. I just need to get my head together, and it's easier here than in my flat. Okay, so the police don't want me, but there's others who do,' he reminded me.

'Perhaps we can do something about that,' I suggested.

'How d'you mean?'

'Just let me know when you're ready; we'll deal with your creditors. And I've a friend called Tim who'd sort you out a front door the Bank of England would be proud of.'

'You sure, Chris?'

'Dead cert. Still got my card?'

He pointed to the wall over his bed. It was pinned up there along with pictures and gardening articles cut from Sunday supplements and a picture of Charlie Dimmock leaning on a spade. Outside, the downpour had lessened. I made to go.

'Wait.' Matt pulled a black-handled knife from his pocket and unfolded its three-inch blade. 'I'm not letting you out of here without some vegetables. I hope you like broad beans, I've a right glut of those . . .'

Chapter Twelve

'So what did you get for the barbecue?' Tim asked, staring into the half-empty fridge. 'He'll be here in an hour, and I haven't wired you up yet, either.'

'Don't be daft. There's not going to be any barbecue. It's purely a pretext to get Gordon here so I can provoke him and you can tape the conversation from the barn. That's why I'm making supper now.' I was shelling Matt's windfall of broad beans at the kitchen table.

'You must be damn certain that Gordon is your man. I mean, what if it doesn't work? How're you gonna explain the lack of food if he doesn't react the way you want him to?'

'Once I've accused him of sexual abuse and Jenny's murder I'm sure he'll have lost his appetite. I can't see us talking about it with chicken drumsticks in our hands. Don't worry about it, Gordon is our man. Only no one ever investigated him properly because he was supposed to have a cast-iron alibi. Except, of course, he hasn't. As Annis said – alibi shmalibi. Everyone thought Jenny was still alive when he left because of the damn flan in the oven.'

'I thought it was a quiche,' Tim contested.

'You're right, it was. But *damn* and *flan* sound better together.' He looked at me as though I'd finally lost my marbles. Perhaps I had. I savaged a few more beans out of their pods and several jumped on to the floor. 'Oh, whatever. There was an hour-long power cut in Poet's Corner between twelve and one. Jenny's hob was gas but her new oven was electric. I noticed the timer was blinking nonsensical numbers when I came into the kitchen. That's because the leccy had been off and the digital clock needed resetting. But the oven itself started up again and cooked the quiche, only it took an hour longer than it should have. We've no idea where Dave and Gavin were at the time but the two girls were upstairs listening to loud music with headphones, sharing Anne's new diskman. They didn't notice the power cut and they didn't hear a thing. And there's something else I remembered. Gordon told everyone he was there because he had to fix a date for the next committee meeting. Purely routine. But when I saw Jenny earlier she had already called a committee meeting for Saturday, when she thought everything would be resolved. After that she was going to take a few days off.'

'Okay, so he's your man. Still, shame about the barbecue,' he insisted.

'That's why I'm fixing up something now.'

'Broad beans make me fart. Good job the girls aren't here.' I had banished Annis and Alison from the house for the day. If there had to be a showdown then I wanted as few people there as possible. Gordon had killed once already, which is why I didn't want any distractions or anyone else to worry about. So I sent them to London to stock up on paint and canvas. They wouldn't be back until much later.

While a pan of new potatoes simmered away I got out the belly of pork, which allowed me to test out my new supersharp Chinese meat cleaver. It made short work of dicing it, which in my present mood was immensely satisfying. While Tim watched impatiently I fried the pork in olive oil in a deep-sided frying pan, then added chopped onions and rendered them soft and golden before adding the beans, a cup of stock, some crushed garlic, cumin and a handful of parsley. Then slammed a lid on it. Nothing to it.

* * *

Tim was right, I had left everything to the last minute so I'd be too busy to get nervous about it. He fixed me up with my radio mike. The microphone itself travelled half-way up the inside of my shirt and would be undetectable, but the transmitter, the size of a cigarette packet, sat heavily and uncomfortably in the small of my back. It was held on with gaffer tape, which started itching immediately. Feeling more like a TV chef than a private investigator I dished up the beans and potatoes, giving a running commentary so Tim could test it out from his hidden set-up in the shed across the yard. Once he was satisfied that the transmitter worked we silently wolfed down our food, snatched gulps of pilsener from big green bottles and listened in to the humid silence in case Gordon arrived early.

With Tim and his tape recorder installed behind a collection of junk in one of the sheds I walked restlessly in the empty yard. Only Annis's Land Rover was parked here, the other cars were hidden in the outbuildings. The sky hung like soft cement over the sweltering valley. I stopped by the stream where it tumbled down into the mossy void where the mill wheel had once sat. The leafy tunnel of the lane through which Gordon would come remained empty. Somewhere across the valley a chain saw started up and fell silent again. The air sat thick and unmoving. It tasted as though I had breathed each lungful at least twice before.

'Nothing so far. Quite peaceful out here,' I said for Tim's benefit. 'I still wish I had my gun.'

Annis and I had rowed about it earlier. It hadn't been easy to convince her to leave in the first place but under no circumstances was she going to agree to it if I waited for Gordon with a .38 in my pocket. In the end the girls had driven off in my DS and taken it with them. When I checked later, the shotgun had disappeared as well.

I knew she was right all along. I couldn't force a confession out of the man at gunpoint. It would never stand up in court. Jenny's murder appeared unpremeditated, committed with an impromptu weapon, so I had no reason to believe that Gordon would turn up at Mill House all tooled up, even if he was wise to my suspicions. And after all, Tim was just across the yard. So what could possibly go wrong?

'I can hear an engine, I'm going inside now. Stay sharp, Tim,' I said to my shirt and hurried across the yard to hide in the shadows just inside the front door. I had expected Gordon's little Volvo to come bouncing down the lane. Instead a huge gun-metal grey Mercedes advanced towards the house. The cautious driver, invisible behind deeply tinted windows, picked his way carefully among the potholes. The car slowed even further, coming to a halt just outside the tumbledown gates of the yard. There it sat, engine softly idling, like a wary animal, ready for sudden flight. After a long minute it rolled quietly into the yard and came to a stop opposite me. I stepped forward out of the shadows, keeping what I hoped was a neutral expression on my face.

Gordon Hines unfolded himself from the driver's seat and stood by the open door, his arms leaning casually on the roof, hands folded as if in prayer. He wore razor-sharp navy blue trousers and a pale blue shirt, open at the neck. An impossibly thin gold wristwatch flashed from under a cuff. Every one of his thinning hairs was immaculately in place and his often wayward eyebrows had been neatly plucked. He had lost every hint of the religious fuddy-duddy. Even his speech had sharpened up.

'Thought perhaps I'd got the date wrong. But I haven't, have I?' he said quietly. 'It's just that your yard looks a little empty for a party.'

'You're a bit early, that's all,' I tried to reassure him. The last thing I wanted was for him to drive off again now. 'Nice car, by the way.'

'You've no idea how nice. Always wanted one of these. No reason not to now.' He reached inside the car for

242

something, then clunked the door shut, walked around the front and advanced. He was holding a bottle of red by the neck like a weapon. 'You might be a good cook, Honeysett, but you're a pathetic liar. I know what game you're trying to play but it won't work. It didn't work for Jenny and it won't work for you. And this is not a peace offering.' He wagged the bottle. 'I just want a decent drink while I set you straight about a few things.'

'Okay, then. You'd better come in.' I stepped back but he didn't move.

'Have you got your posse in there?'

I shook my head. 'Just you and me.'

'That's the way I like it. Lead on.'

Against my better judgement I turned my back on him, though not without keeping his every move in my peripheral vision. Gordon walked into the sitting room as though he knew the place well, checked the dining area in front of the open verandah doors and the passage towards the kitchen. He flicked open the small door to the walk-in cupboard under the stairs and quickly glanced inside. Then he turned the bottle and pointed its neck at me. 'A corkscrew and one glass are required here. I don't intend to share this with you, in case you'd wondered. You're a bit of a lager lout at heart anyway, aren't you.'

'I didn't ask you here to share anything with you, Gordon.' Having to share breathing space with him was quite enough. 'The kitchen's through here.'

He set the bottle on the table and snorted. 'You would have a Rayburn, of course. Style over substance. Just like your paintings.'

I fetched a glass and furnished him with a corkscrew. I was quite happy to let him do all the talking, only so far he hadn't said anything vaguely useful. He got the bottle uncorked, filled his glass, sniffed it and took an appreciative sip.

'You know how I got into charity work? I married a do-gooder. I was never a do-gooder myself. I'd always looked out for Number One. Only I wasn't very good at it. I had a small business but I got squeezed out by the big guys. It didn't matter. Helen had inherited enough money to keep us in quite some style. But charity always got in the way. There was always some good work to do. Pathetic people to rescue. We owned Somerset Lodge but she wouldn't sell it. A million and a quarter just sitting there, infested with deserving nutters. And more well-wishing idiots, like Jenny.'

Gordon's mention of her name made me reach for a bottle of pilsener on the table. It was empty. I got a new one from the fridge and fortified myself with a long cool draught. I had intended to stay quite sober, but what the hell. I stood by the fridge while Gordon stood leaning against the kitchen units by the door, glass and bottle within comfortable reach. He seemed at ease yet never took his eyes off me, registering my every move.

'But don't get me wrong. I loved Helen. I really . . . truly did. When we found out that she had cancer I was more devastated than she was. And it was around then that I went off the rails a bit.' He briefly raised his eyebrows and took a delicate sip of wine.

'Let's get this straight right now,' I said, keeping my voice controlled and as level as possible. 'By off-the-rails you mean you started sexually abusing mental health patients down in Brighton.'

A sharp intake of breath. 'What would you know about it?' A thin smile remained on his face. 'I was not myself then. And it was only one girl. It was a fixation. I prayed with her each time. I helped her atone for her sins. I was trying to help her. We were helping each other. You wouldn't understand.'

It was my turn to snort with disbelief. 'The Culverhouse Trust knew and didn't call in the authorities?'

'They had problems of their own. It was a scandal too many. They couldn't afford it.'

244

'And they were happy to have you on the committee that ran Somerset Lodge?'

'They had little choice, since Helen and I owned the place. They were pretty broke by then. Couldn't afford to buy a place. Finding a new place to rent around here would have been near impossible; they had lost charitable status by then. And I had explained myself well. They understood the stress I'd been under. I had given assurances.'

We weren't doing too badly. An admission of abuse on tape was a start. I only hoped the microphone was picking up his voice across the kitchen. I inched a bit closer under the guise of making myself more comfortable. 'But then it started again,' I prompted.

He gave a single nod. 'Helen was dying. The drugs could no longer suppress the pain. I could no longer bear the pain either.' He gulped what was left in his glass, refilled it and took another swig.

'Jenny found out,' I said flatly. I wasn't prepared for what came next.

'She found out and started blackmailing me. And now you think you can take over. I don't think so.'

'She blackmailed you for money?' I couldn't believe that for one minute.

'Use your loaf, Honeysett,' he said contemptuously. 'Jenny was a real do-gooder. She got a written testimonial from the girl. After my wife died she used it to make sure I didn't sell off the house. I would have to live off my little pension, in my little house, with my little Volvo. And she got more and more ambitious. She started using me to influence the committee. About conditions at Somerset Lodge, the amount of rent charged, working conditions for herself . . .' He trailed off and waved a dismissive hand.

'So one day you decided enough was enough and you killed her.'

His eyes widened. He slowly shook his head. He drew his mouth into a pitying smile. 'Is that what you think? Is

245

that what you got me here for?' He shook his head again. 'I didn't kill Jenny. I've no idea who killed Jenny. *I don't care who killed the bitch but I'm sure glad someone did.*' The dawning of a realization. 'Oh, how unfortunate. You didn't really have any proof of any of this, did you? You weren't even interested. You made me come here to confess to her murder, didn't you? Which means you've probably got a clever little tape recorder hidden somewhere.'

I shook my head slowly, trying to fathom whether I believed him or not. His next move made that rather irrelevant.

'How unfortunate for you.' He reached across the work surface and picked up my Chinese meat cleaver, tested it for weight. 'I hadn't really planned for violence, so thank you for supplying this. I only came to warn you off trying to blackmail me. I'm quite comfortably off now and money buys muscle, if you know what I mean. I really just wanted you to hand over the girl's written statement. The police didn't find it, and I had a very good look for it, here and at Somerset. So I presumed you'd got it hidden some- where. Oh dear. And now I'll kill you if I don't get the tape. And even then I shall probably kill you, I've only just realized that. Oh dear,' he said again quietly, 'this is going to be messy, isn't it?' He took a playful swipe at me. 'Very messy.'

I backed off, looking around for something to defend myself with while keeping more than one eye on the cleaver I had so lovingly sharpened earlier. There was nothing within reach to match his weapon, not even a conveniently boiling pan of water. I was quite sure that Tim had clicked that we were talking about a deadly weapon here but I made myself feel better by spelling it out for him. 'Put that meat cleaver down, Gordon,' I said to my shirt.

'The tape, Honeysett. Where's the tape? Mm? Where's your little microphone? I'm sure you couldn't resist trying to be clever.' He waggled the knife a little and advanced

246

further. He nearly had me backed up into the corner by the stove now and there was nowhere to run.

'There's no tape, Gordon. Just you and me. And I didn't even know about the piece of paper. It was all speculation. I was convinced you killed Jenny. I still think it was you.'

'Think what you like, you'll die ignorant then. Come to think of it, there is no real reason why I can't just kill you and look for the tape afterwards, is there?' he said drily.

'This isn't necessary. We can come to an arrangement here.' I was stalling.

And Gordon knew it. He swung the cleaver in a horizontal arc. I jumped back a fraction too late: the blade sliced into my right forearm which I had raised instinctively to ward him off. Blood appeared instantly through the gash in my shirt which turned crimson in a widening stain. The pain took a few seconds to catch up. Idiotically I wondered how clean I had left the blade. Perhaps this wasn't the moment to worry about germs. I held my arm up and watched drops of blood seep through the material of the shirt, then plop quietly on to the floor. I've always been fascinated by the sight of my own blood.

He noticed that too. 'Hello!' he called. 'I did that to get your attention, man. Now am I going to get the tape of this riveting conversation or what?' He took a firmer grip on the cleaver. Surely this was the moment for Tim to do something heroic? Like save my life again? Perhaps he had decided it would be more sporting to let me get out of this mess by myself, but I was beginning to suspect something more sinister. In fact it rapidly dawned on me that for whatever reason I was probably on my own with this one.

I pulled a dishcloth from the rail of the Rayburn, wrapped it around my forearm and mumbled 'Okay, okay' in a desperate effort to buy my lazy brain more time to devise some sort of strategy. Rushing a knife-wielding man

bare-handed is strictly for TV heroes. In real life you're
bound to come off rather badly.

No such considerations appeared to hamper the
eighteen-stone ball of hatred that flew through the kitchen
door just then and barrelled into Gordon, squashing him
against the kitchen counter. The cleaver fell from his grip
and skidded away across the tiles. The huge figure was
clad head to toe in blue waterproofs, a black crash helmet
clamped over her head. She used it to nut Gordon on the
side of his twisted face, twice, and then again for good
measure while he slid semi-conscious on to the floor.
Despite the biker outfit and crash helmet I had little doubt
as to who my rescuer was. 'Lisa?'

She turned towards me, half as broad as she was tall.
Her visor had detached itself during the headbutting performance. Fierce eyes burned above a fleshy nose and
livid, squashed cheeks. Her voice boomed from inside her
helmet. 'She defended him from his enemies and kept him
safe from those who lay in wait. Not,' she added, and
landed a leather-gloved fist in my face, sending me sprawling to the floor. 'Make yourself small, you worm, or you
shall be trodden on in the realization of my vengeance,'
came her advice.

Gordon lay limp as a rag doll, propped against the
counter. He was still dazed and groaned quietly.

'And they, repenting and groaning for anguish of spirit,
shall say within themselves, this is She, whom we held
sometimes in derision. Hello, Mr Hines.' She lifted a heavy
boot and ground it into his groin. I winced. Gordon
screamed, shocked into full consciousness. 'You were
always pleased to see me before. You told me I was pretty.'
She stepped back and looked around the kitchen, her arms
stiff by her side. Then nodded theatrically, picked up the
meat cleaver off the floor and advanced on Gordon again.
One hand protecting his groin, the other scrabbling for a
hold to heave himself up, he simply shook his head.
'Nononono.'

'Put that down, Lisa,' I said in what I hoped was a reasonable and steady voice.

'Shut the fuck up, Mr Honeysett!' She squatted in front of the scrabbling Gordon. 'There reigns in all men without exception blood, manslaughter, theft and dissimulation, corruption, unfaithfulness, tumults, perjury, forgetfulness of good turns, defiling of souls, changing of kind, disorder in marriages, adultery and shameless uncleanness, remember?' The meat cleaver in her left hand, she began punching him in the face, methodically, rhythmically: 'Do . . . you . . . have . . . any . . . idea . . . what . . . he . . . did . . . to . . . me!?' Under this leather-fisted onslaught Gordon went quite limp, his head on one shoulder, lips, nose and eyebrow split and bleeding. Lisa pulled his right hand from his groin and splayed it on the ground. I thought I could detect a shudder going through her massive body. 'He did unspeakable things to my tits to cleanse my soul, you know,' she said conversationally. The meat cleaver came down and three fingers, severed behind the second joint, jumped away from his hand. Blood spurted immediately. A shock went through his body, his face turned grey and his eyes stared madly. Gordon's breath rattled in and out of his lungs. I realized Lisa had probably punched in his windpipe for good measure. It had to stop, however much both of us hated him.

'Lisa. I know he did unforgivable things to you,' I said without making a move that might invite the attentions of a Chinese meat cleaver. 'And he did kill my friend Jenny. But . . .'

She looked across at me, his second, uninjured hand twitching as she grabbed hold of it and pressed it hard against the tiles for her next operation. She gestured casually with the bloodied meat cleaver. 'He didn't kill her.' She tapped her chest with the cleaver. 'I killed the stupid cow. Didn't mean to, I just hit her too much.'

'Why?' I asked quietly.

'Because the bitch betrayed me. She was supposed to

help me get justice from this pig. She said she'd help me. Then she changed her mind. Said no one would believe me 'cause I'm mad. Keeping the house was more important. The fucking house! What about me? She asked me to leave, just like that. I hit her with that sharpening thing. I was angry.' She nodded. 'I do all sorts of shit when I'm angry.'

She made to have another go at Gordon's digits. Keep her talking. 'If you killed Jenny then how come Dave ended up with the sharpening steel in the lock? Did you kill him too?'

'Dozy Dave? Never. But I saw him die all right. When I came out of the downstairs lav after a quick wash Dave was there, bending over Jenny. Gavin was right behind him, as usual. I told them not to say a thing and scram or I'd wring their necks. They ran out of the door like chickens. Later on I walked up the towpath in Widcombe in case Dave had gone to his therapy session anyway. I thought he might. He did everything like clockwork. I needed to know if they'd told anyone. Sure enough, they were both there. They were arguing. Dave pacing up and down, up and down in front of the lock, waving his arms about, excited, haranguing Gavin about something. And then the idiot paced straight over the side and into the lock. He never stopped talking all the way down, either, the daft sod. Gavin ran off as soon as he saw me. I looked down the lock for Dave but couldn't see him. I still had the sharpening thing, I was going to dump it in the river somewhere. So I chucked it in after him. Satisfied, Mr Detective?'

She turned back to the work in hand, lifted the meat cleaver and struck down. This time the cleaver failed to find its target because a length of two-by-two connected with the back of her helmet, sending her crashing on to Gordon's limp body. She growled, picked herself up and swung around to face her attacker. Tim seemed a little

250

unsteady on his feet but his eyes under the blood-encrusted forehead were clear. 'I've come to repay the compliment,' he said. As Lisa rushed him with a furious grunt, he swung the three-foot length of timber and landed another blow on the top of the helmet. It gave a loud crack. Lisa stumbled another step forward, then stopped, swaying a little. 'I really don't want to hit you again, you know?'

She grunted and shuffled forward, the cleaver still raised in her right hand.

'Oh, hell.' He stepped back and cracked another blow across the crash helmet. Lisa hit the floor like a dynamited chimney, face first. The meat cleaver clattered away across the tiles.

It was a moment of blissful quiet. Gordon was unconscious. His heart silently pumped blood out of his twitching hand into a widening pool around his severed fingers. I was bleeding in more modest fashion into my shirt. Tim rested the length of wood across his shoulder like a workman with his spade and took in the bleeding mess in general and Gordon's severed fingers in particular. 'Bloody hell, Chris. Just as well you never lit the barbecue.'

'It's quite a nasty scratch,' was how Annis referred to my heroic wound. The girls had turned up not five minutes after Tim had restored peace to Mill House. He had a bad headache and probably shouldn't have been drinking after the thwack Lisa had dealt him in the shed. But we all felt the need for a few fingers of scotch before the inevitable police circus descended on us. We sat around the kitchen table and sipped our whiskies while we waited for the ambulance and the unavoidable Superintendent. Lisa was sitting on the floor with her hands expertly tied by Annis. Gordon, grimly quiet, sat where he was with his hand inexpertly bandaged by Alison. 'They could probably sew his fingers back on if we kept them frozen or something,' she suggested.

'Sorry,' I said, jingling the cubes in my glass. 'We're fresh out of ice.'

Acknowledgements

Thanks to Krystyna and Juliet for making this book possible; to Imogen, Veena and Clare for the hard work my manuscript needed; to Matt for answering my inane computer questions; no thanks to Asbo the cat for pouring tea into my laptop.